A Taste for Diamonds

Diane Harding

First ebook edition: Sydney 2018
Publisher: Sydney School of Arts & Humanities
15-17 Argyle Street Millers Point NSW 2000

www.ssoa.com.au

A Taste for Diamonds
ISBN: 978-0-6482036-4-3 print
         978-0-6482036-5-0 ebook

Cover design by Ferdinando Manzo. Text design by Ferdinando Manzo. Typeset in Times New Roman. Printed and bound by Lightning Source as a POD paperback.

National Library of Australia Cataloguing-in-Publication data:

A Taste for Diamonds/Diane Harding.

978-0-6482036-4-3 print

978-0-6482036-5-0 ebook

Fiction – diamonds – Australian fiction – crime fiction – diamond exchange – tango

Dedication

To my family: Fiona, Richard, Cameron, Rebecca, Charlotte, Jeremy and Annika, who are generous and supportive of my writing career.

Acknowledgements

It took a number of people to make my dream of a second novel come true. The most important was Dr Christine Williams, editor, publisher and all round good guy. Without her attention to the smallest of details, the ability to see what would work and what wouldn't, there would have been no book.

Others in the Sydney School of Arts & Humanities publishing team I would like to thank are: Sharon Dean, whose editing is shrewd and all-encompassing; Ferdinando Manzo, who shows his creative flair in the design of the book's cover; Faisal Sayani, who developed a video to promote my books; and Lisa Creffield who works tirelessly behind the scenes in a variety of roles.

There are others who gave me confidence and motivation over the past year of writing *A Taste for Diamonds*: Julie Howard, a talented writer in her own right; the group from Narrabeen U3A Creative Writing – Barbara, Branka, Marg, Leonie, Fae and Margaret; and Dianna, Carolyn and Julie from 'Beyond Words' at the NSW Writers Centre.

Where would I be without my husband in this endeavour? My thanks to Rex for everything – his support and interest and love has kept me sane and happy throughout the experience of writing the novel.

Contents

Chapter 1

'Here, take this.'

Harriett, intent on her phone, felt the cool touch of metal placed in her outstretched hand and as she looked down saw the sparkle of … What? They looked like diamonds!

A brooch like turbulent water, the colours shifting, trembling and shimmering in the sunlight. She looked up, glimpsing a tall, strong male-suited figure moving quickly away around the corner by the Town Hall. Then he was gone.

Disappeared.

Her eyes scanned the area. The neighbourhood of Thames Row was sandwiched between Pimlico and Chelsea, a place for the rich and famous. At this time of the morning the streets were just as crowded as streets in the centre of London, several miles away. There were suits with ties loosened, suits rich and suave, suits looking slept in, and confident arrogant suits. There were people on the way to work with toast in their hands as they hurried along. Others were coming back from early morning exercise, some looking at their watches as they ran. Late again, no doubt.

Harriett walked towards the double doors of the Thames Row Diamond Exchange building.

'Coffee, take away, Harriett?' From across the road, the barista at Bruno's cafe called out to her. Harriett tossed her long brown hair from her oval face, her brown eyes crinkling at the corners as she gave him a brilliant smile.

'Not today. Too busy!' Harriett called back, tucking her lunch box under her arm, and opening the doors to the exchange. She moved slowly towards the electronic gates everyone had to go through to enter and leave the building. No one in the company cared what was being taken in, only what was being taken out.

Two of Harriett's colleagues watched her as she hurried, already late, towards their desks.

'What's your excuse for being late today, Harriett?' Muriel asked with a smile.

'Bet she's got a hankering to work extra hours at double rates,' muttered Janie who hated her job and was always looking for an escape.

Harriett stopped to chat. 'As if they'd ever pay double rates,' she replied. 'They're too mean for that.' She bent down to change her heels to her work flats, smoothing down her calf-length straight skirt, which accentuated her slim build.

'I know,' sighed Janie. 'Just dreaming. Anyway, why *are* you late Harriett? Hatchet-face could be on the warpath, you know.'

'Too bad. He'll just have to put up with it. Besides, I was accosted by a strange man out in the square.'

'What did he want?' Janie asked. 'Did he make you an offer of work as the next movie sensation?'

Harriett laughed. She was not about to divulge anything about the diamond brooch. 'A pity that. I'd like to be famous and rich.'

Harriett gave a little wave as she headed towards the staff lockers and then the diamond sorting room.

She liked Janie and Muriel even though they were the biggest gossips. There weren't many people she was that friendly with at the diamond exchange. Most of her colleagues had families, so they went straight home after work. She wished it were different. She'd love to chat about diamonds. Diamond sorting was a job that required a Diploma of Gems (Diamond Category), with specialisation in cutting, and it took years of work to refine those skills, so it wasn't something you introduced into general conversation.

Harriett was even interested in diamond theft – in how it occurred, and when. There had been a time when she wanted to test the system, see if she could get away with it, find new methods of security and design a newer system. But those days had passed after she discovered that the company executives were thieves in a variety of ways, from stealing diamonds to paying low wages to staff. It was no wonder that many workers chose to put a diamond or two in their bags as they exited. She knew she was at the stage in her job where she saw those petty thefts as a way of people making ends meet.

Today was different though. She wasn't stealing from the company but still didn't want to be caught with such a treasure, as there would surely be questions.

With a sigh, she slipped into her booth. Each of them was a five-foot-high walled cubicle about as big as a cupboard, and inside each cubicle was a computer, a diamond loupe magnifying glass, a secure box for the diamonds and a locked bin.

Nothing more.

Carefully, Harriett took the brooch out of her top pocket. As she did so she also produced a few tissues to hide it, and blew her nose noisily.

Her eyes slid to the second floor glass wall where the executives could look down on the sorters to ensure they were working honestly. Harriett tossed some of the tissues into the bin next to her chair and leaned forward.

There was only one spot where the suits could not see what she was doing. She had discovered it when she was called up several years ago for her one and only so-called 'annual employee assessment' talk. She had stood near the glass and found her cubicle. Before coming up, Harriett had strategically placed her lunch box with its blue lid in view so she could pinpoint the place quickly.

Immediately she noticed that no one could see the back right-hand corner of the desk at all. In a few different places, she had positioned various random items: a pen, a handkerchief, a diary.

Harriett had been working for the company for twelve years. In that time others had left or retired or been fired, but Harriett was still there. It paid to stay quiet and be diligent. She thought she was a trusted employee, although she knew that no one was really that trusted in the company. Over the years she had seen several people hauled upstairs to see 'the man'.

The man was Hatchet-face.

At that moment he appeared by her booth.

'Sorry, Harriett. I didn't expect you to jump in fright.' He pushed back the wavy brown hair that had flopped over his forehead, revealing his intense dark blue eyes.

'That's all right, Mr Symonds.' Harriett nervously clutched her few remaining tissues tightly, hoping no corner of the brooch was exposed.

Mr Symonds' sharp blue eyes gazed at her hands and travelled up to her face.

'Have you got a cold, Harriett?' His eyes slid once again to her hands.

'Just a bit, Mr Symonds.' She touched her nose with the bulging tissues, losing one as she did so. Her mind raced with the thought of what could happen if the brooch's links slipped out between her fingers.

Mr Symonds nodded, displeased as always, his eyes half closed in a suspicious manner.

'Well, carry on, Harriett,' he murmured as he stepped away, taking one more backward look over his shoulder before quietly disappearing.

Harriett hurriedly coughed and sniffed into the tissues as she noticed him turning. *What a suspicious mind*, she thought. *No wonder we all call him Hatchet-face. Always lurking, ready to sling a hatchet at anyone.*

Over the years his wary eyes had uncovered a number of employees who had stolen diamonds. People had been very inventive in their endeavours. Some had hidden diamonds in their mouths, others in shoes, purses or the hems of clothes.

Hatchet-face had found them all.

Sometimes he just suspected them because they looked guilty and so had them randomly frisked, as was the system. Others could not beat the electronic gates that shrilled loudly if a diamond was detected.

The police would be called and the thief would be ushered out unceremoniously through the sorting room and the secretarial room almost as if to say, 'See what happens when you steal from us?'

The company would not know what she was doing. Harriett closed her fist, leaned towards the back right hand corner of her desk and opened her hand.

There it lay. The most beautiful brooch she had ever seen, with about thirty diamonds, all exactly the same size. They were arranged in a waterfall design, cascading down from rare yellow diamonds at the top to white diamonds at the bottom, as if the water had become turbulent at that point.

Harriett estimated that the diamonds alone were worth about two million pounds and in that exquisite setting about another million. There was no guesswork in this estimate. She had been dealing in diamonds for years. Most of the diamonds she handled were mid-grade and mid-sized. Every now and then though, a large diamond made it to her box. After examination, and a report, she would put it aside ready for either cutting into a large stone suitable for a crown or a tiara, or to be used as a square-cut diamond for the rings of the rich, or a radiant diamond for the famous diamond establishments of Knightsbridge.

There were also a lot of chips that were not useful for the company. They went into another bin near her left, to be used by jewellers to make a range of inexpensive necklaces and bracelets. The lid of this bin closed and locked immediately after the chips were deposited. The company still wanted its profit from diamond chips.

Harriett wondered how she could source this brooch. The computer had a software program with every known diamond piece in the world. It would be able to tell her who had owned it through the ages and where it had come from.

The only trouble was that each computer was linked to the

mainframe that the suits regularly checked. Harriett hoped that they would not be checking hers today or she'd have to invent some story to satisfy Hatchet-face.

She figuratively crossed her fingers and typed the words 'brooches', 'yellow diamonds', and 'waterfall setting' into the program … and waited for the computer to work its magic. Up came a picture of her brooch.

It had first been owned by a Russian oligarch, then by an Indian princess, and last by an Italian millionaire. It had been missing for seventy years, ever since World War II.

Harriett closed the screen and shoved her fist into her pants pocket at the same time as taking out another tissue and coughing into it.

Then, trembling with excitement, she opened her box with the password and began to sort diamonds. All the while, her heart was beating faster than normal and she could hardly concentrate on the job at hand.

Within ten minutes Hatchet-face appeared again at her cubicle. What had he seen?

'Have you started yet, Harriett?' His voice was hesitant, although the suspicious look he had for others was replaced with a blush that started at his cheeks and moved down to his neck.

He ran his fingers through his hair again, tossing it back out of his eyes.

Harriett looked at him with a miserable expression.

'Just a cold, Mr Symonds,' she replied – of course Harriett never called him Hatchet-face to his face – giving another sniff and thinking miserable thoughts, which wasn't too hard with him looking over her shoulder.

Hatchet-face looked down at the bin and saw three used tissues, and then looked at Harriett.

'You'd better go home, Harriet. Better not to have germs here.'

Harriett knew what he didn't want. He didn't want a diamond to escape in a used tissue. She gathered up her lunch box, fiddled with tissues and, closing her box, swivelled around on her chair.

Hatchet-face and Harriett walked towards the electronic gates.

She was ready for this test. She had never taken the opportunity to steal diamonds before, but she knew a few tricks of the trade by reading about others who had got away with it. Today, luckily, she happened to be wearing a top with a neckline that formed folds of material like a scarf in the front. In this she had placed one small diamond chip while the brooch was in her pants' pocket. The alarm sounded, shrill and insistent. Harriett looked shocked and glanced down at her hands and body.

The secretaries stopped working. Life was boring if there was no excitement. They were amazed when they saw it was Harriett.

'Stop, Harriett.' Hatchet-face placed his hand under her arm. His face registered a concern for her and the thought that his lovely Harriett would be stealing diamonds.

With a gasp, Harriett noticed a tiny diamond chip in the cowl of her top.

'Oh, Mr Symonds, this must have caught up in the folds of my top and I didn't notice, what with the sneezing and coughing and tissues and all. I'm so sorry. Here, let me give it to you to deposit in my locked box.'

Hatchet-face's serious half-closed blue eyes relaxed as he smiled with relief. He took the diamond chip and ushered Harriett out beyond the gates to the lockers, where she collected her bag.

She walked slowly beyond the lockers, a little unsteady. Her high-heels that made her legs and ankles look so good caused her to become unbalanced, but then, more confidently, she walked through the main lobby with thirty of the best diamonds in the world.

I've done it, she thought, feeling smug.

She staggered past the company lobby and into the soft autumn breeze of the street, still coughing and sniffing. She did this because Hatchet-face, with a thoughtful expression in his eyes, was still watching from inside the glass doors, and she didn't want him to see her smile at getting away with the theft.

In no time at all Harriett was in her apartment only two blocks from work. Still she didn't take the brooch out of her pocket. She was always suspicious of the company, and in particular Hatchet-face. She wouldn't put it past him to place cameras in the apartment. She was sure that the company really didn't trust anyone. So the only place she could go was the bathroom, hoping there would be no hidden cameras there.

Harriett sat on the closed toilet lid and gently uncurled her fist. There was the brooch in all its glory, winking and shimmering at her as if to say, 'I'm yours.'

It wasn't really hers, but on the other hand it had been given to her. Could she keep it or sell it?

There was no doubt about the brooch's provenance and the estimated profit of three million, maybe more in today's market. But what could she do with it? She couldn't sell it as a brooch; it would attract too much attention. So she would have to sell the stones separately. The clear stones would be okay, but the rare yellow ones would attract a huge amount of attention, as there were very few in the world, those that existed known to be on a few specialised custom settings. This was attention she could not afford under the circumstances. Most importantly, how could she dismantle such a wonderful creative piece? It couldn't be done.

Then, as Harriett gazed at it, turning it this way and that to catch the light and wonder of it, she began to want it. She would keep it. She loved it. The artistry was exceptional. The diamonds were magnificent. A sigh escaped her. It was nice to have made a clear and sensible decision. She felt good. After all, she couldn't give it back. There was no one to give it to.

Then she had thoughts she'd been trying to keep at bay since the diamond had materialised in her life that morning. *What about the person who thrust it into my hand? He knows I have it. What does he expect me to do – give it to the company? If he'd wanted me to do that, he could have marched in the door of the Thames Row Diamond Exchange and done it himself. Does he want me to keep it? Surely not. Surely he wants something out of it. So, will he be back for his cut of any profit?*

Her mind raced. *Maybe he doesn't know the brooch is worth millions. Maybe he found it in the gutter and handed it to me, knowing I work there. After all, for twelve years I've been coming in and out that door three times a day – at 9 am, 12.30 pm and 5 pm. Maybe ... maybe ... crap!*

There was no maybe about it. He would be back. She would have to face that when it happened.

But there was an immediate problem to solve. Harriett needed a safe place for her brooch. A bank deposit box was the ticket.

She would only be able to go to the bank at lunchtime tomorrow. She could not take the risk of going in and out of the company gates again. But she could not leave the brooch in the apartment. It would be just her luck to be burgled on the one day she had something valuable for a burglar to take. Harriett pondered this dilemma for a while as she lay on the bed. If they were watching her, she needed to look sick.

She could phone the doctor, the one that was near the local bank. She could stagger out of the apartment tossing tissues left, right and centre, go to the bank after seeing the doctor and organise a deposit box. Then go to the chemist and purchase a few mild pills to take at work tomorrow. Hatchet-face would have nothing to be suspicious about.

Having solved the dilemma, Harriett booked an appointment using an app on her phone and set off – one minute trying to act sick, then worried that she was overacting and trying to tone it down a bit, then concerned that she was being too subtle and ramping the acting up again.

Out on the street, away from the company premises and any colleague who might report to the company that she was not really sick, Harriett began to behave normally.

There she was doing it again! Her subterfuge was working.

Chapter 2

'One, two, three, dip.'

Harriett's leg twisted around George's rump as they danced, and she noticed his plump tummy peeping out of the 'V' made by his shirt buttons not quite meeting at the point where the shirt tucked into his trousers. She then flung her head back until her straight dark brown hair swept across his feet.

He could be trusted to hold her otherwise she would have been on the floor by now.

'Thank you everyone.' Betty, the instructor, clapped her hands. 'That's the end for this term. I hope you all come back next term and join me for the advanced tango class.' She began to herd the group out the door.

Harriett looked at George. He was always slightly out of breath because of his weight, and was a few inches shorter than her, but he could always be relied upon to do his best. Not like Harry who flittered around with Sally, making up his own steps as he went. Or Johnno, who had two left feet and was struggling to keep in time with Jan. Why were all the best male dancers never at classes like this?

'I think we're getting better,' George puffed as he took off his dancing shoes and put on his sneakers. 'Do you think we might even be good enough to enter the end-of-year state championships?'

'Maybe,' Harriett replied, really thinking, *No way, buddy*.

After putting on her coat, Harriett waved goodbye to George, who was going home to Muriel.

Muriel seemed just right for George. She was very petite with blonde, wavy hair and a pixie face. Harriett chatted with Muriel in the secretarial pool every day and knew about her love for George.

Betty came up to Harriett. 'You're doing extremely well, Harriett. I think you could enter the end-of-year English Tango Championships in London.' She patted Harriett on the back and turned away, saying softly, 'I just have to find you a better partner.'

Harriett felt very pleased as she hurried down the stairs to catch the last bus back to Thames Row.

As she watched the dark trees and houses slide by from her window seat, she thought about her life. It had picked up lately with the waterfall brooch now in her possession. The brooch was like a little secret that she could picture holding next to her heart to dream about. When things were not going well she only had to think about it and she felt better.

It was just how she felt when she was five years old and had been given a heart necklace that opened to reveal her mother and father. She had worn it every day and had even kept it under her pillow at night.

She loved her tango dancing classes and her job at the diamond exchange. If her mum and dad were alive, they would have been so proud of her achievements. But her dad would still be saying, 'Have you met a nice man, love?'

He had belonged to the era when women were expected to have a small ordinary job while they waited to get married. Then their real life of looking after a man would commence. *What a crock of piss*, she thought. Still, her dad had been a wonderful father. He had taken her to dance classes and bowling. He had encouraged her to sit by him and hear about his home country – Argentina. She had learned so much from him.

She pondered the thought of a 'nice man', as her dad would have said. Where was he? She'd had no dates for the last six months. Not since Jake had left.

She had thought Jake was going to be forever. She imagined she would marry him and they would find a nice little home in the country and live happily ever after. It was really what she wanted.

She stared at her face in the bus window that had become a mirror because of the darkness outside. She had a nice face, didn't she?

High cheekbones courtesy of her Argentinian dad, clear skin and big brown eyes. She shook her head. Life was what it was; there was nothing she could do about it.

The ride home was slow as Harriett had boarded the last service of the night, and the driver pulled up at every stop. At last there were only two passengers left: Harriett and a middle-aged man. He was lean, with hollow cheeks and thinning hair partly covered by a hoodie, and he kept looking furtively at her.

At the square, she clambered down and walked swiftly past the shopping centre towards the short alley to her flat. Suddenly she heard soft ominous steps behind her. She hadn't noticed how dark it was until then. There were no friendly lights from the houses and flats at this time of night. Two streetlamps beamed downwards, creating a dim pool of light at the base of their metal stands, and making the area outside the light seem even darker … and scarier.

Looking behind her, Harriett saw the other passenger huddled over in his hoodie, hands in his pockets, coming closer, his sneakers hardly making any noise on the concrete pathway.

Harriett walked faster, turned the corner and almost ran to the wrought-iron railing with steps leading to her door.

The man stopped at the corner and flared a lighter for his cigarette. She caught the glint from his eyes as the flame took hold. He seemed to be watching her.

Up the stairs she scurried and into her flat. Then, crouching beneath the window, she moved the curtain slightly to peer outside.

He was still there, but now he tossed his cigarette down, crushed it with his foot, then sloped off down the street.

Harriett sighed. Her fear was all in her mind.

He was just another man going home, she supposed.

*

George arrived home to Muriel, who was watching TV and eating chocolates.

'How was class?' Muriel enquired without much interest, as she poked among the chocolates on her lap.

She looked up at George. They'd moved in together six months before because he seemed genuine and caring, but she was getting a bit tired of his interest in dancing rather than in her.

'Great,' said George taking off his coat and throwing his dance shoes on the floor. 'I think Harriett and I might be in the national championships this year. I might have to have a go at a bit of a diet for it.' He patted his stomach and then took a chocolate out of the open box and popped it in his mouth.

Maybe it's time to move out, back to my own flat, Muriel thought. She'd kept it just in case things didn't work out and had rented it to Janie from work. Janie was a good housekeeper. She had even painted Muriel's flat and redesigned the kitchen. She said she could cook better with the changes.

Muriel wondered if Janie would be happy to give up the flat or even have Muriel as her flatmate as there were two bedrooms. Muriel thought she'd rather share a place with someone who could cook.

She'd have to have a look into that next month.

Muriel noticed George's expression. She could see that he had clocked on to her disinterest. Probably because he'd lost interest in her, too.

George took another chocolate from the box.

He's just more interested in dancing lessons, Muriel thought. *He talks about them all the time. He talks about Harriett all the time and how much fun she is.*

'Guess what?' George spun around. 'Harriett and I learnt a new sequence tonight. One especially for the championship. Our teacher, Betty, must appreciate our skills.'

Muriel sighed. She knew that if he were truthful with himself, he wouldn't be considered as an entry for the championships without Harriett.

Muriel looked up at the ceiling.

'Are you listening, Muriel?' George said.

'Hmm.' Muriel flicked the TV remote several times. *When is he going to talk about us? All he does is go to work at the shoe store, go to tango classes, and come home for food.*

'There's nothing on TV. Let's go to bed.' Muriel sidled up to George and draped her arms around his neck.

'Not just yet, Muriel,' George said, disengaging her arms from his neck. 'I need to write down a few moves for the next class. I might sleep on the lounge tonight so I don't disturb you.'

Muriel sighed. Yes, things were not going well. She might need to talk to Janie sooner than she thought.

'By the way, someone came up to me tonight and asked about Harriett; where she lived and stuff like that. I thought it was a bit strange and he looked, well ...' George shuddered. 'I felt quite scared.'

'What did you say?'

'I told him to get lost. I think I might phone Harriett and talk to her.'

'Good, that sounds very weird. I wouldn't like anyone telling strangers where I lived.'

Muriel turned off the appliances in the kitchen and tidied the lounge. She watched her boyfriend settle down with his phone, an exercise book and a stub of a pencil in his mouth, and then slammed the bedroom door. How distasteful.

She needed to change her life.

Chapter 3

Janie, plump, with peachy cheeks and bright green eyes, met Muriel in the square on Monday morning. They walked together, comparing weekends.

Muriel was quiet.

She turned to Janie, looking sad. 'I might leave George,' she blurted out. 'He's getting on my nerves and the sex is almost non-existent. All he thinks about is Harriett.'

'Oh dear, poor you.' Janie gave her friend a quick hug, then went on, 'That was strange the other day when Harriett was pulled up at the electric gates. Do you think she was stealing diamonds?'

'I wouldn't put it past her. Remember last month when you caused all that rumpus at the electric gates?'

'Yes, it was my black velvet shoes with the red roses on the toes. Those fake rubies near the ankle straps were the problem. I love those shoes but they certainly make the alarm go off. Every time I wear them Hatchet-face has to come to the gates and check them to see if I'm stealing diamonds. I almost want to wear them every day on purpose to cause him trouble.' Janie giggled.

'I'd like to steal one or two diamonds myself. Then I could get rid of George and buy a new flat. In the meantime, though, I'll need to have my flat back, Janie. Would you like to stay on as a flatmate?'

'I suppose, although I like to live alone with my own things and making my own recipes.'

'You could still do that if I was there. Anyway, it is my flat, so stay or go,' she said as she swept her hands through the air, 'I don't mind.'

Janie, chastened, nodded. 'I'll stay until I find something better.'

They walked on, each with their own thoughts, until Harriett joined them near the diamond exchange doors.

Muriel skipped the small talk. 'Did George tell you about the man who wanted to know where you lived?'

Harriett nodded. She was worried that it was the same man as on the bus.

Janie gestured towards the limousine parked in front of the diamond exchange. 'Hey, the big guns are here today,' she whispered. 'They look like criminals to me. See that guy with the cigarillo in his mouth?' She nodded towards a short, stocky man, with a fleshy red-veined nose, thick eyebrows, and a disdainful expression on his face. 'He looks especially bad.'

Harriett and Muriel turned towards the car, but Harriett's eyes went beyond Janie's criminal to the driver. He was the man from last night. The man who had followed her.

She drew in a breath, her mind racing. *Here he is at my workplace*, she thought, *and he's working for my bosses, the ones who look like criminals. Do they all know I have the brooch? Are they keeping their eyes on me?*

Putting her head down and partly covering her face with her hand, she hurried into the foyer of the company. At the door to the secretarial pool, the trio passed Mr Symonds.

'Good morning, girls,' he said.

'Good morning,' they parroted back to him.

Mr Symonds was Neville to his friends and Hatchet-face to his enemies. He knew this because he had often heard it whispered as he came by.

It was part of the job, he supposed. If you are the company inspector, almost a spy, then you were sure to get a negative nickname, although he didn't understand his as he thought he was not bad looking. Not good looking, but not ugly either.

He moved from the secretarial pool, which was made up of five women with Muriel and Janie being the instigators of any gossip, to the diamond sorting room with ten workers of all ages and sexes. He was only interested in one of them. Harriett.

She had been in the job for many years and was a skilled sorter. She was also beautiful, with her long straight hair caught into a knot at the back. His fingers itched to unwind it, play with the silkiness of it. Her brown eyes with flecks of gold entranced him. Tanned skin that glowed invitingly enough to touch. Although he never had touched.

Today Harriett looked very pale and shaky as if something was wrong.

'Are you okay, Harriett? You seem unwell.'

'A bit tired, Mr Symonds. The weekend, you know.'

He nodded and moved away, cursing himself for not thinking of something better to say to her.

He didn't know why he was so shy and tongue-tied around her, but somehow this was the way she affected him. It had taken him three years to say more than good morning.

He knew that whenever he came by her work area, she seized up as if he might find her doing something wrong. *Perhaps she is stealing diamonds*, he thought. Then he corrected himself. *No. Not Harriett. It was a mistake the other day. She just sees me as the enemy like all the other sorters.* He was a creature of the suits who owned the business, and that was that.

In Neville's opinion, most of the executive staff seemed to be a bit crooked. They were always checking up on staff as if everyone else was dishonest except them. Maybe they were covering up some fraud, such as jewellery made with cheap or fake diamonds, like cubic zirconia.

The suits didn't realise he knew so much about precious stones. He had told them he had completed a certificate course to get the job but not that he had been a maker of fine diamond jewellery before that.

Neville had been watching those in charge upstairs for some time.

Mostly they were regular London business types in pinstripes, snow-white shirts and silk ties. They held meetings now and then where copious notes were taken, which were then relayed to their personal assistants to type into reports encased in colourful folders stamped with words such as 'confidential' and 'quarterly finance'.

There seemed more of these regular executives than there were secretaries and diamond sorters. Neville surmised that they were making so much profit they could afford to have a top-heavy business. Every now and then, though, Neville saw a new phalanx of businessmen arrive in a limousine, sweeping importantly through the ground floor workers and up to the first floor.

Neville was almost sure that these men were criminals of some sort. They wore black suits with wide lapels, black shirts with colourful ties, and matching handkerchiefs spilling from their top pockets. They sported pointy-toed shoes and their hair was slicked back with oil. There were suspicious bumps under their jackets. Perhaps they were mafia-related.

This upset Neville so much. *How can these criminal types get away with this kind of activity in a country like England? Where are the police? Where are the politicians making new laws to prevent crime?*

Neville was so incensed that he found himself taking revenge in little ways. Ways that would not be noticed by the suits. Ticking names off on his clipboard to indicate the workers had arrived on time, when actually they were late, was one revenge. Allowing small breaches in diamond sorting and not reporting them to the suits. Letting the secretaries get away with swiping a variety of supplies, which he could sometimes see peeping out of their bulging bags at home time.

All the time though, Neville kept his eye on Harriett. He wished she would notice him.

He would have promoted her if the task had been up to him. But the suits upstairs wanted all the profits for themselves.

Neville took his pen out of his top pocket, and clicked it on and off several times before ticking the sorters' names off his clipboard so they could start work.

All except Harriett, that was. She had been late again and it was only Monday.

Chapter 4

A few days later Harriett was still enjoying her secret gain. She had decided that she was being overly paranoid about the driver of the car. *He just has a job with the company and lives nearby, that's all*, was her conclusion.

She could not be at the bank to look at the brooch every day and she hadn't taken a photo that could be traced to her. So she could only think about it and remember. That soon got boring.

If you have something wonderful, you have to touch it, look at it and talk about it otherwise you may as well not have it, Harriett thought. So she started going to the bank in her lunch hour, just to see it.

On the first day she made the short trek from the exchange to the bank, Bruno, the coffee shop owner, was standing in his doorway. He saw Harriett coming and called out, 'The usual, Harriett?' But Harriett walked on by, shaking her head. Bruno stopped in his tracks with an open mouth. She guessed that her behaviour of suddenly not stopping for a coffee, after all these years of having the same coffee each day at the same time, came as a shock to him.

Also every day that week, the bank manager, Charles, began to look at Harriett in a peculiar way. He noticed she would arrive at precisely 12.45 pm, having taken fifteen minutes to walk from the diamond exchange. By the third day he said good afternoon to her as usual, but this time with a frown.

Harriett tried not to seem different – not too excited, or acting too suspiciously, as if she'd done something wrong … even though, technically, she probably had, considering how the brooch had come to her and that she'd kept it.

Still, it was a wonderful feeling having a secret, and one that was worth millions as well as being related to something beautiful.

Harriett began to feel important, rich, and lovely. This feeling changed the way she behaved. Every morning she brushed her hair one hundred times until it shone, whereas previously she had simply scraped it back into a bun. She carefully applied eye shadow, lipstick … and occasionally a touch of highlighter on her cheeks.

At the end of that week, Harriett sat at her computer and signed into her bank account. The balance seemed healthy.

Soon I'll have enough for a round the world trip, she thought. *Somewhere in the world there must be a 'Mr Right'.*

The brooch was a bonus. She could turn it into cash if needed, so why not spend her savings on some nice clothes? A trip to the centre of London with a credit card beckoned.

Both Harrods and Selfridges had autumn sales for the traditional business attire she craved for her job, and also the sexy, swirly numbers she needed for the tango classes.

That Saturday afternoon, staggering home after a long day of trying on many items including high heels, lacy underwear and sheer hose, Harriett sat at her kitchen table with a celebratory hot chocolate. She had even had a makeup session on the ground floor of Harrods, where all the best brands were set up, and had come home with two hundred pounds' worth of creams, gels, glosses and perfumes.

On the following Monday she dressed in her most glamorous suit. It was mauve and consisted of a jacket that clung to her waist and dipped low at the front, and a bottom-hugging skirt that flared a little at her knees. Underneath, she wore a cream silk shirt. She carefully applied makeup, then slipped into her new beige heels, which featured little straps over the toes.

The secretarial pool women at the diamond exchange gazed at Harriett with open mouths as she strode by with a little bit of a hip swing. Harriett enjoyed the buzz and felt good.

'Wow, Harriett. I like your outfit, especially the shoes,' Janie said. Harriett thought she detected a note of envy in Janie's voice. After all, Janie had a shoe fetish and was often seen wearing designer footwear.

Muriel, with raised eyebrows, smiled at Harriett. 'What's up, Harriett? Got a new boyfriend you want to impress?'

'No,' Harriett replied. 'Just spending my money.' She looked down at the dress. 'It's probably a bit too fancy for work.'

Hatchet-face came into the room when he heard all the talking.

'Good morning, Harriett.' Harriett watched him blush and drag his fingers through his errant hair.

Well, I've captured Hatchet-face's interest today, she thought.

By lunchtime she was across the square in Bruno's coffee shop. Bruno came by for her order. His eyes looked at her admiringly up and down.

He had only owned the coffee shop for a few years. Strong and stocky, with a head of thick black hair, he believed that his Italian accent was a magnet for most women and was always busy chatting up any likely beauties in the hopes of a date.

Before setting up the shop, Bruno had been an influential figure in the Ministry of Defence, involved with war reparations. His job had included recouping treasures seized during any war the British had been involved in since and including WWII, and returning them to their rightful owners. Pictures of Bruno with a few celebrities adorned the walls of his cafe.

More recently, his job became redundant and he was retrenched, so with his severance package he had bought the coffee shop. He was firm in his belief that everyone who tried his Italian coffee would come back for more.

'Harriett,' he said in his slightly sexy accent. 'Would you like to go to the movies with me next Wednesday week?'

Harriett smiled. 'Of course, Bruno, I'd love to.' This was the first date for the new Harriett. The Harriett who was rich, had some beautiful clothes and felt good about herself. The brooch was proving to be a wonderful magic icon.

Lunchtime was almost over when she realised she needed to check her finances. She had spent a lot of money on her recent shopping spree in London's Regent Street. She would just have time to visit the bank on the other corner of the square before going back to work.

Once again, all eyes were upon her as her heels tapped their way across the marble floor of the bank to the cash machine in the corner.

Suddenly, scuttling across the floor to greet her was Charles, the bank manager. Charles had always sat in his glass-fronted cubicle on the mezzanine floor. He'd never looked at her until recently even though she had been banking there for so many years.

In fact, she had rarely seen him with any women. Perhaps he was married or had a girlfriend from another town. But today, there he was.

After checking her bank balance, Harriett turned towards him and smiled. Charles smiled back and accompanied her to the main doors. There he hesitated as he opened them for her.

Harriett stepped forward, eyes flicking up to the opposite side of the street. There was that man again. He was slouched down leaning against the wall, eyes shadowed, but glued to the door.

Harriett's adrenalin spiked, her face became hot and her mind blank. She immediately backtracked into the bank, bumping into Charles who was still holding the door open.

Charles was quite chuffed that she was angling close to him.

'Would you like to accompany me to dinner, say on Thursday evening next week?'

So Harriett nodded and smiled, and they organised times and a meeting place.

By then, she hoped the man had gone and it was safe to leave. She peered through the glass. He was not there. *But something is not right*, she thought, as she escaped into the square.

*

Janie and Muriel were also regulars at Bruno's and it wasn't long before they began to make snide remarks about Harriett, since they hadn't seen her there during lunch breaks recently.

'I wonder if she's meeting someone? A lover, maybe,' Janie suggested.

Muriel grinned. 'Yes, I bet she's got a beau! She's looking very smart, too. That's the first sign, you know.'

Janie leant forward conspiratorially. 'I wonder what he's like? They must have a place to meet nearby, maybe even her flat. Lunchtime sex sounds delicious to me.'

Back in the office, the pair began to rib Harriett about a lunchtime lover, and as Harriett thought this was a better story, a more believable story, than the real thing about a brooch, she didn't deny it. Soon the whole of the ground floor was buzzing with rumours of her secret lover.

People began trying to catch her out. Who was he, this lover?

There must have been a plan hatched by Janie and Muriel, because some people, even those who never normally had lunch at 12.30, began to follow her out the company doors.

'Hello, Harriett. Can I walk with you?'

'Are you lunching at Bruno's?'

'Want some company?'

Harriett could not visit the bank and see her brooch when this occurred, which made her sad and annoyed.

By the following Wednesday evening, though, she was ready for Bruno, having dressed in a slinky grey skirt and a glittery silver top that floated down to her waist. They sat towards the back of the theatre in the comfortable reclining seats of the kind fitted with holders for drinks and popcorn, although the pair had decided to have neither.

The movie was a romance of bygone years: Casablanca. Not long after it began, Harriett could feel cool, long fingers playing with the nape of her neck and curling strands of her hair behind her ears. A frizzle of excitement sped through her body and she turned to Bruno. His deep brown eyes looked like molten chocolate in the dim light of the theatre and his lips pouted deliciously. He leaned towards her until his lips met hers in a soft kiss. Soon they were both panting, and as one, rose and left the theatre for her flat.

As she sashayed up the stairs with his hand on her bottom, she briefly wondered if she had anything other than Nescafe all-purpose coffee to serve him. After all, he was used to having the best ground coffee at the cafe. But in the end, she didn't have to worry about serving him anything, as they came together in a clinch that had her breathless. At once, Bruno bunched his muscles tightly so he could guide her backwards through the open door of the bedroom he had spied immediately on entering the flat. Onto the doona they bounced together, her nose nuzzling his neck and chest, which smelled vaguely of coffee, with him tearing her clothes off in a flurry of lust.

Snuggled down in the doona after Bruno had left, and feeling happy that they had already made arrangements for future dates, Harriett smiled to herself. What a great night, and what an interesting man!

Married to Bruno, she would feel proud that he owned a chain of cafes across London, and she would be by his side as they visited each one. Their home would have a wonderful gourmet kitchen with coffee accoutrements to hand.

Two small Italian children, Bruno and Maria, would be running around outside while she opened the high kitchen cupboard packed with a hundred varieties of coffee. Bruno would come up behind her, squeezing her close with his long fingers snaked around her waist, until she would turn in his grasp to ask if he desired Arabica or Dominica.

'My sweet,' he would say as he ravished her on the Casearstone island bench, 'you are always thinking of me.'

Hmmmm! Delicious.

Chapter 5

By Thursday night Harriett was in a fog of love, the love of being in love.

Tonight was dinner with Charles, the bank manager. His intense blue eyes were mesmerising and he was extremely handsome … for a bank manager. Harriett dressed in her new silk dress, low at the back which indicated she was not wearing a bra, and curling around her knees in truffles of lace.

With a dab of perfume in all the right places, and after pulling her hair into a twist over one shoulder, she was off to meet Charles at the bank.

His eyes lit up when he saw her. He was also 'dressed to kill', as they say, in a modern dinner jacket, his blond hair tamed to perfection.

His hand low on her waist, he guided her to a hole-in-the-wall restaurant called 'The Castle' on the banks of the Thames.

Harriett knew this place had a waiting list of three months, so was thrilled to be going there. She had never been to the restaurant before; she couldn't afford it and not one of her previous boyfriends had been able to afford it.

The old stone castle steps led to a heavy oak door encrusted with iron bands and hinges, and set into ivy-covered walls. Inside, an open fire blazed, its warm light flickering over intimate table settings covered with starched white cloths and a selection of military paintings from the Napoleonic era.

Waiters, solemn and regal, moved quietly around filling up cut-glass stemware, which gleamed in the light. Outside each window, the Thames flowed slowly, picking up the lights from the castle.

A barge floated by; the laughing, happy people on board were clinking glasses, or hugging in quiet corners. Wavelets rippled out from the hull to the edge of the castle wall that bordered the restaurant.

Charles pulled out Harriett's chair, whispering in her ear, 'What wonderful perfume, almost as wonderful as you.'

Harriett smiled at Charles. 'Thank you, Charles. You're very sweet to say so.'

'I mean it, Harriett.' Signalling a waiter, he asked 'Champagne and oysters, Harriett?'

Harriett nodded. She loved this attention.

Charles reached over to hold her hand. 'Tell me about yourself, Harriett.'

'There's nothing much to say. I've worked at the Thames Row Diamond Exchange ever since it opened. In fact, I started work there straight after I finished my diploma. I love handling diamonds.'

Charles turned her hand over and caressed it. 'That's why your hand is so beautiful,' he said, tucking it into his.

In no time at all dinner was served. Charles stabbed titbits of oysters kilpatrick onto his fork and fed her, his eyes never leaving her face. Harriett licked her lips and opened her mouth like a baby bird and swallowed. As oysters slid down her throat, she felt as if she was a cherished courtesan.

They moved to the lamb cutlets, both picking up the bones with their fingers and tearing off the meat with their teeth, then licking their fingers slowly as they gazed at each other.

Finally, they shared a crème caramel. Digging their spoons into the creamy centre, and watching the hole left by their actions fill up with the silky caramel sauce, they again fed each other, spoonful by spoonful.

Around 10 pm, they moved towards the door that would either lead them to the foyer or to the winding stone stairs that led to the accommodation in the turret. Almost without thinking, they chose the stairs, and soon found themselves in a room furnished with a red velvet chaise. With five doors to different rooms to choose from, Charles made a show of withdrawing something from his pocket. It was a key attached to a key ring in the shape of a large number three.

Harriett grabbed the key ring, thinking as she did so, *What presumption! Still, it suits me,* and then moved towards the door marked with the corresponding number.

Grabbing her hand, Charles urged her into the room where she discovered lit candles, soft music, and champagne glasses still fizzing with bubbly, as though a fairy godmother had been and left just a minute before.

Charles sipped his champagne, and then dipped his fingers into the flute glass before rubbing them gently on Harriett's lips. She reciprocated as they moved towards the bed.

Downing the remaining bubbles, and letting their champagne glasses tumble to the thickly carpeted floor, they fell together onto the starched sheets in a feast of wet-lip kisses on eyes and necks. Then their fingers reached for the chocolates they had spied on the bedside table, nibbling and sucking them into each other's mouths.

Further kisses weren't necessary as they melded to each other's bodies and into a nest of soft pillows.

By morning, Harriett, back in her own cold bed, was satiated and in love, or at least in lust.

Charles is a dream come true. He'll be a perfect husband – thoughtful and sexy.

He'll come home with flowers each week and enjoy watching me display them in one of my Orrefors vases.

He'll give me pearls for my birthday and diamonds for Christmas.

We'll have a home built of old stone covered with ivy. It will have a turret room, right away from the nursery wing where the children will sleep with their nanny. The house will be quite close to the most prestigious bank in London, so that Charles can come home to me at lunchtime for a secret tryst and a feast. Dinner will be served by kitchen staff, who will then melt quietly into the background so that we can enjoy our meal.

We'll be known in London's important circles as the couple who are the happiest and the most beautiful.

The two children, a boy called Sebastian and a girl called Petunia, will be clever at school and asked to every child's party, with other parents saying, 'It just wouldn't be a party without Petunia and Sebastian!'

Life will be dramatic and full of spice.

Ooohhh! Wonderful!

*

So much for her night of excitement and blissful dreams. Soon Harriett received a letter.

It was written on plain paper, typed on a computer and stuffed inside a standard envelope. It said: 'I know what you have and I know who you are. Be careful who you see'.

That's all it said. Harriett couldn't believe it.

All her precautions, all the times she had given the impression of having a lover, and letting people from work follow her had been wasted.

Even Hatchet-face must have heard the rumour about a lover because he had made a point of stopping by her cubicle several times that week with a weak smile on his lips and his fingers brushing back his hair.

But the letter changed everything. Who had sent it?

Harriett thought through a list of people who knew her and who might have seen her receive the brooch and hide it at the bank.

There was the guy who'd given her the brooch of course. But why would he send a message like that? Of course he knew who she was and what he'd given her. Doh!

What about the people who'd noticed she was behaving differently? There was Bruno, Charles, Janie and Muriel and probably just about everyone at work, including Hatchet-face.

And what about the limousine driver? Perhaps she wasn't

paranoid after all. He had been nearby many times. Was his presence a threat?

The letter wasn't really anything at all, no request for money or for the brooch. Perhaps she should just ignore it. Maybe she should just file it away and carry on with her life. Her ordinary life and her secret diamond brooch rich life.

Perhaps the letter writer knew nothing about the brooch? Maybe he or she was just fishing for information after noticing how differently Harriett was behaving? Perhaps, from now on, Harriett should really start hinting strongly about the existence of a lover? If anyone at work had written this letter because he or she suspected Harriett was keeping a dramatic secret, a secret perhaps linked to something illegal, the idea of a lover might throw the person off, maybe by convincing him or her that Harriet was just having a fling?

With that thought in mind, Harriett jumped at the first opportunity to reply to Janie's frequent innuendos.

'Been meeting your lover again, Harriett?' Janie whispered.

Instead of telling Janie to get lost, as she usually did, Harriett raised her eyebrows and looked flustered.

'Got several on the go?' Muriel muttered. Harriett stifled a giggle, aware that Muriel would really love to have several on the go, even though she seemed to still love George.

'Stop it,' she hissed, looking around to see that no one was listening, 'He wants to remain anonymous.'

Muriel and Janie stopped typing and gasped.

Had she gone too far? Even Harriett could see that was a mad thing to say. But, no, they took this information as the truth instead of rumour, with eyes that lit up wildly, and glanced around.

Probably searching for the next person to tell this new information to. If it wasn't for the letter, Harriett would have laughed at the ridiculousness of this conversation.

But she managed to contain herself, and was just turning to walk away when Hatchet-face came up to her with one of his almost-smiles.

'Good afternoon, Harriett.' He caught her glance, his eyes an intense blue.

Harriett looked back to see Muriel in shock and then in understanding. It looked as if they had flushed out her secret lover all by themselves.

Harriett could see they were bursting to tell someone as soon as she and Hatchet-face walked away, Harriett to her booth and Hatchet-face to another diamond sorting room.

If everyone thinks Hatchet-face is my lover, maybe they'll leave me alone, was Harriett's reasoning. *After all, no one wants to cross Hatchet-face. On the other hand, will my reputation as a nice girl be ruined, because no one would ever, ever, ever go out with Hatchet-face, let alone have sex with him? Ugh!*

Harriett had a lot on her mind, but decided she couldn't worry about it all now. She had work to do and a serious manner to adopt in her efforts to avoid Hatchet-face's advances … not to mention a letter to ponder – a letter that suggested difficult times were ahead.

'Good afternoon, Mr Symonds,' she replied as she walked to her booth.

Chapter 6

That night when the buzzer for the apartment complex sounded, Harriett ran down the stairs quickly to answer it, not thinking about who it might be.

There was Hatchet-face, looking expectantly at her. He was holding a box of chocolates and a bottle of wine (Harriett noticed it was the cheap wine from the pub on the corner). She looked past him to see if anyone she knew was loitering outside and would see them together. No one seemed to be there.

What could Harriett do but invite him in? In fact, she grabbed the arm that was holding the bottle of wine and yanked him in the door, shutting it with a bang.

They stood there in the foyer looking wildly at each other and panting from the sudden exertion.

Then Harriett took charge. 'What are you doing here?' she yelped.

Hatchet-face looked aghast. 'Janie said …' he began, and then stopped as he looked at Harriett's face glaring at him.

Oh no! Janie had somehow told Hatchet-face that she, Harriett, was really interested.

They were still standing there looking at each other warily. How could they both get out of this situation gracefully? After all, he was still her boss.

At that exact moment the door buzzer sounded again and Harriett reached behind Hatchet-face and pulled the door open. As she did so, Hatchet-face moved forward to get out of her way and they bumped into each other, both of them reaching out their arms to steady themselves.

And there they were, in a not-to-be-forgotten embrace while Harriett's bank manager, Charles, stood on the doorstep with a letter in his hand.

His first look of shock was quickly replaced by a look of resentment and jealousy. He stuttered, 'Mr Symonds, Harriett – ah, Ms Langer, sorry, didn't mean to interrupt a tryst.'

A tryst! What was that?

'I'll just leave this letter I found on the floor of the bank with your address on it. Thought it might be important, and as I was walking by I …' He trailed off now, as his eyes looked from Harriett to Hatchet-face. Perhaps he could see that she hated Hatchet-face. Harriett didn't want to ruin her wonderful relationship with Charles.

'Mr Symonds, sorry,' Charles gulped. 'I didn't know you'd be here. I was going to catch you at the meeting tonight. In fact, I'm on my way there now. Perhaps we can walk together?'

A meeting! Harriett thought. *Hatchet-face was going to a meeting with Charles!*

What was he doing here then? And with wine and chocolates and a look on his face that intimated he was hoping for sex. Was he ready for a quickie before the meeting?

Harriett closed her eyes tight. Then opened them, grabbed the letter, the wine and the chocolates (*Never leave wine and chocolates behind*, she thought) and ran up the stairs to her flat, slamming the door behind her, leaving Hatchet-face and Charles to sort out whether they were going to a meeting or not.

The wine and chocolates Harriett plonked on the kitchen bench while she tore open the letter. Another one. This one more specific.

'I'll tell unless we split the profits fifty/fifty.'

Maybe Charles had seen who had dropped it? Harriett needed to talk to him.

Grabbing her purse, she rushed down the stairs and out the door, following the two of them, who were now on the next block. They turned the corner as Harriett rushed to catch up, and went into the basement of the Town Hall. Yes, they were going to a meeting. Harriett wondered what sort of meeting both Hatchet-face and Charles were likely to be involved in.

As she rushed down the hallway Harriett bumped into another man coming from the same room.

'What meeting is that?' She gestured to the room at the end of the hall.

'That's "How to Become a Successful Male Model",' he replied. 'But first I'm going to the other one in the adjacent room.'

'What's that one about?' Harriett asked, trailing him as he spoke and bemused about the meeting both Hatchet-face and Charles were going to. Would they give up their day jobs and become models?

'It's called, "Using your Diamonds as an Asset",' he said. 'Here it is.'

Now her ears pricked up at the title of this meeting. It was just what Harriett wanted. And this guy was very nice. He was lithe, tall and intelligent looking, and he gave her a great smile as he said, 'Why don't we go in together? We can share the ideas we're interested in and talk about them over coffee afterwards.'

Yippee, Harriett thought. *Another really nice man!*

They pushed the double doors leading into the room and chose seats at the back. The room was already full. This lecturer must be really great.

An organiser at the microphone blew into it, murmuring, 'One, two, testing, testing.' He then cleared his voice and a scream erupted from the mic, causing everyone to flinch.

'I'd like to introduce our speaker, Kevin Coates. He's an international expert on diamonds, and we're lucky to have him here with us tonight.'

Harriett looked up at the stage, half expecting one of the suits from her office to step forward. But her breath left her. She was stunned. The person walking towards the mic was the man she had glimpsed walking away after giving her the waterfall brooch. She was sure of it.

Later, in the coffee shop with her new friend, Tom Brown, Harriett was restless. She had tried to talk to Kevin Coates after the meeting, but he had been surrounded by people who wanted to talk assets and she couldn't get close, let alone bring up her questions.

Tom and Harriett sipped their coffees. Harriett liked him. He was interested in diamonds just as she was. Harriett liked to travel and so did he. They compared places they had been and told stories about travel difficulties and pleasures.

Harriett was fidgety, though. Hatchet-face and Charles were on the other side of the shop talking animatedly. As they hadn't been in her lecture room they were probably talking about the best ways to become a male model.

Harriett looked critically at them. Hatchet-face was not bad looking as long as he didn't open his mouth. The 5 o'clock shadow on his jaw was quite fetching. There had been a lot of frisson when they had clutched each other in the foyer of her flat. As for Charles, he had a square jaw and wonderful blue eyes too, and that could work in a photo shoot. He had certainly caused a flutter in her chest when he had looked at her on their date.

Harriett turned back to Tom. He was very nice too, with his brown hair curling up from his white collar while his hand toyed with his glass of red.

Harriett wondered what he thought of her. She was soon to find out.

'Let's go for a walk along the waterfront,' he said, looking intimately at her.

Harriett smiled. 'Sure,' she said. 'The night is ours.'

On the way, Tom told her about his background. He had been interested in diamonds since he was small.

'My mother, who is quite a celebrity, has a number of ancestry pieces in the shape of tiaras and necklaces. I've spent hours going through my mother's jewellery boxes. When I left university I wanted to start my own business. I thought diamonds might be the way to go.'

By 10 pm they'd walked and talked their way back to Harriett's door. Tom smiled at her and said, 'Want to come dancing with me on Saturday night?'

Harriett nodded brightly. It was a beginning.

A quick kiss and he was off down the street. Harriett watched him go. He had struck just the right chord with her; she felt she could get hooked with this one.

It was several years since Harriett had had a serious boyfriend. The one before Jake had lasted a year and she'd kicked him out because he wasn't committed to her ... and had chosen to demonstrate this by having affairs with other women.

Harriett ran up the steps to her apartment as if on air, collapsing on the lounge with the chocolates. Her dreamy state was interrupted by the strident sound of the phone.

She picked it up thinking it was sure to be Tom with a romantic goodnight.

But it was not.

'Get rid of him. He's no good. They are all no good,' came a voice.

'Who is this?' Harriett said angrily.

'It's Kevin Coates. Did you hear me?'

Kevin! The diamond expert who had put the waterfall brooch in her hand.

'If you mean Tom, he's nice. So are Charles and Bruno. Why did you give me the brooch?'

'I had to. It was the only thing I could think of. Anyway,' he said angrily, 'they're only befriending you to get to the brooch.'

'No, you've got it wrong. They're interested in me. And anyway, how does anyone know I have the brooch? And how do you know that I know Tom?'

'You're ...' There was a sharp breath at the end of the phone. 'Someone's coming. Got to go.'

The phone clicked.

Harriett yelled into the empty phone, 'You're what? Who? What's going on here?'

Harriett had a headache. Was Tom after her brooch? He could have taken the punt that she would be at the Town Hall to go to the Diamond Assets meeting and organise to accidently meet her there?

And what about the others?

There were no drugs in Harriett's medicine cupboard, so she ran down the steps and along the street to the chemist that was next door to the coffee shop. Bruno was just locking up and came over to her as she was heading to the headache section.

'Haven't seen you around much, Harriett,' he commented, actually leering at her.

'Been busy,' Harriett said as she picked up Aspros, Herron and Panadol. Surely one of these would help.

'Saw you with Kevin Coates a short while back. Didn't know you knew him.'

Her head jerked up at this. Was he the one sending the letters?

'Do you know him?' she asked. 'Where does he live?'

'I don't know, but yes, I used to work with him in a government business recouping art works and jewels that had been requisitioned by troops.'

'What a change – from art and jewels to coffee,' Harriett said, thinking that he might know about her brooch.

'Yes, I wish I'd made a better choice. Business is hard, lots of hours and not much profit.' He looked pensive and sighed. 'Well, see you next Wednesday for our date. Or maybe even sooner.'

Harriett paid for her pills and ruminated as she walked home. *Sooner? Bruno could be in on this. He seems to be telling me something in a roundabout way. Or will he just see me at the cafe?*

And her thoughts didn't stop with Bruno. Tom Brown could be someone to worry about. Certainly Kevin thought so. And now that Harriett thought about it, Charles could be too. It did seem to her a bit over the top that a bank manager would deliver a letter that had fallen on the floor in the bank rather than give it to an employee to deliver, or have it mailed to her. Besides he might not have found it on the floor at all, he might have written it. Still, he could simply have wanted to see her again.

Should she go with her gut feelings? Harriett had always done that before. She tossed her hair back angrily. She'd work it out.

In her flat she sat on the lounge and took a couple painkillers with the rest of the box of chocolates.

No one seemed to be who she thought he was. In fact, Janie and Muriel were fast becoming the two people Harriett liked most in the world.

She decided to walk down to the wharf to enjoy the brisk late autumn breeze off the water. It was several blocks away from her flat and the breeze might blow her headache away.

The wharf stretched out over the river, which had widened there to form a lake surrounded by fishing boats and pleasure cruisers. The vessels bobbed on the dark water, twisting and turning with the tide, the lake dark and foreboding, just like the night.

A shadow beside the river wall moved slightly. She squinted. Was that someone standing there? The shadow shifted again and a hoodie moved into the light. He was there. That man. Suddenly Harriett realised how dark and lonely the area was at this time of night. She needed to get away.

Hurrying down to the corner and to the lighted area, she stumbled a little before picking herself up and moving swiftly on. When she reached the light and felt safer, she looked back. There was no one there.

Perhaps this was a portent of things to come. She would think about it all tomorrow.

Chapter 7

At 8.30 pm on Saturday, Tom was at the front door at the bottom of the stairs. He had tight jeans and a thin jumper that showed off his six-pack, glorious arm muscles and an exceptionally tight derriere. Harriett was thrilled. She had chosen a snug black top with a short red skirt and black tights. Her hair was caught in a ponytail that swung from side to side as she skipped down the stairs in ankle-high leather boots.

Soon they were in the midst of the crush at the Town Hall, both of them showing off their dance steps.

Through the crowd Harriett spied a familiar face, the limousine driver. He was looking her way and as soon as he spotted her looking at him, he turned away.

She stopped dancing and nudged Tom, pointing, her hand suddenly becoming shaky.

'Do you see that man? Do you know him?'

Tom followed her finger. 'What man? There are at least ten men over there. Give me a clue.'

'He's thin and weedy, and rather scary.'

Tom laughed. 'I can't see anyone like that.'

Harriett looked over to where the man had been. He was not there.

'I guess I made a mistake,' she mumbled. 'I must be seeing things.'

At the start of a slow guitar piece, they moved together and danced as one, hips stuck to hips, arms entwined. Tom waltzed Harriett out the door and they hurried back to her flat. *Thank goodness I cleaned up the bedroom*, she thought.

Her memory of the previous Thursday with Charles and its thrilling climax consumed her and she turned halfway up the stairs to kiss Tom deeply. Tom caught on at once and picking her up carried her the rest of the way. At the door Harriett fumbled for her key. But Tom, in a mighty rush, grabbed it and unlocked the door himself.

Once inside they sank to the floor, rolling over and over, discarding boots, jeans, shirt and skirt as they went. With hardly any finesse, Tom was upon her while Harriett succumbed, curling her arms around his neck and melting into his shape.

Later, as they showered together, with slick soapy water cascading over Tom's bunched hard muscles, he muttered words of satisfaction and they agreed to catch up again the following week.

'I've so enjoyed this. Let's meet at the Town Hall. Perhaps another walk to the river and back to your flat?'

He glanced at Harriett hopefully, rubbing his hands up her arms and pulling her towards him for a last kiss.

After he'd left, Harriett tidied her flat and boiled water for a cup of tea. She sat with her hand on her chin and dreamed.

Tom could make an excellent husband. We'll have an attic studio in the centre of London, with exposed beams and the new industrial metal look. Original paintings from new artists will grace the walls with a safe behind one or two of them. I can see it all. Tom will go off to work as a diamond appraiser and occasionally bring home diamonds, just for me.

Our two children, Julius and Celia, will be wise to the London scene. They'll go to museums and gallery events every weekend unless they're off to Prague with us for a diamond lecture.

Yes, Tom will be a wonderful husband and father.

It all seems soooooo good.

*

There he was again. The limousine driver.

Harriett was in the perfume aisle at the chemist and noticed him lingering nearby. He seemed to be picking up boxes of aspirin and placing them back again.

He's not really buying anything. He's watching me, she thought.

A shiver of fear ran through her body. Rather than stay in the store she hurried outside, leaving her selected purchases behind.

At Bruno's she took a chance to look back. He was not in sight. *But of course he won't be visible if he's following me*, she thought. Nothing seemed innocent any more.

Harriett had seen the man around so many times she was becoming alarmed. Common sense told her that she saw most people who lived and worked locally about once a week, so why was this different?

She mulled this over. It was because of the focus of his gaze when she caught him nearby, and even the way he looked away quickly when he noticed her looking back. There was something frightening about him. Something evil in his stance and his face.

Something aimed at her.

As she walked towards the square, Harriett met Charles who stopped her with a 'Good morning, Harriett.' She blushed as she thought about the night they had enjoyed.

Slowing down to reply, he pinned her with his cool blue eyes and said, 'I have two tickets to a show next week. Would you care to accompany me?'

Harriett looked into those blue eyes and agreed.

By lunchtime, Harriett was back in the coffee shop ordering a latte. Bruno came over to her table with the steaming drink as well as a pastry on the side. She looked up, impressed with this largesse.

'Harriett,' he whispered sexily, 'I wondered if you would like to come to the movies again tomorrow night. That new Denzel Washington one is on at The Empire, Leicester Square.' He gave her an inviting look.

'Of course,' Harriett replied, thinking of the great evening she had had with Bruno the previous week. 'That sounds lovely. I'll meet you at 8 pm at the theatre.'

Bruno nodded and went off to serve others.

Wow! Three dates in a row, if she counted Tom Brown's invite as well. Harriett had never been so lucky. All she had to do now was wait for Hatchet-face to ask her out as well.

*

There is an old, old saying, 'Careful, or you might get what you wish for', and of course Harriett had been wishing all her life to be surrounded by men wanting her, loving her, entranced by her – and she was now being pursued by three men. This was bliss. There was Bruno Ginelli, Charles Foster and Tom Brown.

And so the halcyon days of Harriett's new femme fatale life began.

Her employers at the Thames Row Diamond Exchange didn't need to wonder about her pretend multitude of lovers now. She had them. They turned up at her door with flowers, chocolates, wine, tickets to shows, and invitations to dinner or picnics in the country. And even a lovely romp in the hay just by chance as well!

Harriett now spent more time on her phone diary than ever, making sure all her commitments didn't overlap.

Perhaps I'm in heaven, Harriett thought.

Hatchet-face was the only exception. He could now see that she had a plethora of dates and kept his distance. *Ha*, Harriett laughed to herself, *serves you right for believing Janie.*

She wondered which one of her new boyfriends she would like to zip off with on a trip to Paris, along with the waterfall brooch.

And then she'd be dead!

Goodness, where had that thought come from?

Of course it had been lurking at the back of her brain for days. Kevin Coates thought Tom Brown was after the brooch. Charles Foster might be sending her letters about the brooch, ready to blackmail her or do away with her. Bruno had also given her an obscure message that suggested he knew something. Even Hatchet-face was still hovering near her cubicle on a daily basis. Could he know something too?

How sobering.

And what about the limo driver? Owning that brooch could prove very dangerous.

*

A fortnight later Harriett was beginning to feel exhausted. Three lovers a week was just too much – along with a full-time job, her tango classes with George, and trying to find out more about Kevin Coates and the strange man who was following her.

She found herself starting to make small mistakes in her decisions about the size, quality and suitability of the diamonds she was handling. She needed a break from men or at least lusty men who turned her on.

She wanted her bedroom to herself. To change into her pyjamas when she came home from work, eat a jam sandwich for tea instead of a three-course meal, sit up in bed under the doona and watch *Downton Abbey* or read a John Grisham novel.

She wanted to be alone.

Harriett mused about which celebrity had said this in the 1940s. She'd always thought that was a silly comment, but now she understood completely.

Hatchet-face had come by her booth a number of times. As usual he had that almost-smile on his face, his gaze searching hers while he pushed his hair back from his forehead. Harriett didn't like it. Why hadn't he sacked her? Other people had been fired for making fewer mistakes.

Her private life was also getting complex.

Keeping Charles, Tom and Bruno from seeing each other at her flat was one thing. Remembering who she was with in the throes of lust and saying the right name was another. Soon she was calling everyone darling just to be on the safe side.

Putting up with phone calls from Kevin Coates was the last straw.

The brooch was now a jinx, a bad luck thing. She didn't want it.

*

One morning, Harriett woke to a beam of thin winter sun on her bed. She stretched and looked at the wardrobe, considering what to wear.

The wardrobe door was slightly ajar and several of the drawers gaped open with clothes bulging out of them.

She frowned. Had she left them that way? It wasn't like her to be so untidy even though life had been hurried lately.

She scanned the room. The top of the chest of drawers under the window was different too. The photos, perfume and jewellery had been moved slightly to one side as if someone had not put them back properly. The third drawer down which always stuck, was open. Someone had opened it and hadn't been able to close it again.

Harriett panicked. Her heart thumped in her chest and she took shallow, grating breaths.

Had someone been in her room when she was asleep or while she was out the day before? Fear of strangers in her home, and in her bedroom in particular, swamped her mind.

She lay there looking up at the ceiling, imagining someone standing there next to her bed, looking down at her while she slept, probably holding a gun ready to shoot if her eyes opened, or to slit her throat with a knife or even strangle her with a stocking.

He'd have moved to the wardrobe and opened the door to rifle through her drawers, especially her underwear drawer – the sexual deviant! Then around to the other side of the bed, once again looking down on her, opening her chest of drawers and finding one drawer stuck, and changing everything around just so she'd know he'd been there, and then, on silent sneakers, leaving.

She sat beside the bed clutching her doona, shaking and feeling vulnerable.

Someone wanted the brooch and knew she had it.

She leant over to pick up the phone on her dressing table and called the police.

*

The two constables were huge. Wearing shiny black boots and looking incredibly bulky due to the weapons they were carrying, the men seemed to take up all the space in her lounge room.

'Show us where it happened?' one said.

Harriett stepped into the bedroom and pointed. 'He opened the wardrobe door, see?'

The constables looked at the door slightly ajar. Harriett could read their expression, which seemed to say, 'Is this it? This is all you've got?'

She turned to the chest of drawers. 'He opened this drawer and couldn't close it, and he moved things around on the top.' Harriett moved the photo frame a few inches back to the original position.

Both constables sighed. Was this really a crime or just a person who forgot how she left things?

'That jewellery was taken out of the box there, too.'

The constables perked up at this. Here was a possible jewellery crime. 'Is anything missing?'

'No,' Harriett said. 'Nothing is missing.'

Dutifully, the constables tested for fingerprints, took photos and checked all the windows and doors.

'Best get new locks and an alarm,' they said as they left.

Harriett phoned the rental agency, arranging for new bolts for her door, and then sat down to wait.

She needed to find Kevin Coates and give the brooch back to him.

At Bruno's cafe, waiting for the bank to open, she warmed her hands on the coffee cup. Suddenly anxiety attacked her and coffee splashed over the rim, dribbling down the sides of the cup, which clattered when she returned it to the saucer. She pulled a newspaper towards her and began to read. On page two was a photo of Kevin Coates with the following article:

> Kevin Coates, local diamond expert
> was taken to hospital last week with
> a fractured jaw and a number of
> abrasions to his body. He told police
> that several men burst into his home
> and attacked him. Coates is to be
> released from hospital this morning.

Bruno came over with a coffee pot. 'Have you read this about Kevin Coates?' He tapped his finger on the paper.

'Why would they do that?' Harriett looked up.

'He's into diamonds in a big way. Perhaps they were looking for something he had.' Bruno topped up her cup and moved away.

Could it be something to do with the brooch? She thought back to when it had been given to her. It seemed this had happened around the same time as she'd begun to suspect she was being followed.

He must have told them that she had it and that's why someone had been in her flat.

She had to get rid of the brooch that very day.

Chapter 8

I need to go to the cops, Harriett told herself. *I'm in danger.*

She collected the brooch from the bank safety deposit box and walked past the Town Hall to the police station.

'The men who accosted Kevin Coates came into my flat but couldn't find anything. They'll be back – and maybe they'll hurt me to find out where it is.'

'It's certainly beautiful.' The constable moved the brooch about to capture the glitter of the diamonds. 'And it's worth about three million pounds, you say?'

Harriett watched the constable write his report and place the brooch into a safety pouch.

'When you called us to your home the other day about a burglar, why didn't you tell us you had this brooch? That would have been a reason to worry.'

'I … I don't know. I guess I was scared.'

He examined the report from the other constables. 'You say you think someone has been in your flat looking for it?'

'Yes, little things were moved. You wouldn't know it if you didn't live there. I also have these letters that someone sent me.'

The constable clipped the letters to the report.

'Forensics won't be able to do anything with these. Why didn't you hand the brooch in immediately?' He looked suspiciously at her.

Harriett blushed. 'I wanted to keep it. It seemed no one wanted it. So I put it in the bank.'

There was silence.

Harriett looked at the constable. She shrugged and sighed. 'I knew it wasn't the right thing to do.'

'Too right it wasn't. It's almost theft.'

'I'm worried that the people who broke into the flat will not realise I don't have it now. They may come after me.'

'Well, now. That's what happens when you do the wrong thing. We will be announcing it on the police bulletin tomorrow and sending a copy to the diamond trade to find the owner.'

'What if they don't see these notices?'

'You're welcome to talk to the press', the constable replied. 'That's if you want to.'

Harriett decided to do just that and contacted the local papers. Reporters went to her flat, took photos, interviewed her and left.

The article would be in the paper the next day.

She was free. Free from danger. Unless the criminals didn't see the article. Now she could also prove that her lovers really liked her and wanted her. She decided to stagger her dates with each man so she had time for herself.

It wasn't long before Harriett noticed a difference.

The days following were difficult. She felt as if she was sometimes normal Harriett and sometimes scared Harriett.

Normal Harriett enjoyed work and went out at night with her lovers. There were times when she forgot her troubles.

Scared Harriett came to the fore at night. Sometimes she was fearful of opening the door to her home to discover it had been vandalised. Always she turned on every light and searched all the hidey-holes in the flat. When it was time for bed and she had turned off all the lights except the bedside lamp, she found she could not sleep. More than two hours later she realised the lamp's light was too bright and was keeping her awake, but when it was turned off, she was kept awake by the dark.

Keeping her eyes open to try and penetrate the dark was taxing. She often ended up falling asleep in the early hours of the morning and waking up late for work. Her eyes looked sore, with threads of red radiating out to their edges.

The normal Harriett loved being with Tom, Bruno or Charles and enjoyed the intimacy.

But the scared Harriett began to see that she was inviting her lovers home for intimacy but also because she couldn't stand to be alone or to come home to an empty flat after a night out.

Soon her paranoia started to affect her relationships.

If Tom said, 'I like your necklace,' she saw it as a way for him to find out about the brooch.

If Bruno said, 'My cafe needs an injection of money at the moment,' she immediately thought he was trying to get the proceeds of the brooch.

If Charles said, 'Where do you keep your valuables, Harriett?' it seemed like a way to discover the brooch.

Everything was spoilt.

A few days later in the coffee shop, Bruno sent a barista over with her order and a message that he had to work late and couldn't meet her at the movies at present. As Harriett went into the bank to make a deposit, Charles scuttled away so he would not have to say good morning to her. Tom had texted to say he couldn't meet her and would ring sometime. At work, though, Hatchet-face was just his usual slimy, suspicious self. At least someone was the same.

Although he did look different.

He had slicked his hair back with a quiff at the front. Harriett could imagine him becoming a model. He had that sultry look that was so 'in' today and could walk well with a bit of a swagger, even if it was only to discover what she was doing.

Harriett had been abandoned by all three suitors in one day. They were not interested in her, the femme fatale, only the diamonds.

Everyone had seen the paper.

'What an amazing find, Harriett!'

'Do you know who owns it?'

'Didn't you want to keep it?'

'I saw your photo in the paper.' Hatchet-face stopped to speak to her as she walked through the sorting room. 'What was that about?'

Harriett told him about finding the brooch but not about having it in her booth.

'A brooch worth three million pounds, Harriett. Easy come, easy go with you, is it?'

'It wasn't like that at all, Mr Symonds.' Harriett was flustered. 'I thought I was in danger.'

Hatchet-face held up his hands. 'Okay, okay! Just a joke! You did the right thing. Diamond thieves are some of the most villainous in the world.'

'I saw that guy with the cigarillo and the limousine driver the other day. They definitely looked like criminals.'

'They probably are, Harriett. Best to keep away from them. Did you see who gave it to you?'

'No. I thought it was one of the suits at first and then that diamond expert, Kevin Coates.'

'Good grief, Harriett. He was beaten up recently, wasn't he? Was that about the brooch, do you think?'

Harriett just looked dejected.

'Pity it wasn't yours, though.' He grinned, his blue eyes crinkling wickedly.

Harriett blushed. If only he knew.

*

That night Harriett sat in her flat, drinking cheap wine and contemplating a lonely, single non-life, with no brooch.

The buzzer sounded downstairs. It could have been anyone for any of the flats, but she still ran down the stairs hoping that one suitor was left.

It was Hatchet-face.

'Ah, Harriett.' He looked shyly down at the ground. Then taking a breath, he looked up at Harriett who was tapping her foot in exasperation.

'I know that you saw Charles and me at the modelling workshop.'

Harriett nodded.

'Well, the whole series of workshops are nearly finished and the best one of us will be given a job as a model. I want it. It's an audience participation thing, so votes will come from the judging panel as well as the audience. I was hoping you might come and vote for me.'

'But,' Harriett said, 'I've never seen you model anything.'

You might be terrible, she thought. But quickly following that thought she had another. *Hatchet-face will owe me if I do it and that might come in handy at work one day*.

'Of course I will,' she replied, registering his disappointment at her pause. He brightened up at this, thanked her and turned away for home, after telling her that the final would be held in January, on a Wednesday evening.

'I know it is only November but it's always safe to get in early.'

Throughout the next weeks, Hatchet-face met Harriett at the electronic gates with a faint smile each morning and ushered her out each afternoon. Sometimes during the day, he would come by her cubicle for a chat, thrusting his fingers through his wayward hair. By now Harriett was well and truly over this mannerism he seemed to do compulsively. But she was beginning to like him. He wasn't so bad when he talked about things other than security and didn't fiddle with his hair.

Muriel was still keeping a close watch on what Harriett was doing but Janie seemed to be ignoring her. Harriett wondered if any of her previous boyfriends had anything to do with that and her suspicions were confirmed when she saw Charles waiting for Janie at the end of the day one Tuesday. He gave Harriett an embarrassed look. Another time she saw Bruno hovering over Janie with coffee and pastries at lunchtime.

Everyone and everything was more enticing than romps in the hay with her.

Chapter 9

On a whim, Harriett decided to visit Oxford to see a Shakespearean play. It would keep her mind off her lack of male admirers, the loss of the brooch and any criminals that might still be following her. Although she hadn't noticed the limo driver since she'd handed in the brooch to the police.

Her car, which she hardly drove in Thames Row, needed the drive to keep it ticking over.

On reaching the roundabout to Thames Row and turning right, she noticed a sporty car that was almost across the middle line and going fast, too fast.

As the car swept forward Harriett pressed her horn, sharp and loud. The car swerved and carried on while Harriett lifted her two fingers in the universal 'up yours' salute.

At the same moment her brain registered that it was Mr Symonds in the other car.

She groaned. It had to be him of course. Just her luck, although maybe he hadn't seen who was driving.

The next morning, she knew better. Harriett moved through the electric gates and into the sorting room. Mr Symonds stood in her path.

'Good morning, Harriett. Did you have a nice drive yesterday?'

Harriett stiffened and then, remembering the near collision, became angry. 'You swerved almost over the centre line, Mr Symonds. You could have caused an accident.'

This was the most Harriett had ever said to Neville and although it was said in an angry manner, he was pleased she had spoken to him. He decided to keep the flow of conversation going.

'I was well within my side of the road, Harriett. You were too close to the middle. Had you been drinking?'

'I don't drink,' Harriett retorted. Then, thinking that statement wasn't entirely true, added, 'Not when I'm driving, anyway. I was not over the line, you were. So once again, Mr Symonds, *up yours!*' She flipped him a two-fingered gesture and flounced off to her booth, groaning at her audacity and the possibility that it would get her sacked.

Neville Symonds just walked away with a smile.

The next morning, Hatchet-face sidled up to Harriett again.

'Did you know that in days of old when the English and French fought each other with bows and arrows, the English used the two-fingered gesture to say "up yours" to the French? They were really saying, "We are the better archers as we still have our two fingers, rather than having had them bitten off by the bow strings as they were released".'

Harriett stood with her mouth open. Was Hatchet-face giving her a lecture on English history? How amazing. Or was he flirting? More amazing still.

She didn't know which was the most disturbing.

A tradition seemed to be establishing itself, if you could call 'twice' a tradition. When Harriett passed Hatchet-face the next morning, she murmured as she went by, 'Got any fingers left?'

Hatchet-face turned slightly as he moved away in the opposite direction, 'Yes Harriett, two,' and held up two fingers in the gesture.

It wasn't long before the tradition escalated. Every time they passed each other, and that was at least twice a day if not more, one of their hands made the appropriate gesture. Sometimes it was made down by their side; sometimes it was as they brushed their hair back from their faces; sometimes it was when they crossed their arms. No matter what the action, the gesture was always visible peeping out from their arms.

If Hatchet-face was busy with meetings on the first floor, she began to realise that she missed this rather flirty interaction. She was getting used to his sense of humour and fun.

*

It was getting close to Christmas. The air was chilly. Thick jumpers, boots and hats had been rescued from the back of the wardrobe. Muriel, Janie and even Harriett were full of Christmas cheer.

'I love everything about Christmas,' Muriel said. 'The tree, the lights, the carols, the presents – everything.'

'I do, too,' Janie said. 'I've already made my Christmas cake and puddings.'

'So what about our work party?' They had taken on the job of organising something for the company. 'Should we have a theme or a dress-up event?'

'I could dress up as Jamie Oliver,' Janie enthused.

'You mean the TV chef? He's a he. Is that who you want to be?'

'I like his cooking,' Janie said petulantly.

Harriett looked at both of them in amazement. 'Well, it's only just a work Christmas party. It doesn't take much figuring out. Let's choose a pub and ask them to cater for it.' Harriett stood up. 'Whatever you like to do, I'll help. But I need to go. I'm tired. See you tomorrow.'

Scrabbling around in her wardrobe at home she found the box she wanted on the top shelf at the back. In it were her photo albums.

Sitting cosily on the lounge she flicked through them, starting with herself as a baby at Christmas time. What a wonderful life I've had. A loving mum and dad, nice school friends, good grades and a good job.

It was just that she was restless. It would have been nice to have someone to share things with. Someone to love and be loved in return.

The only thing she had to look forward to was her weekly tango class. Although this term was proving to be a challenge, as George wasn't the best partner.

She picked up the remote and clicked on the tango DVD she'd been given by her teacher. The choreography was magnificent, the dancers wonderful.

She was filled with an envy she didn't know she had. She

sighed. How could she ever think she could be as good as these dancers? She was just a suburban worker who went to the local tango classes.

I want something more, she thought. *Something creative and fulfilling. Sitting in a sorting booth isn't quite enough anymore.*

*

Muriel and Janie continued talking as they hurried home. The cold of winter was now beginning to seep into their bones.

Janie said, 'I like the idea of a theme. What about making it diamonds? That would be appropriate for a diamond company event.'

'That's a great idea. I like it. What about a bar with cocktails?'

Muriel nodded in agreement.

'I wish George was interested in this. He's only keen on his tango dancing with Harriett.' Muriel turned to Janie and made an annoyed face, her lips puckering and her eyes crossing.

'Are you going to leave him at last?' Janie asked. She had heard Muriel moaning about George and his shortcomings for the past month or two.

'I might,' said Muriel. 'I met a nice man at the hall while I was waiting for you.'

'Who is he?' Janie was all ears.

'His name's Tom and he seems to be in a modelling class. He's very handsome. I peeped in the class the other day and guess who else was there?'

'Who?'

'Hatchet-face. He was in the class too. I nearly fell over when I saw him. I quickly closed the door so he wouldn't see me.'

'What a strange thing for him to do.' Janie was excited. She couldn't wait to share the news with the secretarial pool.

'How come you didn't tell me before, Muriel?'

Muriel shrugged. 'I guess I was so rapt in thoughts of Tom that I forgot.' She sighed. 'Still, he hasn't asked me out on a date yet, even though I've been hanging around the hall around the time he always comes along.'

Janie said thoughtfully, 'I think I saw him with Harriett once.' She looked at Muriel's pinched face and added, 'But that was a long time ago.'

Muriel brightened. 'I hope not, because I'm really keen. I might ask him out myself next week if he doesn't get around to it.'

'Good idea,' Janie said. 'If we always leave it to the blokes to ask for a date we'd never get anywhere.'

*

Harriett arrived home to see a parcel on the doorstep of the block of flats.

Picking it up, she yelled up the stairs. 'Parcel for someone here. Anyone expecting something?'

A neighbour came to his door. 'Not mine. Is there a name on it?'

Harriett turned the parcel around. 'No, nothing.'

'Well, open it and see what it is.' The neighbour came down the stairs, curious to see what it was.

Harriett tore off the wrapping and gazed fearfully at what was inside. There was a doll. The sweet little lips had been covered with bright red lipstick that leached onto the pink cheeks. A large garish plastic brooch had been pinned to the dress.

It was a warning, Harriett knew. In the doll's hand was a note. Harriett picked it up and opened it. 'Get the brooch back,' it said.

'What's that all about?' The neighbour looked at Harriett's white face.

'I don't know,' Harriett whispered. She dropped the doll in the bin near the door and hurried upstairs, curling up on the lounge in fear.

Chapter 10

Diamonds was the theme, and the pub, 'The Frightened Deer', was keen to help.

Janie climbed the stairs to the room in the pub hired by the diamond exchange company. It was away from the regular drinkers. She walked to the special corner allocated to the cocktail bar.

She had surrounded it with curtains so they could be opened at the right time.

'Come and see,' Janie grabbed Harriett's arm. 'It looks fab. You know, we'll be behind the bar from now until the party opens at 6 pm, don't you?'

Harriett had tried to put the doll out of her mind all week. The police had been no help, even after she'd recovered it from the bin and presented it to them.

'There are no fingerprints on it and no other clues. I suggest you ignore it as we have the brooch now,' a constable explained.

Harriett tried to look interested in Janie.

'Yes,' Harriett moaned. 'Two more hours.'

'There's a lot to do,' Janie announced. 'Muriel should be here by now too.'

At that moment Muriel appeared. 'I've made bar aprons for us. Look.' She held up three black bar aprons with the words: 'Diamonds are Forever', 'Diamonds are a Girl's Best Friend', and 'Diamonds mean Love'.

'Perfect,' Janie said, putting an apron on and moving behind the bar.

She took charge. 'Right. We have to put up the signs advertising our cocktails and make a few ready for the mob.'

An hour later the bar looked spectacular with comic signs, cocktails, and a scattering of fake diamonds on the bar itself.

'What are we going to do for the next hour?' Harriett sighed.

'Let's just test these cocktails to see if they are as good as they look,' Muriel said.

'Good idea,' Janie said. Sometimes these fancy internet drinks don't work as well as you think.

Harriett handed them the 'Dream Diamond' cocktail made with vermouth, cranberry juice and lemonade.

'Hmm, very nice, but it needs more vermouth to give it a kick.' They tried another one with extra vermouth.

'Great,' Janie said. 'Now let's try "Diamond Ginger" with vodka, limes and ginger beer. I think we've been a bit cautious with our liquor. Let's make them double strength.'

According to Muriel there were just four more to try: 'Ring of Fire', 'Grand Carat Diamond', 'Death by Diamonds' and 'Million Dollar Diamond Baby'.

It wasn't long before Muriel was telling jokes and Janie was confessing to them about her latest love.

'You know I have a new boyfriend called Charles and he's oh, so handsome.'

'Me, too,' said Muriel. 'Tom is a great dancer and a businessman. I'm leaving George at last. I just have to find the right time to tell him. Then it's back to the flat with you, Janie.'

Janie looked crushed. 'I wish you wouldn't. I've got Charles now and I might want to bring him home. I don't want to find a flatmate there.'

'Too bad Janie. It's my flat and I need it too. I might have Tom with me. You can find something new.'

'What a friend you are.' Janie turned, slapped her hand on the bar, fake diamonds bouncing and the nearest drink splashing onto Muriel's face and dress.

'Shit, shit, shit, my new dress. You've ruined it. I'm going home.' Muriel flounced off, leaving Harriett with Janie, who was suddenly sobering up.

Wrapping her head in her arms on the bar, Janie groaned. 'Now our bar is ruined.'

Harriett, who didn't normally drink this much, was feeling very sociable, but slightly dizzy every time she moved her head. Janie was more concerned about the bar than Muriel's feelings or dress.

It was 6 pm. They could hear people arriving, shedding their coats, scarves and hats, and chatting about the holidays to come.

'Time to open up,' Janie slurred.

Harriett and Janie grabbed the curtains and swished them aside with a clattering of curtain rings.

'Ta da!' they shouted.

Everyone turned at the sound of their voices and began to laugh and shout out encouraging words, as they lined up for a cocktail, discussing merrily which drink they would have and why.

'This is so good,' Janie exclaimed, perking up now that the bar seemed to be a success. 'It has set the mood for the night to come.'

Neville noticed Harriett immediately. She was still sitting, smiling inanely behind the bar with her 'Diamonds are a Girl's Best Friend' apron.

He strode over. He was feeling good. The company was closed for the Christmas and New Year holidays. Six days with no work.

'Hello, Harriett.'

Harriett's eyes tried to focus. There were two Hatchet-faces in front of her. She blinked until there was only one.

'Hello, Hatch, ah, Mr Symonds.' She gave him a brilliant smile which was most encouraging for Neville.

He took her arm firmly. 'Like to dance?' He nodded to the band area, where a few brave souls were hopping and bopping already. He guided her out from behind the bar and onto the dance floor.

Harriett held on tightly to Neville and was surprised when he began to dance smoothly.

'I didn't think you'd be able to dance so well,' she said, glancing up at him. Neville just raised his eyebrows and did a twirl. Harriett, who was not expecting this, staggered and almost fell. Looking very embarrassed, she tried to pull herself up straight and dance properly. Her serious, intent look made Neville smile.

He guided her over to the balcony, which ran the length of the pub.

Once out in the fresh, chilly air, Harriett stood against the rail. She watched the moon's silvery path cross the grassy area, the car park and the stand of oak trees beyond.

'I think I'm a bit tipsy.' She turned to find herself looking at Neville's shirt front as he had moved directly behind her.

'Look at the moon,' she waved her hand vaguely in the air.

Neville pulled her closer. 'Hmm, nice,' he said with a double meaning intended.

He slid his hand down and cupped her bottom. Harriett snuggled into him. 'Cosy,' she thought. She felt her body begin to tingle and warm up with the feel of his arms around her.

Neville moved one hand up to the back of her head, and angled her towards his kiss. Softly he touched her lips with his, then licked her lips gently. As soon as he felt Harriett press her lips to his, he deepened his kiss, his tongue exploring her mouth tenderly.

Harriett was entranced. He was warm and strong. His kiss was firm and loving. She moved closer and felt the frisson she had felt before with him. She had been waiting for this closeness for some time. When all her lovers had disappeared she had been bereft. Now here, unexpectedly, was that feeling and it was with Hatchet-face.

He bent his head and began to give her little kisses on her neck, on her ear and finally on her lips. A soft kiss, a gentle kiss, and then as passion overtook him a hard meeting of mouths and tongues until they both ran out of air.

She leaned back and opened her eyes. He was handsome. She

hadn't realised it before. She let her hand caress his cheek. She hadn't realised his kisses would be so good and he was her boss.

Boss!

She jerked back in alarm. This was her boss kissing her, a lowly employee. She was just a cliché. How could she have done this?

She tore out of his embrace and ran back inside and straight to the ladies' room.

Neville stepped back. What had he done wrong? He watched Harriett run into the pub as if he were poison.

Janie had been on the lookout for Harriett, and followed her. There was Harriett sitting on a closed toilet lid, curled over her knees, sobbing. Janie squatted down next to Harriett, hands on her arms. 'What is it? What's wrong?'

'I've been such a fool, Janie. I was kissing the boss. What a cliché. The boss takes me out on the verandah and kisses me, a nobody, an employee. I'm so ashamed, even if his kisses were wonderful. I'm just so silly.' Her sobs became louder and more erratic.

'No, you're not silly. You've just had a bit too much to drink. Too many cocktails, I think, that's all. He's to blame. He could probably see you had been drinking and still took you outside. Forget him.'

'I can't. It was so nice. He'll just think he's got me where he wants me. Wherever that is.' She wailed.

'At least you don't have to see him for six days. By the time you go back to work he might have forgotten it. And you can just be a diamond sorter as usual and he can just be Hatchet-face again.'

Harriett sniffled and nodded. She could do this.

Janie took out her phone and texted George.

'Muriel mightn't want him but I do. George is going to take you home.' They hurried down the stairs onto the footpath where George had just pulled up in his car. Janie helped Harriett into the back seat where she collapsed, checking first that she had her key with her.

Once inside her flat and alone, Harriett sank down onto the bed, pulling the doona up over her, curling into a ball and sobbing.

He was Hatchet-face.

He was her boss.

She liked him, even loved him.

He was a louse.

*

Harriett wasn't interested in anything during the six-day holiday.

If the truth be told, she was frightened to go out. The strange man might be out there, or even more frightening parcels.

Besides, she had nothing to go out for.

Christmas Day was very lonely as she had rejected several requests from friends to join them for Christmas lunch.

'Come out with us,' Janie, who had made up with Muriel, pleaded. 'Especially on New Year's Eve.' But Harriett had refused.

On Christmas morning she sat at home, looking at the small tree she had decorated the previous week. There were no presents under the tree. She had no one to give anything to, and although she had bought herself new soft leather boots for winter, she didn't even open the festive bag they came in.

After a quick email wishing a 'Happy Christmas' to Betty, the tango teacher, George, her dance partner, Janie, and Muriel, she cuddled up on her lounge, in the pyjamas she had been too sad to change out of, and sipped a cup of hot chocolate.

Her thoughts kept coming back to Hatchet-face and his kiss.

She realised she had begun to warm to him after the 'up yours' incident and its subsequent interactions. She had discovered he had a wry sense of humour and that he had a softer side than the one he showed normally at work.

And there was this frisson she always felt when near him. Her body didn't lie. She'd never felt that same way with any of her other boyfriends, even though she had enjoyed their company and lovemaking. It had really meant nothing more than her own body and mind being excited that she had men interested in her.

This feeling was different. Her heart felt heavy and sad.

It must be love, she thought.

I'm in love with my boss! A man who might just want a fling with an employee. A man I've christened Hatchet-face. A man I've discovered as personable, serious but fun loving, warm and loving, does his job properly. A man who makes my heart pound and can kiss like ... like ... a man who loves me.

She sat up in wonderment, and then slumped back down in despair.

But he's gone.

Either I've signalled I've rejected him by running away, or I've assumed, because he's my boss, that he's insincere without giving him a chance to show me otherwise.

The day was ruined and so was the rest of the week.

New Year's Eve was just like Christmas Day – quiet and lonely.

However, there came a time by that afternoon when Harriett began to pick herself up.

She couldn't be like this forever. It was a new year and she needed to make some resolutions she could stick to. First, there was her job. She was a professional, she could do it well. Second, she would go back to tango lessons with a new energy and plan for the championships next summer. Third, she would not pine for Hatchet-face or anyone else. She would rely on herself.

By the next Monday, the first day back to work, she was ready to go. She would be cool and distant when she met Hatchet-face. She would show him she was in charge of herself.

Chapter 11

As Harriett walked through the doors of the diamond exchange, she immediately noticed Hatchet-face with his clipboard. She lifted her chin and walked towards him with a cool, calm, professional look. Her manner suggested that if he remembered the incident at all, it was just a party romance, a Christmas mistake.

It seemed to work. He hardly came near her at all, and when he found himself near her, he just nodded and said, 'Ms Langer'.

Until the next week, when others were talking about the modelling competition, she had forgotten that she had promised to attend and vote for him. Could she back out? *No*, she thought, *I won't be that shallow. Besides, he might see that as an indication that I was troubled about his kiss.*

The Wednesday of the competition arrived and Harriett could see that Hatchet-face was on tenterhooks.

He had obviously had his hair cut and styled, his skin glowed and every now and then he would do a turn using some swift and fancy footwork that might be needed in the show.

By 7 pm she was seated in the main room of the Town Hall in the front row. The lecturer gave a preamble that went on for much too long and then invited all the participants to come on stage one at a time, to model a variety of clothes and then pose for photo shots.

Harriett looked at her voting form. She was just about to fill in Hatchet-face's name straight away, when she realised she had forgotten his first name. She couldn't remember it at all. She had been calling him Hatchet-face or Mr Symonds for so long.

'Now,' said the compere. 'There are nine models. Each is

clothed in casual dress, formal wear and finally a wedding suit.'

Harriett sat entranced. All of them were gorgeous. She could have dated any one of them. And a couple of them she had!

Charles was first and did well. Then, out of the blue, Tom appeared as one of the contestants. Harriett went into a bit of a dreamy state remembering the wonderful time she had had with both of them. It wasn't until the ninth contestant had strutted his stuff that she found she had missed Hatchet-face's turn.

What was his first name and what number was he? She flipped the flyer over. Luckily, all the contestant's faces were on the back with their names and numbers. At last she could write down Neville Symonds. That done she could hand in the flyer with her vote to the official collecting them.

The compere gave another long speech. Then the official came up to the mic to announce the winners.

He cleared his throat. 'This is the tenth year we have run this event in the boroughs surrounding London to give everyone the opportunity to try for the job. Each time we have found a new and exciting model. This, though, is the first time there has been a tie for the winner. In this case we will be awarding two opportunities for work as a model.'

And the winners are: Charles Foster and Tom Brown.

Claps and whoops of happiness mingled with the groans of disappointment that followed. Harriett was sorry for Hatchet-face. *He was very good*, she thought, *even though I didn't see much of his section, but obviously he didn't have the audience following*. She could see now that Muriel, Janie, George and a clutch of coffee drinkers and bank tellers had boosted the votes for Charles and Tom.

Hatchet-face came over to Harriett. 'Thanks for coming and voting for me, Harriett,' he said in a downbeat tone.

Harriett tried to look casual about his disappointment. Somehow though, she seemed to radiate an attitude of sternness.

He looked down to hide his sadness, and Harriett was suddenly overcome by unhappiness for him.

'You know, the two winners had lots of coffee shop and business people to help them win.' She didn't mention that none of the diamond exchange people would have voted for him, even if they had come to the event.

By Thursday Hatchet-face seemed to be over his disappointment.

There was quite a buzz in the sorting room as the company was about to host Marilyn Monroe's famous diamond and ruby ring, said to have been given to her by Jack Kennedy. The exquisite setting, with rubies surrounding a perfect solid diamond as the centrepiece, would be on display in the showroom and was worth an estimated ten million pounds.

It was also known that Hatchet-face had handed in his resignation the day before. What a shock! Harriett decided he wasn't over his disappointment at not winning the modelling contest after all.

Most of her colleagues in the sorting room and the secretarial pool were looking at Harriett to see what she thought about this, as they still believed Hatchet-face was one of her lovers.

Several people sidled up to her.

'What do you think of Hatchet-face leaving after all these years?' Harriett just made a face.

'You know he didn't win the modelling competition so he probably doesn't have a job to go to.'

'I wonder what he'll do now?'

Harriett tried to look nonchalant and uncaring, although she too was shocked that he would leave after all these years.

*

Harriett sat on a seat in the park near the river embankment. The trees' branches wafted across the area, changing the shadows on the ground and creating light and shady shapes.

She looked out at the Thames sluggishly passing by, sometimes oily and dark, sometimes sparkling silver.

Where was she going with her life?

Tom, Bruno and Charles were no longer her lovers. She didn't have any lasting friends in the sorting room. They kept changing, moving on. Hatchet-face was now not showing any interest in her after his kiss at the Christmas event and had decided to leave.

The brooch was gone but the criminals she thought were following her were probably still a threat of some sort, which could not be fixed by the police. Her finance account was low because of the purchases she made when she thought she could use the brooch as an asset.

She still had enough though to leave the diamond exchange and go somewhere. But where? Her first thought was Argentina. Her dad had always talked a lot about his home town and shown her photos. She had started learning tango dancing because of him. She loved it.

Was it within her budget? Maybe she only had enough cash to go to York. This was where her mother came from and it was not far away Also, there would be no language difficulties. She could easily get a job in a jewellery store in York or even a nearby diamond factory.

That night Harriett came to her decision. Twelve years at one job, even though she had loved it up until a short while ago, was not very adventurous. Charles and Tom had taken a leap to change their careers. Even Hatchet-face was taking a chance. She would use the last of her money to try it. It was her time to go as well.

The next day Harriett resigned too.

The executives showed no emotion when she handed in her letter of resignation. The sorters and secretaries, though, were most intrigued. Muriel whispered to her what everyone was thinking.

'Are you going off with Hatchet-face?'

Harriett shook her head.

His leaving party was going to be a bigger affair than hers. It was down at the pub at night so that even the 'suits' could attend.

Harriett's was just going to be a lunch at the coffee shop with a few of her close colleagues.

Nothing special.

Chapter 12

Neville was sick.

Sick of people calling him names behind his back because of his job. Sick of being in the same job and going nowhere. Sick of never really attracting and holding Harriett's interest.

Once he had wanted to be a famous designer of diamond jewellery. The diploma course had led to a small business in a cheap studio to fashion beautiful pieces. He had also made fakes for the very rich who mostly kept their real jewels in the bank and wore their fakes to events. He had been so good at it that even the owners of the real jewels could not see the difference. In time he had sold a few of his best and most creative pieces, but the cost of then procuring diamonds to make the next piece became too expensive. He needed a job just to eat and pay rent. So he had joined the Thames Row Diamond Exchange.

Every day he had seen Harriett at work he loved her more. But until the "up yours" incidents she had paid no attention to him. And then the work party. He had thought she was interested then, but somehow it had turned out badly.

Perhaps he should not have expected Harriett to like him. After all he was her boss.

It was Charles who had suggested they join the modelling classes and he had found they were just what he wanted. Unfortunately, he hadn't won the contest and was still at the diamond exchange, going nowhere. That was why he had handed in his resignation.

He needed to finish up the work in hand during the two weeks before he left.

At the beginning of each day he usually spent some time

reading his emails and responding to correspondence. There were clients who needed to be contacted; there were potential employee references to check; there was the task of engaging and training new employees in diamond sorting; and there were directives from the suits upstairs.

It was one of these directives that had intrigued Neville.

The famous Monroe diamond and ruby ring was coming to the Thames Row Diamond Exchange showroom. It would attract customers and boost sales.

Neville set about preparing the display case in the main showroom to enhance the ring. As he was working, he considered how a thief might steal the ring and what precautions he should take to avoid this occurring.

It was during an afternoon break while Neville was sipping his coffee that he overheard two executives speaking. They obviously thought no one was near as they seemed to be discussing a theft.

'It wouldn't be difficult. Especially if we can lay the blame on one of the staff.'

Neville was shocked. What were they planning to steal and who were they going to blame?

'I think a staff member who is going to leave in the next few weeks would be the best bet. Anyone investigating the theft would immediately suspect one of them. You know the staff. Who's leaving the company?'

Neville strained to hear the voices. He knew a few of the suits, the ones he had dealings with, but not all of them. He could not recognise these two voices.

'Symonds is one of them leaving, but I think he's been here for so many years he would have had the opportunity to steal before this. George, the cleaner is another, but he's almost seventy years old and can hardly shuffle around anymore, so I don't think the police would see him as a possible suspect in the theft of a ring as important as this one.'

A ring. They were going to steal the famous diamond and ruby ring!

Neville sidled over to the slightly open door to hear better.

'What about Celia Dawson. Her husband has just left her with three children and little money. She would be a suitable suspect. Anyone else?'

'Langer, the diamond sorter is leaving. She could definitely be the target.'

'That's a great possibility. She's been here for twelve years and she's the right age to want to steal diamonds.'

'This is a good choice. We were keeping our eyes on her when Kevin Coates admitted he'd given her the brooch.'

'Pity we had to rough him up a bit to find that out.'

There was a silence, presumably as they thought about Kevin Coates.

'I'd like to get back at her for that. Remember I had Garcia search her flat? Turned out she'd put it in the bank and she handed it in to the police anyway. Coates steered us wrong there – he's becoming a bit of a liability.'

'She's also a good choice because she's already had dealings with the police. They might re-think her innocence. Let's see if we can find something of hers to drop near the ring display.'

'I'll get Garcia to find something suitable in her flat tonight. Perhaps a cigarette, if she smokes, with her DNA on it. We'll talk again tomorrow and start setting things up.'

Neville heard their chairs scraping back and footsteps moving down the corridor. He quickly scuttled quietly back to the kitchen door in case one of the men came his way.

This was terrible. They were about to blame a worker for the theft of the ring. That worker could be a woman with three little children or more likely, his wonderful Harriett.

He needed to tell someone. Who could he tell? He hadn't seen their faces and their voices were muffled and hard to recognise. The culprits could be any one of the suits in the company. Even the CEO. He didn't think it had been the CEO's voice he had heard but he could still

78

be one of the thieves. In fact, all of the suits could be in it together.

Telling the police was the obvious solution, but Neville's imagination began to work overtime as he thought about the consequences of doing that. He would not be able to tell them much at all, so they would have to question all the executive staff. That might result in the people finding out he was the one who had heard or seen something. He could well imagine his life being at risk then.

Of course all the staff would deny it and the police would be left thinking he was just making it up, especially as he was leaving. The suits might even turn it back onto him by saying he was just angry that they had not offered him more money to stay or a more secure and important position.

He could not think of a solution. Taking care of it himself was the only way out.

'I have to save Harriett,' he told himself as he shaved.

As he dressed he asked himself, 'How do they plan to do it? Could I beat them at it?'

Was he prepared to steal? In his depressed and angry mood of the morning, his mind had latched onto the fact that the upper echelons of the company didn't appreciate him, and he hadn't had a raise in years. He could also see now that they had no compunction in blaming an innocent worker. They deserved to lose this time.

Placing a copy of the ring in the display case would be the way to go. He had access to this area and could easily do it, especially as he knew he could make a copy that would not be uncovered for some time, maybe never. At home that night, he began to fashion the replica based on the photograph he found on the internet and an accumulation of suitable gems that he had collected over time in his previous career. He was a skilled designer and if he worked all that night and the next day, he could do it.

He would make sure that Celia Dawson was safe. Perhaps he could suggest she take this time off as holidays owed, before she left to organise her family life. Then she could not be there to blame.

Of course, that would leave Harriett as the thief. It seemed that the suits were after revenge because she had handed in the brooch. Harriett and the police didn't even know the suits were part of this.

As he walked to work he murmured, 'I will need to make the exchange so clean that there will be no forensics to discover. No one from the company to blame.'

The electric gates always posed a problem. How could he do it? Janie could be helpful. He had realised that Janie was hiding small diamonds in the faux ruby settings on her fancy shoes and getting away with it. The shoes always set off the alarm at the gates whenever she went home. Everyone had come to expect that to happen and laughed when it did or called out to Janie, 'Got your fancy shoes on again today?' He needed to usher her out the gates at the same time, so that no one would be aware that he had a diamond too.

Neville considered the places that would hide a person who had just stolen a 10-million-pound ring and be able to fence such a famous piece for cash.

The place was obvious. South America.

On further research it seemed that the South American organised crime syndicate, which the company dealt with, was a haven for diamonds. So Neville considered another company in the vicinity would be the best. He would have to be cautious, even disguise himself so he could remain an enigma. The general reputation of 'mafia gangs' as killers was well known.

He drank the last of his coffee and slammed his cup down on the saucer. 'This is it. Argentina!'

He wanted to take Harriett with him. Would she go? He had always thought she was an adventurous person. But what did she really think of him? He had hoped they had made a connection, especially when they had touched. He might be lucky.

Since deciding to make a copy of the ring, he'd worked on it for two nights. He used most of his savings to purchase stones resembling as far as possible the special ring's stones but of much less value, ensuring the facets on the large diamond were right, as well as the number and colours of the smaller diamonds surrounding it.

The next day when he checked the display, with sleight of hand he substituted the fake ring for the real one, which he hid in his desk.

His neck was aching from the hours he'd spent at home leaning over his workbench, and his eyes were red and watery from the fine detailed work.

Of course no one said anything, not to him.

He was secretly satisfied and overjoyed when the executives came down to examine the display.

'Is the security on this ring sufficient, Mr Symonds?' one fellow asked.

Neville wondered if this person was trying to get information which would help in the theft.

'I believe so, sir. The display is locked with a key pad and the CEO is the only person with the password, which he initiated on his phone.'

'Who handled the ring before it went into the display case?' another suit asked.

'The security team from the London office came with their own bodyguards. They only let me take it to place on the plinth in the display case at the last moment.'

He blanched as he remembered the risk he had taken when he'd used sleight of hand to exchange the ring for the fake one. 'The only time that ring could be stolen was before it even arrived at Thames Row.'

'Good, good, nice to know it is safe and can't be stolen from here,' another said.

They all examined the replica murmuring, 'How wonderful!' 'What skill!' 'What exquisite cutting!' as they admired it.

Meanwhile the real ring sat snug in his locker for the next two days. He needed to get it out. Janie would be the best help.

He ambled into the secretaries' room and up to Janie's desk. When would she wear her shoes again?

In the end he had to encourage her to wear them.

'Janie, are you coming to my leaving party this Friday? We are going to the pub straight from work.'

Janie, who had never known Mr Symonds to take an interest in her, suddenly perked up. Here was another possible date.

She immediately answered, 'Of course, Mr Symonds.'

Neville needed her to wear her fancy shoes. 'What about wearing that lovely red dress with your fancy shoes that always sound the alarm when you're going home?' He joined Janie in a laugh about that.

Janie was tickled pink. Mr Symonds had noticed her dress and shoes. What a surprise! She gave him a sultry under-the-eyelashes look that was her signature method of flirting, and pursed her lips.

*

On Friday, everyone who was going to the party turned up better dressed for work than usual. Janie's red dress was a hit with several of the men in the sorting room and had even captured the interest of a couple of the suits.

At 5 pm the diamond exchange staff began strolling out of the main gates. Neville had been hovering near Janie's desk for the last hour, making sure he didn't miss her. As Janie picked up her bag to leave, he joined her.

'Let's go out together, Janie.' He said brightly. 'In any case I have to be here with you to make sure the alarm is turned off after your shoes go past.

Together they moved to the electronic gates. As predicted, the alarm sounded.

Everyone looked around, noticed Janie and her shoes, gave a grin and carried on out the doors. Neville turned off the alarm at that moment, nodded to Janie, and after walking through himself used a remote key to reset the alarm.

He was outside … and had the ring.

Now all he had to do was enjoy his farewell party.

By Friday evening, Harriett had her termination pay in her pocket, a short reference that said nothing about her work and skills, a calligraphy pen set and a bottle of wine wrapped up with a farewell card.

She was unemployed.

Hatchet-face had not even bothered to say goodbye to her.

Harriett thought: *He's just another one of those fickle types*.

Chapter 13

That night Harriett was again disturbed by the shrill sound of the bell downstairs. She had no boyfriends left so she ignored it. Suddenly the voice of one of the tenants floated up the stairs to her ears.

'It's for you, Harriett.'

Harriett opened her door and there was Hatchet-face looking up at her. She ran down the stairs with a quizzical look on her face. Had he come to say goodbye now, even though he had ignored her all day?

He held flowers and wine (still the cheap stuff from the pu in his arms. Harriett glanced behind him to see if anyone was loitering outside and then yanked him in just as she had done before. They stood in the foyer breathing heavily and saying nothing.

'Harriett, I am so sorry for whatever I did at the Christmas party. I thought you were enjoying my company but,' he shrugged, 'obviously not.'

Harriett stared at him. He was not her boss now and didn't have to show any interest in her. So was this real? Did he really like her?

Shyly, she said, 'You were my boss. I thought you just wanted to flirt with me, like bosses do.'

'No, Harriett. I …'. He looked down, gulped, thrust his fingers through his hair and then looked straight at her, 'I love you, and want to marry you.'

Harriett held on to the railing of the stairs in case she fell. She was overwhelmed. He wanted to marry her. Even though he didn't have a job and neither did she.

'Oh, dear,' she replied in a hushed voice. 'I do. I mean, I will. Yes.'

Neville laughed. His face split into the widest grin.

'Thank you, Harriett. I was worried that you hated me after the Christmas party. Especially as you ignored me when work started again.'

Neville took a breath. Now was the time to confess about the ring. He couldn't start off any relationship with Harriett without being honest.

'I've got something for you. I hope you don't think I've been rash.'

He pulled out a box from his pocket.

At first Harriett thought it was going to be more chocolates. But no, the box was little and velvet and looked like …

An engagement ring!

There it was, nestled in the open box in all its majesty. Of course, Harriett had seen one like that before. It was the Monroe ruby ring, with the rarest of all diamonds, the ring that the suits had been talking about all last week, the one displayed in the bullet proof glass cabinet on the main floor. It was as big as the scoop on a coffee spoon, the diamond square cut and surrounded by rubies in leaf shapes that cascaded around the band. It was the most glorious thing Harriett had ever seen and easily worth 10 million pounds.

'Is this a fake, a copy? How did you get it?'

'A bit of hocus pocus,' Neville grinned.

'It's beautiful. Is it really for me?'

'Yes, Harriett. I stole it for you.'

'Neville,' she said slowly, 'you didn't steal it, did you? It's just a fake.'

'No, Harriett, it's the real thing. An engagement ring.'

'I can't take it.' She thrust it back into Neville's hand. 'I can't marry a thief. You're just joking, aren't you?'

The grin on Neville's face slowly disappeared as he looked at Harriett.

She raised her voice angrily. 'How could you spoil this moment. I've always wanted a romantic proposal not one that ends in you telling me you stole a ring.'

Neville began to realise that he had gone about his proposal the wrong way. He had to start again.

'Oh dear, Harriett, I'm sorry. Let me start again.'

'I love you and want to marry you. I've loved you for a long time but could never get up the courage to ask you. You seemed too wonderful to ever consider marrying me. But today I am not your boss anymore and this seemed the last opportunity I would have to tell you how I felt. Please marry me.'

Neville looked beseechingly at Harriett and reached out to touch her face, running his thumb along her cheek and finally clasping her neck and pulling her closer to meet his lips.

Harriett sighed. This was the proposal she wanted, and Neville was the man she wanted. She parted her lips and kissed him softly.

'But I need to start our relationship with the story about this ring.'

Harriett looked at Neville's serious and intent face. 'Yes, you do. I can't marry a thief. So, what about the ring?'

'I heard the company suits talking about stealing the ring and blaming one of the workers who was leaving.'

'Who? Who were they going to blame?'

'At first it was Celia Dawson, and then it was you.'

'That's terrible. Poor Celia. You know her husband left her with three children and that's why she had to resign. She needed a part time job so she could be home for them after school. As for me, why me?'

'Harriett, there seems to be some connection with the brooch you had. Evidently it was theirs and Kevin Coates took it, then gave it you.'

Harriett clutched Hatchet-face's arm. So the man following me was from our work?'

'What man, Harriett?'

'I was being followed and then I gave the brooch to the police. How could they do that? What did you do about it?'

'I took the real ring and substituted a copy.'

'Why didn't you just go to the police straight away and tell them who was planning the theft?'

'I didn't know who it was! The police would talk to the company and might say I overheard them. Or the suits might guess I was the one who overheard them as I am the only other person who goes to Level 1. I couldn't take the risk, and I didn't want Celia or you to be blamed. So I made a copy and took the real one.'

'But what difference will that make? They'll just steal the copy and still blame someone.'

'But once the ring is stolen, the police will be called to investigate and I've made sure there is no evidence for blame. It will be discovered to be a fake. Then the theft will be foiled. And I will have turned the blame away from the staff and at the same time ruined the company, a company that would do such a thing as blame staff.'

He looked coyly at Harriett.

This was shocking. How could the company suits be so devious and despicable? It seemed that Neville's solution was going to work.

'But what about the ring? This ring? The real one? What will we do about it? We can't keep it.'

Neville fluttered two airline tickets in front of Harriett. 'That's why we're going to South America, as soon as you agree. Then we can sell it'

'So you want to keep the money instead of the ring?'

'No, I don't. I want to find some worthwhile charity to give the ring to.'

Harriett frowned. 'Yes, we could sell it and give the money to some organisation like St Vincent de Paul or African Relief Fund or that French medical group in Syria. That sounds good to me.'

'Right,' said Neville. 'That's settled then.' He looked beseechingly at her. 'Will you come with me, Harriett?'

'Yes. When?'

'Now Harriett. Now.'

He looked so sweet and so concerned. 'Can I just wear it for a little while?'

He grabbed her hand and slid the ring on her finger. Harriett gazed at him, then turned and ran up the stairs, with Neville following. At the top, she twisted her head around to him and said, 'What am I going to call you?'

'Darling, if you like,' he grinned, 'or Neville, or even …,' he paused until she looked around at him, '… Hatchet-face, if you like.'

Harriett covered her mouth with her hand. 'Oh dear, you knew! Sorry, Neville,' she breathed.

In the bedroom, he found her suitcase, took it down from the top of the wardrobe and she began to fill it with clothes and underwear. Then she went into the bathroom and came back with toiletries.

'Passport?' Neville asked.

'Got it.' She glanced at her ring, turning her hand this way and that. 'I love it. I love you. Let's go.'

They ran down the stairs with Harriett's case and by the front door he picked up a backpack that she hadn't noticed. Then out the door to a waiting taxi that Neville must have arranged earlier.

Harriett sat next to him with her hand on her lap looking at her diamond. As their hips touched, Harriett felt that frisson in her body again. She had felt this before when they had bumped together. If she went with her instincts she knew this was right, even though they might now be fugitives from the law.

This was Hatchet-face, no, Neville. She must remember to call him that now they were engaged.

At the airport, they sailed through ticket collection. No one noticed them. Then they floated through customs as there was nothing to declare, with the ring simply an extension of Harriett's body. Finally, they twirled with ease through boarding and eventually settled on the plane to Buenos Aires.

Harriett looked at Neville with a question. 'Buenos Aires?'

He smiled. 'I have contacts there. And it's good for diamonds.'

First they clicked their seat belts and adjusted their seats. Then they found their pillows and blankets and were given a pre-take off glass of champagne, that is, the real thing, French champagne available in business class. They watched the steward point out the exits and how to put on masks and safety vests.

The engine roared and the enormous aeroplane set off slowly down the runway, eventually picking up speed until its front lifted into the air.

As the plane levelled off above the clouds, Neville clasped Harriett's hand gently in his. Maybe all his dreams were coming true at once.

Harriett's body jolted from her head to her toes with love.

'Harriett,' he whispered.

'Neville,' she purred.

Chapter 14

When the plane landed, Neville and Harriett hefted their bags from the carousel and hurried through customs to the outside world of Buenos Aires.

They had been a little worried as they waited at customs. There were a few visitors who had been hauled aside while customs officials were opening cases and fumbling through the contents, their bodies being searched with a remote detector. Would the customs people notice her ring? They both relaxed when nobody did.

The streets were thick with people, vehicles and smells that were foreign to both of them. Neville seemed to know what to do and where to go, so they ended up in a hired bomb of a car tootling along the outskirts of the city. The houses were small, packed close together and did not have any landscaped grass out the front, as Harriett was used to. Everyone seemed very poor, and everything old and run down. She hoped that this was not where they were going to live. She'd given up everything to come with Neville and didn't want this.

Soon though, they were out in the beautiful countryside where haciendas sat squat on acres of rich land, and old gnarled trees shaded the wooden rockers on their verandas.

Neville drove into a circular drive and stopped at a front porch that led to a breezeway and then into a villa. It was beautiful. *This is more like it*, Harriett thought.

'What do you think?' Neville turned to her.

Harriett just smiled.

They busied themselves with luggage and clothes and exploration. When they came to the bedroom Harriett gave a gasp. Tall windows overlooked the lawn and down to a lazy river lapping the bank. Cool tiles covered the floor in a chequered pattern, meeting two large terracotta pots at the corners. A native rug in reds and browns was spread over the bed, while fluffy white pillows cascaded from the bedhead.

Harriett turned to Neville to exclaim her delight, but instead was captured in his strong hands and her head angled to his lips.

'You are beautiful,' he sighed.

She was on fire. They shuffled close together to the bed. All the while, she felt sweet wet kisses on her neck. As the backs of her legs hit the mattress she was suddenly tossed onto the native rug with an, 'Oof.'

Harriett bounced gently on the bed springs which squeaked and groaned. She was in raptures, a femme fatale at last. She lay on her back panting and waiting to be ravished. At last her dream was coming true, and with Hatchet-face of all people. Harriett made another mental note to call him 'Neville' from now on. Or 'darling'.

He grasped both her wrists and pulled them up over her head as he covered her body with his. He slid his hands along her arms to her fingers, slipping the ten million pound ring off her ring finger and into his palm.

With a leap he was off the bed and walking out the door, saying 'I'll be back as soon as I've changed this into hard cash.'

Harriett couldn't believe it. What about a bit of hanky-panky? She lay on the bed, bereft, looking at her naked finger. Had she been too trusting? Was he leaving her already, now that he had the ring? Was she just a stooge who was needed to wear the ring on the plane? Would he now abandon her in a strange country where she knew neither the language nor the customs?

Harriett sat up on the edge of the bed and cried.

Had he meant anything he had said to her? About loving her?

*

Neville gunned the car, his mind intent on getting to the Buenos Aires

True Diamonds Exchange head office in the city in time. He shook his head trying to dislodge thoughts of Harriett alone in the hacienda looking sultry, beautiful and ready for sex. But there was nothing else to be done – he had to reach the office before closing time.

He checked that the ring was still in his pocket then gazed at the seat behind him, where he had placed several necessary items.

The head office was probably filled with suits similar to the important guys he used to see upstairs in the diamond exchange in Thames Row.

His fears about criminal connections in the Buenos Aires True Diamonds firm almost frightened him to death.

It was one thing to plan, design and swap the ring in the showrooms at home, but an entirely different undertaking to face the bosses in an unknown country. Especially bosses who might think killing was just part of a tough day at the office.

But he couldn't put it off. He didn't know when the suits at Thames Row would discover the fake.

His thoughts raced back to Harriett. She had willingly embraced him in the Hacienda, for the first time showing her love for him, and he had promptly left her there. He wanted to stay and make love with her but was panicking about the whole theft of the ring, even though he had done it to save others. Maybe it would be discovered straight away and the authorities would be onto him immediately. He had to get rid of the ring before that happened. He should have stopped to talk to Harriett about this. Instead he had just rushed away. What a fool he was!

Finding a parking spot a street away from the diamond traders firm, Neville shoved cotton balls into the sides of his mouth, high up in his cheeks, to change the shape of his face but still allow him to talk easily. Then he smoothed a small fake tattoo on his neck. He had been lucky to find one in a reject shop that said, 'Diamonds are Forever'.

Thick tinted glasses with black frames and a cloth cap pulled low on his head completed the disguise.

He was ready.

The Buenos Aires True Diamonds company and the Thames Row Diamond Exchange had always been in competition. There had been several incidents made public over the years with the newspapers attributing blame to one or the other company. Both no doubt had ways of washing their profits clean, Neville thought, as he approached the Argentinian company's store, hoping it might do a deal since it was in competition with the English firm.

As confidently as he could, he strode into the shop and straight up to the reception desk, using a booming voice to ask for the manager.

The manager nodded from his nearby office, beckoning Neville in. He looked just as Neville had imagined he would: tall and dark-haired, with a supercilious smile. He stood to greet Neville, waiting for him to speak.

No niceties here, was Neville's thought. *No customer service either.*

He gulped and cleared his throat. 'Good afternoon. Do you exchange diamonds for cash?'

The manager nodded. 'Yes, we do. But only exclusive diamonds. What do you have to show me?' His diction sounded perfect as he looked Neville up and down, perhaps debating whether such a scruffy person would have anything worth selling in his possession.

'A wonderful diamond ring with an exquisite setting has come into my possession. It is worth perhaps 12 million pounds. I'm hoping to exchange it for cash.'

The manager seemed bored until Neville produced the ring from his pocket, allowing it to catch the overhead light in the room. Its fame was notorious to those in the trade.

'That's from the Marilyn Monroe collection?' He squinted at Neville, who nodded. 'How did you come by it?'

'As you may have heard, it was being displayed at a diamond exchange in London and I understand security was not as tight as it might have been.'

The manager's eyes lit up.

I hope he's tempted by the thought of outwitting his rival company, Neville thought.

'It won't be discovered missing for some time, I can assure you. Time enough for you to find a buyer who is prepared to pay what this incomparable piece is worth,' Neville reassured the manager.

The manager held up his loupe, closely examining the ring for authenticity.

The greedy look in his eyes bodes well, Neville thought.

'Alright, come with me.'

They walked down a small passage through several empty rooms and into an office with no outside windows. Two security guards followed them and were asked to close the door and stand guard.

Neville wondered if this was the start of his demise. His thoughts ran wild: *I could be bumped off here, carted to the port for disposal and never be heard of again. Harriett would be all alone in Buenos Aires, with no idea of what's happened to me.*

First, the manager took up a tough negotiating stance, explaining that there were certain risks involved in disposing of such a ring, even though he had to acknowledge that it would be extremely appealing to several of his clients worldwide.

'You understand,' he said, 'that this is a precarious situation. There should be no need for me to explain the utmost secrecy that needs to be maintained. And the figure you have given me as its value might be the official figure, but it's another figure altogether that would be accepted in these extraordinary circumstances. Let's get real.'

Neville soon realised he was out of his depth. The fact was that he was beginning to shake a little, even while he assumed a stony expression. He didn't give in immediately, but soon realised that, figuratively, he had his back to the wall and would have to accept a lower figure than his initial expectation. The manager was calculating, but not outright mean. They settled on a sum closer to half of the ring's official value.

Once the deal was settled, the manager opened a floor-to-ceiling safe and extracted many large boxes of notes. Neville watched as a machine counted the notes and they were clipped into bundles quickly and efficiently. The cache he received looked enormous now as it was all in pesos.

Neville handed over the ring and, with two suitcases in his hands, he was ushered out into the street alongside a security guard, who walked Neville towards his car. Clutching the suitcase handles tight, Neville flung the 'luggage' into the boot of his car and sped off the way he had come. The tension over the deal still pulsed through his body.

I've done it! Harriett will be over the moon! he thought. *We might live happily here in Buenos Aires or even go somewhere else. The Bahamas, for instance, or even Australia. We'll find a charity that needs an injection of cash and at last feel good about what we've done.*

Neville removed his disguise as he reached the hacienda. Then, after swinging the cases out of the boot, he hurried to the front door of his haven and to Harriett.

*

Two hours had gone by and then another four. The day had quietly become evening and the rowdy sound of cicadas had filled the night air. Harriett had not moved.

The sound of feet crunching on gravel alerted her to someone coming. She hoped it was Neville and ran to the front door.

He strode in with two large suitcases, which he plonked on the bed. With a flick of each wrist, he flipped open the catches to reveal the contents: money. A lot of money, all in 500 peso notes, with bundles clipped together. The cases were stuffed to the top. Of course she could not work out how much there was, as the notes were all in South American currency. But she knew it was a lot.

'Ta da,' Neville sang, waving his arm over the cases. 'Over five million pounds, all in the local currency,' he announced with a satisfied grin. 'What do you think of that?'

Harriett was still upset. How could he leave her without saying why? It was if he didn't even notice that she was upset or unhappy. All he was concerned about was his money. But where was the rest of it? The other five million? Uncertainty obviously showed in her expression.

'I had to bargain, and that's not so easy with stolen goods,' Neville explained. 'We settled on a fair price. In fact, it didn't take long before I realised I didn't have much choice. No questions asked.'

Harriett looked hard at him. He was still her Neville and she loved him. She just had to get over this glitch and move on.

'Yummy,' Harriett declared and leapt on him, wrapping her arms around his neck. She was still hoping for a continuation of her femme fatale moment.

But no, it was not to be.

'Sit here,' he said. 'And start counting. I want to make sure we weren't conned.'

Well, this is nearly good enough, Harriett thought, *as my next two favourite things besides love and sex are counting money or handling diamonds.*

Each bundle totalled one hundred thousand pesos. So there was a lot of counting to do to reach the five million pound mark. Harriett's head was spinning within half an hour.

Neville explained how he had chosen the company from among his former employer's contacts in South America to sell the ring. Companies only dealt in cash so the transaction was less likely to be traced but, even so, he had to get to a bank the next day to ensure its safety.

'Can we keep just this amount to spend?' Harriett asked him, waving a bundle in the air.

'Of course,' he grinned and she put the bundle in the pocket of her trousers.

Then they looked around for a likely hiding place until they were able to go to the bank the following day. It was lucky that would be Monday as banks in Buenos Aires did not open on Sundays.

The best place for the money to go was under the mattress, with them sleeping on top of it. So their night was spent in a very uncomfortable way with rustling paper, and dips and gullies that they kept falling into as they turned over trying to get comfortable.

There was no smooching and no cuddling as they were too alert to noises that might mean robbers. Every time a tree branch rustled or the wooden floors creaked or an animal plodded by in the fields, they were rigid with fear until the sound subsided.

By 2 am they couldn't stand the noise and discomfort any longer. So they moved to the floor, Harriett placing all the soft pillows in a nest for them to sink into.

This was the first time Harriett had been this close to Neville without his pants. He was wearing just his boxer shorts and she had on her lacy bra and panties. Suddenly a tension fizzed between them. Neville reached out to Harriett, clasping her hand, turning it over and kissing the inside of her wrist. Then he moved up her arm with nips, licks, kisses and tiny bites, until he reached first her neck and then her lips.

Harriett moaned in ecstasy. Neville was not as common as Tom or as slick as Charles or as foreign as Bruno. He was real and warm and loved her, which he began to whisper over and over as he explored every inch of her.

Harriett was enraptured, almost bursting with her love for him.

'I never thought you …' she began.

'Neither did I …' Neville interrupted.

They smiled at each other as they began yet another attack on each other's flesh.

Afterwards, they lay curled together in the pillows until the sun came up. So early, quiet and sultry, it felt like the beginning of a wonderful Buenos Aires day.

Neville sat up, saying that they needed to bank the cash. 'I bet it would surprise you how quickly people here discover you have money.'

Chapter 15

It was probably her lack of sleep, the love she had for Neville and her heart-beating fear, which led to the mistake Harriett made that day.

They began the morning collecting all the cash they had lain on the previous night, smoothing it out and making sure it was all re-bundled in the paper wrappers – even though they'd run out of time to count it all – and then stacking the bundles back in the suitcases.

With every stack laid down, Neville leant over and gave Harriett a kiss, so the completion of the job took several hours. A weight had been lifted off his shoulders with the sale of the ring. Now he could concentrate on Harriett.

At last the suitcases were closed with a snap. Harriett sat on the bed, tears overflowing down her cheeks.

'What's the matter, my love?' Neville knelt in front of her, holding her hands together and warming them.

'My beautiful ring. You gave it to me and I treasured it.'

Neville shrugged. 'Sorry, my sweet. We needed the money. We needed to sell it. It was never really ours. The cash will be given to a charity. It was the only way, otherwise we would have begun our lives together as thieves. Now …'

He found himself lost for words but Harriett came to his rescue. 'Now we have each other. Forever.'

By early afternoon the cases were packed and the couple set off. They travelled back into the port of Buenos Aires in the same beaten up car with the two suitcases in the boot. It was fifteen miles to reach the city area, one of the ten most populated urban areas in the world.

Neville, who had studied the map of the city, wanted to go to the barrio, a district called La Boca. It was the most colourful barrio in Buenos Aires with lots of tourists milling around, where they could more easily hide themselves and their cases. It would also have banks that took significant amounts of tourist dollars and would not be fazed by their large amounts of cash.

They parked the car in a multi-story car park and, taking a suitcase each, walked briskly onto the street and across the road to an exchange booth. In careful Spanish, Neville asked for the whereabouts of a bank.

The man in the booth chewed on his cigar, looked at them and their cases, moved his cigar from one side of his mouth to the other and eventually waved his hand to the left with a flick that seemed to say 'around the corner'. They hurried off, past a shop and a small group of locals.

Within seconds, one of the locals came up to Harriett and, while her attention was concentrated on where Neville was leading, the man sprayed something on her arm. It stung like hell and she put down the case, keeping it close to her leg as she began to rub and scratch her arm. It smelled like mustard.

Her arm was soon stinging and the pain became unbearable. She gazed at it becoming red and lumpy.

Harriett was immediately surrounded by portenos, the local port people, who jostled her and commiserated with her in Spanish. One, then another, came to pat her hand or hold her arm and offer cream to soothe the spray, all the while talking loudly and waving their arms in front of her face as if to help her. And help they did, helping themselves to her suitcase.

Almost as soon as they had gathered around Harriett they vanished, and she was left standing alone and without a case.

Harriett screamed. 'Stop. Stop them.' She waved in the direction that the group had disappeared.

All this time, Neville had been one step ahead and when Harriett was surrounded, he backed away clutching his case to his chest.

Realising it was a scam he tried to push his way back into the melee and grab the case, but the crowd thwarted him, nudging and bumping his body this way and that, throwing him off balance, digging into his side and back with elbows and hands, as well as waving them in front of his face, so that he had to bat them away while still holding onto his case.

'Harriett, get your case! Hold on to your case!' he yelled over and over, his voice harsh with concern. But he could tell she did not hear him.

As the crowd of portenos began to melt away, he shifted his weight to the arm with the case and slammed it over and over into their arms, legs and heads.

But the group was too strong to give in to such tactics, pushing and shoving back. And also too wily to reveal the whereabouts in the crowd of Harriett's suitcase as it was handed from one to another. Soon they had left him behind.

He raced after the group calling, 'Stop those thieves. Stop them.'

A few tourists reacted immediately, leaping forward to look for the most likely thief. Others, mouths open, stared at Neville, not able to take in the import of the incident. He rounded a corner and scanned the people moving casually, laughing and taking photos. There was no sign of the portenos or the case.

Confusion played over Neville's face and he had a feeling of being out of control. His breath was harsh and laboured. He couldn't think straight, or even at all.

'Neville,' Harriett gasped, running up to him. 'They've stolen my case. Help me. They did something …'

Neville spun around. He was wet with sweat and limp with exhaustion, his body still shaking from the shock of the attack.

'I can't help you. They've gone. How could you have been so utterly stupid as to put down that case with all the money?'

'I couldn't help it. See what they did?' Harriett held out her arm, which was red and sore. Small bubbles were appearing like sunburn blisters. Blood trickled from the blisters as she scratched her arm.

'Please?' Her voice was faint.

Neville was so furious he could hardly talk. His fingers gripping his case were white with tension.

'I can't believe you could be such a stupid bloody idiot.'

'We can still be okay and give your half to charity, can't we?' Harriett pleaded.

'What, you think that's okay then? To lose nearly three million pounds? Like it's just nothing. I can't think. It's so stupid. I can't stop thinking about your stupidity. I have to get away. I thought we could be a couple forever, but this is too much.' He backed away from her. His hands shaking, his eyes wild. He raised one hand onto his head, his eyes blinking as he stared from side to side, stripped of self-control and any sense of sympathy for Harriett's injury.

'I have to think, get away and think.'

'We're going to stay together, aren't we? Neville?'

'You've wrecked it. I stole millions to save you and the other staff. I never imagined this. To do some good, I thought. It was a theft, even though it was done for good. Do you realise that? Do you? I could have been caught and gone to jail. I still could.'

He was shouting. His breath caught in his throat. His body bruised, his face too, and his chest heaving from the delayed shock and fear he'd had for his own and Harriett's life.

'Neville, I love you. Please don't leave me?'

'I'm so angry I can't stay here with you. I have to get away.' He began to walk away. 'Or I'll say something I'll regret …'

Harriett ran after him, reaching out her arm to touch his shoulder. 'Neville?'

'Let go.' He shrugged her hand roughly away.

'But Neville, please. Can't I fix this? I'll do anything.'

'Just get lost, Harriett. You can't fix anything.' Spittle speared the air in front of him. 'You can't even hold onto three million pounds for just a couple of hours.'

'I can. I will. Give me another chance.'

'Another chance? I don't have another three million pounds to give you so you can lose it again.'

Harriett stopped, her arms by her sides. She called after him. 'So is this the end, Neville?'

Neville kept on walking unsteadily, not answering. His anger filled his body and his mind. He had never felt like this before. The combination of designing a fake, swapping it for the real ring, asking Harriett to come with him and dealing with what he thought were mafia bosses, and finally the crowd attack, had sent his body and mind into a spin. He could no longer control himself. He had to hit out at someone and that someone was Harriett.

Harriett stood, bereft, as Neville disappeared along the street.

She stared at the space where Neville had been. Absently, she rubbed her arm, the physical hurt outweighed by the pain of her realisation that Neville had left. A couple of tourists who had tried to find one actual thief came over to her to suggest she call the police.

In a state of shock, Harriett nodded and agreed, but just stayed there as they returned to their friends, satisfied they had helped – and besides, it wasn't their concern anyway.

A cacophony of sounds assaulted her ears as it swirled around her. Voices, car horns, street vendors, laughing children.

But she heard only silence.

She was all alone. Her emotions shattered.

*

As Neville had stormed away from Harriett, he'd thought he could hear her saying sorry, sorry, sorry, over and over. With one arm heaving the suitcase along, he slapped his free hand onto the side of his face, trying to get rid of the sound of her voice. Striding around another corner, he noticed two banks opposite each other. He chose one and hauling his case onto the counter, he concentrated on organising the deposit.

'I want to deposit the cash I'm carrying in this suitcase.' His hands shook as he tried to unfasten the clasps. 'Can you help me?'

'Of course,' the teller said. Noticing how tense his customer was, and the size of the case, he ushered him into a private room.

Various papers were placed in front of Neville for him to read and sign. The bank teller gazed at Neville. He was most suspicious. 'Are you all right, sir?'

'Not really,' Neville said. 'I've had a bit of a fright out in the square. Someone tried to rob me. I need a moment to compose myself.'

'I'll get you a cup of coffee, sir,' the teller said, leaving Neville alone for a few moments.

Neville took some deep breaths, trying to stop the shaking in his hands and the coldness that racked his body. The teller returned with coffee and the manager, as he had checked the suitcase and was amazed to see so much cash. He knew the manager needed to be in charge of the transaction. After a while, Neville was able to make up a reasonable story to reassure the manager that the money was legitimate, before signing papers to complete the deposit. He wasn't sure that they really believed the explanation but he could see that they were keen to have such a large deposit, so they just looked the other way.

It took over an hour to count the cash and complete the transaction. By that time, Neville was much calmer.

But he was dismayed at the way he had treated Harriett. He loved her, he knew. It was just the heat of the moment that had caused him to say what he did. He needed to find her and make it right.

He was not sure where she would have gone, but if he drove around the surrounding streets he might find her, he hoped.

*

Three million pounds gone, as if it had never existed, and Harriett felt she was to blame. There was no way to get help to recover it. It was tainted money and she could not go to the police. How could love last when one person in the partnership, that is her, had lost three million pounds.

Harriett, too, had not been able to gather her thoughts together. It had all happened too fast. She looked around her, then wandered over to sit on the side of a fountain, along with a number of other tourists.

What would she do now?

An hour later, and still shaking, she put her hand into the pocket of her skirt and her fingers fumbled, finding money. The 10,000 pesos that she had put aside the night before could help her. She began to think again. She wasn't rich, that was for sure, but she had something at least. Perhaps she could catch a freighter from the port to another country where she knew the language.

Argentina's home language was predominantly Spanish, but was also influenced by the large population of Italians who had migrated to the country over decades. She knew neither language.

But before finding out how to leave the city, or the country, she needed to find Neville to try to talk to him one more time. And say sorry again. She hurried off, and turning a corner, saw two banks. Which one might Neville have chosen?

Standing with her hands pressed to the glass doors of first one bank, then the other, she could see nothing of him. So she wandered back to the square and sat once again on the rim of the fountain.

'Can you take my photo?' A tourist leaned over her, holding out a camera.

Harriett just shook her head and turned away.

Perhaps Neville has gone to the multi-story car park and I'll find him there,' she thought. She raced up to the level where they had parked, but the car wasn't there. *He must have doubled back and taken it. Now what will I do?*

She hurried back to the first bank she had seen. Fortunately, the staff all spoke English because of the multitude of tourists they dealt with every day, so she began to explain to several what had happened and ask for help.

A kindly man in the bank sat her down in the lounge area. He made her a cup of coffee then listened to her story.

'I was in the square and these people sprayed my arm. Look.'

The bank teller examined her arm sympathetically.

'They took my case and money. I don't know what to do.'

'This terrible thing is very prevalent in the barrio where all the tourists stay. Just today another customer was robbed there.' His view was that the portenos' leaders were to blame. 'You are lucky you did not try to fight them or they may have knifed you.'

He looked sad, thinking of the morals of some of his compatriots.

'What can I do now?' Harriett asked. 'Where can I go for help?'

'There is an embassy for English people just nearby. You should go there.' He found the address in his computer, and wrote the directions on a piece of paper for her. With a small wave and a gentle, 'Good luck to you', he watched her leave the bank.

Harriett found his directions were easy to follow and she soon found the embassy.

Like most embassies, it was located in an imposing building with guards at the gates. The British flag was flying from the flagpole on top of the building, and this gave her renewed hope. Getting some attention was more difficult. There were several lines of people all needing help. A couple of them seemed to have been conned just as she had. They were pulling up their sleeves or holding out their arms to show how they had been attacked with mustard spray. Everyone seemed worried and the staff were trying to stay calm and help as much as they could.

Harriett despaired again. Her plight seemed hopeless. There were so many people ahead of her who looked as if they had more important issues than hers, particularly as she had caused her own problems. But eventually she came to the front of the line, where a weary assistant listened to her problem.

'There's not much we can do to get your suitcase back. Do you have a return flight ticket to England that can be transferred to today?'

Harriett sighed. She'd already realised that she had no return ticket, no credit cards and not enough cash to purchase another ticket. All these were in Neville's wallet.

Woeful, she shook her head. The assistant felt tired. Why did these people not think out their essential plans before setting off on their travels?

'It's not our policy to lend money. The only thing I can do for you is to give you one week's rent in the barrio area so that you can contact relatives or friends at home to assist you.' Harriett took the address of the rental place and left to find it.

It wasn't far away. As she scuttled along the winding streets she kept an eye out for more of the portenos and their mustard spray. She felt so afraid and alone. She hadn't realised how much she needed Neville.

Chapter 16

A dark doorway opened between two shops that had seen better days, and led upstairs to several rooms. They all opened out from a bare wooden landing that smelt of fish and fat and cigarettes. One of the doors was Harriett's. Carefully, she opened it with the key provided by the embassy. As the door swung open she was faced with an almost empty room that was dusty and plain. A bed butted up against the far wall. It had a thin mattress with a blanket folded on top. There was a chest of drawers, a table and chair.

The room was cold and ugly and depressing. She sat on the bed and cried. Everything was gone. The money was gone – and although that was terrible, and her fault, it was not as bad as losing Neville. He had disappeared and so had his love.

After a while, Harriett's tears subsided into sniffles. She felt empty inside and like a shell of the person she had been. She needed to get herself up and out and try to recover.

On the landing, as she was locking her door, she met another woman coming up the stairs, holding a baby in her arms.

'Hello,' the woman called. 'I'm Sylvia. Just arrived?'

'Yes,' said Harriett. 'Are you next door?'

'Sure am. I'm just moving in. I got stuck here because my fiancé left me with the baby.' She jiggled a fat happy baby in her arms. 'Now I have little opportunity to get home. What about you?'

'I was conned. They took everything I had.' She began to cry again.

'Never mind. Come and have a coffee. The shop is just next door.'

Soon Harriett had told Sylvia all about her own fiancé.

'He ran out on me when I was conned. I guess he didn't really love me.'

Of course she didn't say anything about the ring or the money.

'What's your fiancé's name?' Sylvia asked.

Harriett thought quickly. Even though he had left her, she didn't want anyone to find him with all that money, so she answered, 'I've blocked his name from my mind, so don't ask.'

Sylvia looked in sympathy at Harriett. She held her hand and squeezed it. Harriett thought, *She's so nice. How could anyone have left her in such a predicament?* The baby, Jacinta, who was in a carrycot on the floor next to the chair, gurgled happily and waved her arms in the air.

Harriett was impressed that Sylvia was able to carry on through all her troubles.

'You've had a bad day, Harriett. I've got myself a babysitter coming tonight. It's an opportunity to go out and have some fun. Otherwise I'd be stuck in that ghastly room every night. Why don't we go down to the corner?'

Her face had lit up. Her eyes smiled at Harriett. 'You and I could have a great time together. There is something special on tonight that I think you'll like. Do you know the Milongas?'

Harriett shook her head. 'What is that?'

'It's street dancing,' said Sylvia.

'Do you mean everyone dances in the street?'

'It's a bit more complex than that. It's tango dancing. People gather around a dance square drinking coffee or just waiting, hoping to pick up a dance partner.'

'I'd like that. I learnt tango in London, you know.'

'If you are any good you might get a dance.'

'I wasn't bad. My teacher entered me in the British Championships.'

'Wow. If a man catches your eye, you nod and join him'

Harriett sighed. 'No one would seek me out dressed like this.'

Sylvia glanced at Harriett's clothes. 'If you take off this shirt so your midriff top shows up better you could be okay.'

'Oh yes,' Harriett agreed, getting into the spirit. 'And if I split my skirt up to my thigh and tie my hair back in a low bun, I could look the part. Can you lend me some makeup and a brush, please?'

'Of course. We'll get you looking great.'

Harriett stuffed her worries about Neville and the money into the back of her mind. She needed to forget and move on.

That evening, between a hollow feeling of depression without Neville and an excitement about the Milongas, she managed to spruce herself up and brush her hair.

They set off down a narrow alley to a square where people were gathering. They joined them.

The day was waning and the ornate street lights flickered. The air in the square was tense and smelled of cigarettes and coffee and perfume.

Sylvia looked at her transformation and laughed. 'You look just like a tango dancer.'

Sylvia explained what to do. 'Just wait here and maybe you'll get a dance. Especially the way you are dressed.' She sat down at a cafe table nearby and showed Harriett where to go.

Harriett loitered near the wall of the cafe, trying to strike a pose that suggested she would like to dance.

There were several men all with heavy-lidded sleepy eyes perusing the women. One man was looking directly at her. He stood, proud and dark-haired, on the edge of the dance square, clothed in a grey pinstripe suit of a 1940's vintage.

Harriett's eyes opened large. He flicked his head, she nodded. Then they strode towards each other; he pulled her close while she carefully floated her hands onto his shoulders in the dance position. They paused, then, leaning forward, he moved smoothly into the tango.

In the alley, the band had been waiting for these first steps. There were two men in Latin shirts and vests; their black hair slicked greasily back from their foreheads, one with a thin moustache. Three women ranging from their twenties to fifties stood tall in long black dresses. The band began to play.

A solitary streetlight captured them as the man and Harriett stepped out slowly, the only two dancing. The violin bow scratched across the strings from top to bottom – slow, haunting, all jarring, whining and screeching in discord, while the double bass kept the beat with deep, pulsing vibrations.

The music, 'Quejas de Bandoneon', evoked hot, steamy, courtyard cobblestones, and sultry evenings and mornings. It spoke of lovers falling together in a passionate embrace.

The piano accordion joined in, staccato, sharp, with an odd syncopated rhythm. And then a flute, with trills filling the spaces between chords, and a tinkling melody began which Harriett imitated in small toe-twisting steps.

All eyes were upon the couple as they swept into the twists and twirls and for them the crowd became a blur of rich whirls of colour.

The violin player lowered her instrument, leaned forward to the mic and added her voice of exquisite clarity and pain to the twilight.

She sang the story of Argentinian love and Harriett was transported to another time. A time when she was a courtesan, when tango was new and danced to the smoky air of spices and cloying scent. The song rose into a crescendo, battling with the instruments, then tapered into the sweet melancholic sound that told of love gained and lost. The music stopped as suddenly as it began and Harriett walked out of the square to stand against a wall, panting slightly from the exertion and the excitement of it all.

Sylvia whispered 'Wow!' to Harriett, who turned to find her partner coming towards her.

'Do you speak Spanish or Portuguese?' he asked. Harriett looked quizzically at him. Sylvia translated for her. Harriett shook her head. She had only rudimentary Spanish learnt from her father. The man began to speak in English, asking where she had learnt to tango.

'In London,' Harriett said, still short of breath. 'I took lessons every week and was going to compete in the British Championships.'

'I am Antonio,' he said, 'and I'm looking for a partner to dance in the theatre. You would suit me. Are you interested?'

Harriett's mouth opened in surprise. 'Why would I suit you? What about all these wonderful local girls looking so capable and so Latin?'

Harriett's first thought had been: *Is this another con?*

Antonio could see her concern and began to tell her about his theatre group.

'I'm with a national tango troupe and came here tonight to see if there was any new talent. You fit me. Fitting together is almost as important as being able to dance.'

Harriett remembered George and his valiant attempts to partner her and easily understood that fit was important. She had moved into this man's arms as if they'd belonged together.

'Can you just ask me to join like that?'

'You'll still have to audition, but if I say you are good they will listen.'

Harriett thought for a moment as Sylvia looked warily at Antonio.

He seemed nice. He was certainly handsome and well-dressed and could dance. Perhaps this was her chance.

Her next question was, 'Do I get paid?

'Of course,' he said, and proceeded to tell her about the company's payment scheme, the shows they were doing, and the start-up wages she would receive.

There was not a moment to lose. Harriett agreed and accompanied him to the theatre nearby, saying goodbye to Sylvia, who was still looking a bit concerned.

'I'll tell the embassy about the room.'

A little bit of her wondered if this was another con or whether Antonio was a rapist or murderer. But she shrugged these feelings away because she needed a job and she hoped this was one she could perform in this foreign land.

Perhaps, after all, she had fallen on her feet.

Chapter 17

Neville had rushed back to the car in the most despairing state he had ever been in. He sat behind the wheel, again shaking with shock. Harriett had fallen for the simplest trick in the book. Leave your bag and someone will take it.

He had loved Harriett – still did. But he needed to come to terms with his anger. With clutch grating and gears groaning, he set off to find her. Driving endlessly around in circles covering the same ground at least ten times, he realised that it was hopeless and set off to find a hotel.

He had a sleepless night. He tossed and turned, sheets twisted around him as he replayed the angry conversation they'd had, blaming himself for his anger.

Yet it wasn't until the next morning that Neville began to doubt his own role in the attack on Harriett. He had seen a car when he parked at the hacienda the night he had brought home the money to Harriett. He had seen the same car on the way to the city the next day.

It was then he considered that he may have been followed from the diamond trader's office where he had cashed in the ring. So he made his way back to the square.

Looking around, he saw a group of portenos lounging against a cafe wall. He thought they were the ones who had accosted Harriett. He could see them examining each of the tourists that passed by, checking out their bags and vulnerability. He couldn't go up and expect them to talk to him. They would probably knife him.

He waited until one of them leisurely sloped off to buy cigarettes from a nearby shop.

Now was his chance.

Holding his pocket knife in his hand, Neville moved up behind the man. He put on his Hatchet-face look. The one that had scared all the employees in the diamond exchange. With a growl he said, 'Tell me what you did with the suitcase yesterday.'

'What suitcase?' echoed the man, in English.

'The one you stole from the girl after spraying her with something.'

'Oh, her! Pretty girl. Well, we didn't get anything. The suitcase was empty.'

'No, it wasn't empty.'

'It was. We gave it to the man who hired us to get it and when he opened it, there was nothing in it.'

Neville was flummoxed. Had Harriett conned him? Had she taken all her money out of the case and put it somewhere else? No, that couldn't be. He'd been with her all night.

'He showed us the case later and there was nothing in it.'

Neville heard those words and realised. 'You mean he didn't open it right there in the square?'

'No, we had to disappear quickly and meet him at another place when it was safe to do so.'

'Well, you've been mightily conned yourself. He's secreted away anything that was in the suitcase in that time so he didn't have to pay you. Who was he?'

The man looked shocked. 'I don't know. Just a guy who asked us to do a job.' He pushed past Neville back to his group, and Neville let him go. There was no use talking to the gang out there, as they probably didn't know anything. And his risk of injury was too high.

So Neville had been right. The job was fixed. And the business he'd sold the ring to was determined to get its money back. He had not been so clever after all. In that case, Harriet was not to blame entirely. They had been too slick for her. He saw that he was in large part to blame.

He had left Harriett in anger, and didn't know where she was.

She might be alone, cold and hungry, or even in danger.

Where would she go? What would she do?

He walked slowly back to his hotel. He could have walked the streets again, but that seemed a futile exercise. He needed to rest and think.

The next morning it occurred to him to try the British Embassy.

The line at the embassy was long and ranged from people who'd had money or passports stolen to people who had lost their tickets home. Neville finally got to the head of the line and asked about Harriett Langer.

After some conferencing with other assistants, the woman in charge came back to him. 'Harriett did approach us and we gave her money for rent for one week to tide her over. You can find her at this address.'

Relieved, Neville rushed out and down the street to where Harriett was living. He bounded up the stairs to Harriett's door and knocked loudly, keen to apologise profusely to her and take her in his arms. There was no answer. And after knocking several times he decided to sit on the floor at the door and wait for her.

Half an hour later, a woman holding a baby came struggling up the stairs. She stopped when she saw Neville.

Neville sprang up from the floor and smiled at her, hoping to put her at ease.

'Hello, I'm Harriett's fiancé and I've come to visit her.'

Sylvia glared at him. This must be the man who had left Harriett without any money. That was just like her fiancé who had left her with a baby and no money. They were all the same. Thinking only of themselves. She hated men. He didn't deserve Harriett.

'Harriett's gone.' Her smile looked nasty. 'She won't be back.'

Neville gasped. 'Where has she gone? Did she leave an address?'

Sylvia didn't want to tell him that Harriett had gone off to the tango troupe, that she'd found a better life. She was going to dance the tango that she loved. She had told Sylvia all about her tango lessons in

London. She didn't need such a rotter as this man.

'I think she's gone home.'

'You mean to England?' Neville enquired.

'I suppose that's what she meant. She said she was going home.' Sylvia hoisted the baby higher on her hip and opened her door, disappearing inside with a goodbye.

Neville stood on the landing, feeling bereaved.

How could he find her now? He would have to go home too. Perhaps she had persuaded some of her friends at the diamond exchange to send her money for a ticket. That was it. He'd go home to London.

As he walked back through the barrio to his car, Neville noticed the same portenos again lingering on the corner waiting for a victim.

Taking out his wallet, he went up to the fellow he had spoken to earlier who was again standing separately from the rest of the group.

'I want to know who hired you to scam my girl?' The man looked down at the notes in Neville's hand.

'I don't know. He just offered to pay us, that's all.'

'Can you describe him for me?'

With shoulders lifted in an 'I might or might not attitude', he described a man with a scar similar to the the man at the Buenos Aires True Diamonds Exchange store who had paid cash for the ring.

Taking out his phone, Neville thumbed the True Diamonds Exchange Facebook page and scrolled down to find pictures of the Board of Directors.

'Is this him?' Neville asked the guy, pointing to the photo of the man he'd dealt with, Lautaro Rodriguez.

'Yes, that's him.' Neville handed over the money wondering if he was still being scammed.

Lautaro Rodriguez's Facebook page mentioned his skill at buying diamonds, and that he'd only been back a few weeks from a trip to Australia where he'd searched for suitable roughs to be transformed into highly-prized diamonds.

The page advertised that he would be interviewed that evening at a leading television studio about diamonds in general, and the roughs he'd bought, in particular.

Neville's mind began to spin as he walked away.

Here's a man who has hurt Harriett, he thought. *Rodriguez has probably used the money he stole from me to purchase the roughs. He deserves to be brought down in some way.*

It wasn't long before Neville had an idea. He looked on his phone for the address of the TV station and, after purchasing a wig and suitable clothes as a disguise, he hurried there that evening. Once through the front door, it was easy to get inside the studios' area as there were many workers bustling in and out with technical equipment, designer clothes, files and make-up.

Neville walked confidently down a corridor, looking into each recording studio for Rodriguez and his interviewer.

Reaching the right studio, he hung back but saw through a two-way mirror that the interview was under way. Rodriguez was showing the female interviewer two roughs he had bought as he explained how diamonds were extracted from them.

'Roughs come in all sizes. These roughs are quite small, but we can still extract about three to five gem-quality diamonds from them through cutting and polishing. The largest gem-quality diamond ever found is the 'Cullinan', and it was cut into several stones, the biggest called the 'Cullinan I' or the 'Great Star of Africa', weighing 530.4 carats. Along with 'Cullinan II', it's owned by the Queen of England as part of her 'Crown Jewels'.

The interviewer turned the roughs over and over in her hand. 'These are quite cloudy in places. Can you show the viewers how they become beautiful diamonds?'

Of course, Rodriguez said, as the pair moved over to a stand where several diamonds which had been through the process of being cut and polished were on display.

Neville would never have a better chance. The interviewer had placed the roughs on the coffee table next to the chairs where the interview had been conducted, and now seemingly forgotten. As the studio cameras were turned towards the display stand for close-ups of the polished diamonds from different angles, Neville quietly walked towards the table and swooped down to remove the coffee cups and also the roughs.

He was out the door in seconds and on the way to the airport within five minutes.

Once inside the Buenos Aires international terminal, holding a ticket for the first plane out of the country with connections to London, he found a tourist shop with just what he was looking for, a plaster model of 'El Obelisco', a famous landmark in Buenos Aires. He also bought some glue that enabled him to fasten the two roughs, which at that stage looked just like pretty stones, around the plinth that the obelisk stood on.

Neville looked at his handiwork. This would get him through Customs back home in England. He just had to hope that as he'd been wearing a disguise he wouldn't be detected.

Whereas back at the Buenos Aires television station, Rodriguez was experiencing total dismay and anger at having had the roughs stolen from under his nose. And, as he discovered from the studio CCTV footage, they'd been taken by the man he thought he'd outwitted, who'd been dressed in disguise.

Rodriguez phoned Joaquin Garcia. 'I want that man. Find him, torture him and kill him. Kill him several times over. I won't be thwarted by that punk.'

*

After a harrowing time at Heathrow Airport Customs, moving along the 'nothing to declare' line, Neville caught the Tube to a city hotel with a great sense of relief, as well as optimism that he would be able to track down Harriett within a day.

He thought about how it was only a few weeks before that he had set off with Harriett, as his fiancée. And now look what had happened.

The next evening he was back in Thames Row. It looked exactly the same as before, with employees rushing out the door of the diamond exchange, heading for home. He saw Muriel waiting to be met by Tom on the Town Hall corner.

He sighed. If only Harriett would come magically out of the door as well.

Muriel spied Neville and called him over. He shook hands with Tom and gave Muriel a kiss on the cheek. She was flabbergasted and held her hand up to her cheek.

'I thought you'd gone away.'

'I did,' Neville said. 'But now I'm back. Have you seen Harriett?'

Both Tom and Muriel looked at him with curious expressions.

'I thought you'd gone off with her as she left at the same time as you,' Tom said.

Neville just shook his head. He could see that they knew nothing of Harriett. He changed the subject.

'What are you doing here Tom? You were a winner at the Model competition. Didn't you get that job they promised you?'

Tom sighed. 'I did, Neville. But it only took me a week to discover it was much too time-consuming. You had to be available every hour of every day. So I declined. I thought a better idea was to start an agency myself. So now I own Tom Brown Theatrical Agency,' he said proudly.

Muriel looked up at Tom with a smile. 'And I'm his secretary. It was just part-time in the evenings at first until the business took off,' she explained.

'You know,' Tom said, 'you were very good in that competition. Maybe you'd like to join my agency.' He handed Neville his card. 'I could probably find lots of work for you. I know Harrods is looking for a model. It'd be better than going back to the Thames Row Diamond Exchange, mate.' They both shuddered at the thought.

Neville considered the offer for a few seconds. Harriett was not here in Thames Row; Muriel would have known if she was. He needed a job to keep his mind off her and get back to normality. He'd always wanted to be a model and here was Tom offering him work without him having to go out and find it.

'Great, yes, I'd love that. I'll come around to see you as soon as I can and sign on.'

He waved goodbye and set off to find a local place to stay. *Sometimes bad things can lead to good things,* he mused.

The next morning, he needed to go to the bank. *I might see Charles today*, he thought. *Even though Charles was keen on Harriett and used to make me jealous, I still like him.*

Inside the bank he arranged a deposit so he could draw on it to arrange to rent a flat, and installed the roughs he had stolen in a safety deposit box. Then he asked to see Charles.

'Sorry, sir, Charles doesn't work here anymore.'

'Oh, why not,' Neville enquired.

'He won a competition a few weeks ago and has left to become a model. We know he got his first job at Selfridges and was quite a hit with the ladies.'

'Well, good for Charles,' said Neville thinking that he might have just as much opportunity as Charles now that he was going to be a model. He wondered if Tom was Charles's agent too.

Chapter 18

Harriett and Antonio walked together to a hotel near the theatre.

'I'm sorry, Antonio,' Harriett said, 'but I have no money. It was all stolen in a scam.' She told him about the mustard spray and how things had turned out.

'I've heard about such things and I feel sorry that you have had to suffer this in my country. I'll pay for your accommodation until you receive your first wage and then you can pay me back. And now we have to find a practice room to prepare for an audition,'

'You're pretty confident I will get into the company, aren't you?'

'Of course you will. Besides I am about to coach you.' Antonio could see that Harriett didn't have the same confidence in her talents as he did. 'It's alright, Harriett. You'll be great and they will hire you.'

There was nothing else for it. She had to go with this opportunity.

The next day Antonio ushered Harriett into a practice room and began teaching her the steps of one of the dances. At the end of the practice session, Harriett's calves ached and her toes were covered in blisters. She hobbled to her room.

'Methylated spirits,' said Antonio. 'Soak your feet in metho and they'll toughen up.'

'I think I'd rather drink it and forget about dancing altogether.' Harriett laughed but she obeyed Antonio anyway.

Just three days later Antonio decided she was ready. 'I've arranged an audition with the director, Constantino, and his creative team. Let's go find a company costume for you. Something sparkly, I think. And maybe taking a new stage name might be helpful to you.'

Harriett decided to give it some thought as she pulled her hair back and slapped on new makeup she had bought from a local shop with the little money she had borrowed from Antonio.

To begin the audition, Antonio stood beside Harriett with his hand on her shoulder. He whispered in her ear, 'You'll be great. Just focus on the music.'

And it was true.

As soon as the music began, Harriett became a sultry tango dancer acting out the story of a naïve young girl who becomes a confident woman. After the climactic end, Antonio and Harriett stood on stage, puffed from the exertion of the complicated steps, as they waited for the result.

The director and his team huddled together, finally saying that yes, Harriett could join the company.

The couple adopted a casual attitude as they walked out of the stage door but once outside in the heat of the Argentinian sunshine, they turned to each other.

'We've done it!' they called out together.

With whoops of joy and a crazy impromptu dance they cavorted down the street together, Harriett finally realising that Antonio also had ambitions to be the greatest, and had chosen her to help him. Their arrangement was mutually beneficial.

Now Harriett had to find her room in the hotel arranged by the company for all their performers. It was a small room on Floor 15, neither bigger nor better than the one she had been given by the British Embassy. Still she had a job now and she loved it.

Her mind drifted to her father and she thought, *I hope you are proud, Dad. I'm a tango dancer now and live in Argentina, your home country.*

That night, after going to bed and lying awake for the longest time, making lists in her head, Harriett finally jumped out of bed and started to write. There was a new passport to get and a new stage name to call herself as well as a new bank account where her wages could be deposited.

After making the list, she sat chewing on the end of her pen. This list was mostly about the legal requirements, but what did she want for herself?

She could hear her dad's voice. 'Find a nice man, Harriett, and marry him.'

She tore off another page of her note book and started a new list. 'Number 1 – find a nice man.'

Immediately she thought of Neville. *He had been a nice man, thoughtful, gentle, and in love with me. Until he wasn't.* She sighed and wrote, 'Number 2'.

Then she thought hard for a moment. *What would I like? What do I want?* And then it came to her.

'Number 2 – buy diamonds when I'm rich.'

Feeling very satisfied, Harriett underlined this point. She had always loved diamonds, and working in the Thames Row Diamond Exchange had given her the skills to know how to tell a good diamond. To own one would be her personal indulgence as soon as she was rich.

Both lists went on the bedside table before she snuggled down under the quilt, closed her eyes and slept, dreaming of Neville.

*

'Harriett, Harriett.'

She swung around at hearing her name and saw Sylvia hurrying towards her with baby Jacinta in a stroller.

'I need to talk to you,' Sylvia called out.

Harriett stopped with a smile. 'Hello Sylvia, it's nice to see you again. Let's go to the coffee shop over there. I have a few minutes before the company warm up begins.'

Sylvia sat with Jacinta on her lap while Harriett ordered two coffees and a water for Jacinta.

She noticed Sylvia's worried face as she patted Jacinta's head and tousled hair. 'Is anything wrong Sylvia? Can I help?'

Sylvia looked around to make sure no one was listening. 'I had a visit from a very frightening character who was looking for you. Not you, the tango dancer, but Harriett Langer. Here's his photo. I took it as he walked away so it's a bit grainy.'

Harriett squinted at the photo. It was a bit fuzzy but she could still make out a strong, broad-shouldered man of about fifty with a thin moustache and a scar.

'What did he want? I don't know anyone here in Buenos Aires except people in the theatre and you. And they only know me as Rosa.'

Harriett had already taken measures to change her name. Accompanied by Antonio to assist in verification, she had opened a bank account in the name of Rosa La Boca and used it as a stage name. Even Antonio now called her Rosa and had almost forgotten her old name.

Sylvia leaned in to whisper. 'The man said you had a ring that was his. Do you, Harriett? Do you have a ring?'

Harriett was shocked. How did a stranger know about the ring, which would surely mean he also knew about Neville?

She began to scan the area, frightened.

'No,' she said. 'I don't have a ring. In fact, until I got this job I had no money or valuables at all. You know that.'

'What about your fiancé, Harriett. Where is he? Perhaps he has the ring?'

Harriett shrugged her shoulders. 'I don't know where he is.' She felt cold with fear. Someone was still after her and Neville.

After Sylvia had left, Harriett walked slowly to the theatre, thinking about 'moustache man'. Who could have found out that she and Neville had the ring? Was it someone from the Thames Row Diamond Exchange who had discovered the fake diamond and believed it was she who had taken the original? Or perhaps Neville had been caught and was in prison.

Whatever the situation, she needed to formalise her documents. They were looking for her as Harriett Langer. Although she had taken the name of Rosa and had a bank account in that name, she needed a new birth certificate and passport in the name of Rosa La Boca.

She set about chatting to some of the dancers at the company. It wasn't long before she found a carpenter in the props department who knew what to do.

As soon as the company warm up was over, Harriett was off to find a forger at an address she had been given. Along a narrow lane, she found a small uncared for place between two factories. She was ushered into a tiny room scattered with papers and half-completed documents.

In hesitant Spanish, Harriett explained what she wanted, writing down her new name, her new date of birth, her new country of origin and a new address. She had decided that making herself an Argentinian and using the theatre address would be another way of foiling anyone looking for her. She then paid over all the money she had, promising to bring more when she picked up the documents.

Now I'll be safe, she thought.

Back in her room, Harriett worried about Neville at first. Had he been discovered? Was he in jail? But soon her worry gave way to anger. He had abandoned her, so it served him right if he was handcuffed to a wall with only bread and water for sustenance.

Harriett hurried back to Sylvia's flat the first chance she had. Ideas about this stranger she had named 'moustache man' had flitted through her mind until she'd come to a decision.

'If he comes back, Sylvia, phone me immediately and I'll come if I can.'

'If you can't get here Harriett, I'll follow him for you.'

'No, Sylvia, I don't want you in any danger and especially not with Jacinta.'

Sylvia just nodded but when Harriett had left for the tango company, she thought about it. There would be little time for Harriett to get away and follow this man, so it was up to her. She had always wanted to be a spy and now was her chance. She would even be a better spy with Jacinta in her pram. No one would suspect a mother with a baby. Besides she had her blond wig to wear.

Scrabbling around in the wardrobe she found the wig. It was designed as a long plait which hung over one shoulder. Just the thing. It changed her look entirely.

By Tuesday no stranger had approached the flat and Sylvia and Harriett had just about given up worrying when 'moustache man' appeared on Sylvia's landing as she was searching for her key.

'Hello,' said Sylvia. 'You again!' *Thank goodness Jacinta is playing with the boy downstairs and his mother is looking after them,* she thought.

'Are you still looking for someone?'

'Yes, Harriett Langer. Has she returned to her flat?'

'I haven't seen anyone,' Sylvia said, casually. 'If she returns I can give her a message. Although, you know her flat was given to her for only one week? So she's probably moved on. You could leave a message under her door.'

The stranger baulked at this. 'No thanks,' he said, as he proceeded down the stairs.

Opening the door to her flat, Sylvia grabbed her wig from the stand near the front door, and her phone. She shoved the wig on her head and ran down the stairs after 'moustache man'. There he was strolling down the street looking in shop windows and not seeming to have a care in the world. She could easily keep up with him whilst using her best spy tactics such as hiding in doorways and crossing the road a number of times.

She was able to surreptitiously capture several photos of him on her phone. Some from the side and others front on, as he crossed a street. It wasn't far to the True Diamonds Exchange, where he disappeared through the front door.

Looking around, she saw a small café nearby and settled herself inside to phone Harriett. Sylvia knew that Harriett would have finished her warm up by then and may have time to meet her.

Soon Harriett was hiding inside the cafe with Sylvia.

'He didn't look around at all,' Sylvia said, feeling proud of her espionage skill. She pulled up the photos on her phone and together they examined them closely.

'He looks a bit nasty,' Sylvia said.

'Hmm. Yes, he does.' Harriett agreed. 'Can you email this one through to my phone, Sylvia?'

Sylvia sent it to her.

'I think you'd better go home now, Sylvia.'

'Can't I stay with you? I have phoned my friend and she can have Jacinta until evening.'

Harriett didn't want Sylvia to know what she was up to, or about Neville and the ring. It seemed best if she left.

'He may not have noticed you properly this time but if he comes out and sees you here an hour later he may become suspicious.'

Sylvia nodded. She was disappointed but realised Harriett was right.

'Why don't you tell me where your fiancé is, just in case something happens to you.'

Harriett laughed. 'Nothing is going to happen to me.'

Left alone, Harriett considered what to do. She needed to get into that office to see what information they had about her and Neville.

On the left of the building was a car park with several cars in it. She wondered if any of the staff left their keys in their cars. There was a slight chance she might find a spare office key, especially if they always arrived after the office was open and only needed it for emergencies. It was worth a try.

Casually she sauntered past the cars. Just as casually, she peered into the driver's windows. One had a key in the ignition with two keys attached. Of course – one of the keys could be a key to a front door at home and the other an office door key. Yes! This might be her chance. Reaching through the driver's window, she unclipped the keys and moved away quickly.

It was a strange intuition she had followed, and so far it had paid off. She thought that perhaps after the show that night might be the best opportunity to get into the office.

Chapter 19

There were five curtain calls that night, so Harriett did not get back to the True Diamonds head office until about 2 am.

She stood in the shadows for a while, watching the building and surrounding area. There were no cars in the car park and no cars on the street. Had the person who had lost his door keys not noticed, she wondered.

After a short time, she walked to the office doors and tried the first key. It worked. Suddenly she thought of security alarms and cameras, but looking up she didn't see any cameras on either side of the building and even the building next door. Good.

What will happen when I open the door? They're sure to have alarms located at a security centre. This won't work, she thought.

Then she had another thought.

She had heard that some security companies were slack. If the security staff came running and found that the alarm had just gone off because of some fault, they were hesitant about carrying out a thorough check a second time. Perhaps she could take advantage of this laziness.

Harriett turned the key in the lock and opened the door. Next to the door was a box with a red flashing light. This must be the alarm. Immediately she hurried back out the door, locking it again. Her figure merged into the shadows of the bushes around the car park, and she waited.

Within minutes a security detail in a van arrived. Dressed in black, with guns on their hips, they approached the building, unlocked the door and went inside, turning on the lights as they went.

Harriett understood enough Spanish to make out what was

being said.

'Nothing here. All clear.'

'Let's reset and go make a report.'

Before long Harriett was alone among the bushes. Once again she went to the front door, unlocked it and entered, shutting and locking the door from the inside and looking around for a place to hide.

In the third room was a large cedar desk that was just the place to squeeze under and not be seen. She was nearly caught as the security detail was there again as it turned out, turning on lights and calling, 'All clear,' in each room. Footsteps sounded down the corridor and someone hesitated at her room. Light flooded the space as the boots clumped across the room and to the front of the desk.

With her eyes shut tight and her body curled into a ball she tensed every muscle and almost stopped breathing. Maybe her fear was so intense that the security man could feel a presence. Footsteps clumped to the file cabinets at the side of the desk and she heard the man shake them, then he moved back to the door, paused, turned out the light and disappeared down the corridor.

'Nothing here,' she heard.

'There must be something wrong with the system. We'll report it and have someone come out tomorrow.'

'Let's use our door clamps to make it safe for tonight.'

Harriett could hear hammering and drilling noises towards the front area. She hadn't counted on them doing something that would keep her locked inside. Finally, the front door slammed and Harriett was alone inside a company building, probably owned by the criminals who could kill her when they found her, because there was no way out now, she thought.

She was still frozen in place ten minutes later. The noises at the front suggested that the security men had gone after locking her in, but she was afraid that they had also left someone inside to watch the place. They might even have suspected someone was still inside and were pretending to go so she would leave her hiding place and be caught.

Eventually her stiff limbs needed to uncurl, so she crawled out from the space under the desk in the dark room.

She searched in her pockets for the torch she had brought with her, her eyes adjusting to the grey-dark inside the room because of the street lighting outside casting a glow from the high windows. The quiet was deafening. Her ears strained to hear anything, her eyes drilled into the black to see, and her heart thumped loudly in her chest. She needed to move.

She crept to the front door to see what the drilling had been about.

Across the doors were metal braces, clamped to the wall and the door handles. She would have no way out from there. Surely there would be another exit. Surely Buenos Aires must have fire exits similar to England.

I'll find them after I discover the files, she thought.

The fanciest office looked promising, with grey metal filing cabinets stretched across the back wall. They all had locking mechanisms at the top but the keys were dangling from them. Administration was obviously not strict here.

Cards in slots displayed on the front of the filing cabinets detailed the contents, so Harriett moved directly to the cabinet with M to S. She would look for Symonds first. Almost straight away she found his file. Taking it out and opening it on the desk, she scanned each page.

There were copies of Neville's passport with his photo, airline tickets, a rental agreement and a car hire contract.

Harriett was amazed to discover his full name was Winston Churchill Neville Symonds. No wonder he called himself just 'Neville', a name she had never been keen on. Still, there was an advantage in using the full name, making it harder for anyone to find him.

It seemed they had been wary of him when he tried to cash the ring and had checked him out later, in their plan to foil him. *It's obvious that Neville was not such a good thief or he would have realised they would want to find out who he was and how he had come by the ring,* was

Harriett's conclusion.

Next she went to the file marked A-M to find her name. It was not there. If they hadn't discovered her name, why was the stranger looking for her?

She went back to Neville's file where she discovered a page with copies of airline tickets and passports for herself and two other women who had been sitting on the other side of Neville during their flight to Buenos Aires.

We all look pretty much the same, she thought. *Travel clothes, hair tied back, coats and backpacks. The private detectives they hired to obtain this information had obviously thought he hadn't travelled alone but were unsure who was with him.* This was in her favour, she realised. Especially as she had a new birth certificate and passport. She would be safe. But Neville wasn't. They would eventually find him, may have already done so, and kill him or torture him for the rest of money.

She wanted to protect Neville but was unsure about what to do.

She sat for a while, trying to put her thoughts in order. Could she possibly change his name slightly so they would end up looking for someone else?

The front page of each file had a summary of its contents. There was no way she could change Neville's details on the tickets or contracts inside, but she could change the summary on the first page. That way anyone checking the details might only read the front page.

If she could get into a computer, she might be able to cut and paste his name so that it read slightly differently.

She moved to the closest computer on a nearby desk. If the files were not locked with a password, maybe she could get into the right file. She tapped the space bar and up came the desk top. This person hadn't even turned it off.

I might have been a diamond sorter in my last life and a tango dancer in this, but I'm also computer savvy enough to scramble this, she thought.

Harriett searched for 'Symonds' and up came the papers. First she had to change the name slightly. They might remember the beginning of the name but often don't remember the spelling at the end. Quickly, she deleted the end of 'Symonds' so that it now read 'Symens'. Then she saved it to the file, deleting anything with Symonds on it.

The summary now read: 'Winston Churchill Neville Symens'.

Copies of the documents – the airline ticket, the rental agreement and contract for the car – were easy to change with 'XXX's across vital details, and then save. But she could do nothing about the passport. Neville's photo and name stood out boldly. She could only hope that they wouldn't look too closely at this.

She printed off the pages, and after screwing up the old papers and placing them in her pocket, she arranged the new papers in the file with the passport at the back.

Finally, she took the adhesive name off the front of the manila folder and replaced it by writing the new name. With a last flick through the file to check all was complete, she leant on the passport photo and name page with her arm causing the page to crumple slightly, making it harder to see the correct spelling and a clear photo. Then she placed the file in the cabinet again under Symens.

Now it was time to leave. She looked up the hall to the front door, then down towards the end of the passage. There should have been an exit sign somewhere.

Nothing. Perhaps this was the result of poor management. Maybe they were just so confident of their office staff they had become slack about security.

She began to search each of the rooms down the corridor. At the very end, the corridor opened up into a big room with booths, high windows and a bathroom at the end.

Harriett recognised it at once. Hadn't she spent 12 years in just such a room? But there was still no exit sign.

Maybe she could climb up to the windows and get through that way, she thought. But on a further examination she could see they were too small. She would be caught there and discovered in the morning.

The bathroom might offer a better exit. Inside on one side were hooks where the diamond sorters' white coats were hung, with toilet cubicles on the opposite wall. But still no exit.

Harriett slid to the floor and sat there with her eyes closed. Her head was beginning to ache, and her stomach to flutter with tension. It had been such a good idea but she hadn't thought it through well enough. She had been over-confident. Thought herself so clever. There was no way out.

Leaning her head against the wall, she looked up and saw the trapdoor in the bathroom ceiling. This would be better than nothing. Maybe she could get out on the roof somehow.

There was a cord hanging down next to the trapdoor which, when pulled, became a ladder. Now she could climb up and see what could be done.

Feeling shaky, she climbed through the trapdoor, at the same time pushing the small door up and onto the rafters of the building. It was very dark and she struggled to get her torch out in such a confined space. There were no gaps or loose boards in the ceiling. No way out.

Of course, she could hide but that didn't help her to get out. Then, as she looked down at the coats on hooks, an idea came to her. She was a sorter, wasn't she? And a good one at that. She could hide in plain sight.

She nutted out the idea in her head. If she stayed there until most of the staff arrived, then put on one of the coats and walked out to the booths, she could stay there all morning until the staff went for morning tea or lunch and leave with them.

It was such a good idea that Harriett began to feel better.

She shimmied down the ladder, took one of the coats, and climbed up to the ceiling again. Pulling the ladder up after her took some doing and then closing the trap, she settled down to wait.

Chapter 20

It had been 2 am when she'd first entered the True Diamonds office. Now it was 4.30 am. She had four more hours to wait. She stretched out along the wooden beams and tried to get comfortable.

At 8.30 am she heard noises below. The security company was back with the owners or managers to discuss the alarm system. Then staff began to arrive, walking down the corridor to the sorting room. Harriett could see a tiny sliver of the room through a small crack in the trapdoor and the open bathroom doorway.

Both men and women were shouting hello to each other across the room, shrugging into white coats, putting their belongings under their desk and settling into their booths. It was all pretty normal to Harriett.

She needed to wait until everyone was sitting at their desk before coming out. Finding her half way down a ladder would be a disaster.

By 9.30 am everyone was working quietly. The trap door groaned a little and the ladder snapped into place. She hadn't noticed these sounds in the night.

She shimmied down the ladder, repositioned it and the trapdoor as quickly as possible, hoping no one wanted the toilet this early in the morning.

Now she had to find a booth. This was the only problem with her plan. Would there be any spare booths? In Thames Row there were always booths that were empty because there was always someone who was away on holidays or sick. She crossed her fingers in her pockets and sauntered confidently along the row.

About three quarters of the way along was a spare booth. Harriett paused and checked with the woman next to her.

'Is this booth available?'

'Who are you?'

'I'm Chica – just filling in for today.'

She hoped her Spanish was sufficiently natural.

'Yes, that one's O.K. No one is there.'

Harriett sat down and organised her box. The woman next door was watching her closely. *She won't catch me out, I can sort like the rest.*

She began to grade the stones in the box using her loupe and placing them in the chute. After a while the suspicions of the woman were allayed as Harriett showed her skill and she stopped watching her.

By 11.30 am the woman was talking to her like a colleague.

'Where do you live?'

'La Boca.' Harriett blurted it out before she could think though whether it was a good idea to give that kind of information. 'I've got a rented flat there. What's your name?'

'I'm Martina. Where did you work before this?'

'Just in the other diamond store and, um, in an international company.' Harriett hoped there was another store in the True Diamonds company and another international company in Buenos Aires.'

'Oh, I used to work in the other diamond shop here too. Did you know Lota?'

Blast. She would know someone. 'No, I didn't. Sorry.'

They settled down to work again. Harriett wondered how she was going to escape after lunch. That would be most noticeable. She needed an excuse to leave.

Quietly she pressed the button on her mobile and waited for the ring tone.

Then after a hello, she listened closely, then said. 'Oh she has? Goodness! Is she alright? They've taken her to hospital. Oh, dear. I'll come as soon as I can.' She listened for a moment. 'I know it's my first day here but this is more important. I'll just have to cancel the work. See you as soon as I can.'

Martina had forgotten her work and was watching Harriett.

'What's happened?'

'I have to go. My mother has been taken to hospital and I need to be there.'

'What about your job? You've only just started.'

'I know. I need the money too. But I can't leave my mother in hospital. She has no one left but me.' Harriett hoped that her emotional response would appeal to Martina. 'I'll just finish this box of diamonds and then leave. It will be lunch time by then. I don't want to let the company down.'

Martina nodded at this. She was obviously tuned into mothers and company loyalty.

It was then that Harriett decided that the company was shoddy and disgusting, just like in Thames Row. But, worse, this company was searching for her with perhaps the intention of killing her. They needed a wake-up call.

So – she would steal a diamond, she decided.

She searched her mind for the ways she knew others at the Thames Row Diamond Exchange had been successful in stealing diamonds.

She knew of a perfect way. Swiftly, she palmed a small diamond into her hand. *I'm not greedy*, she thought.

She stood, turning to Martina. 'Just need the bathroom, Martina.' She hurried down to the end of the row searching for a person with cigarettes. Three booths down, there was a young woman with studs in her ears, lips and nose. Her hair flopped over her face and her fingernails were coloured black with nail polish. On her desk sat a carton of cigarettes.

'Give me a cigarette, love,' Harriett said in her hesitant Spanish. Without looking up, the girl flicked the carton over to her. Harriett slid a cigarette out and replaced the carton. 'Thanks love.' Then she hurried to the bathroom and hid in a toilet.

Carefully, she took some of the tobacco out, poked the diamond down as far as she could, and replaced the tobacco. Then she went back to her booth.

As the bell for lunch sounded, Martina scrabbled for her lunch and bag. Quickly, Harriett took her cigarette and put it to her mouth. She would light it when she was near the door.

In the meantime, she tidied her booth, wiping down the desk, the box and the loupe, to avoid any fingerprints being discovered. She had nothing to gather.

A group of women was just beginning to walk down the corridor and Harriett joined them. As she got closer to the door, her hands began to tremble from nervousness.

A few suits stood by the door watching everyone leave and keeping an eye on their electric gates. She just needed to get past them. Almost at the door, she asked a woman for a lighter, someone she'd seen lighting up a cigarette earlier. The woman fumbled in her bag and brought out a lighter with a metal tip. *My lifesaver in case the alarm goes off*, Harriett thought.

Harriett flicked it with her finger. Nothing happened for a few seconds and she was almost at the front door. Then it caught and the flame soared. She casually inhaled, and moved forward, keeping her hand to her face. Immediately a beep sounded.

'Hey, you. Where are you going?'

'Who, me?' Harriett's voice was barely a squeak.

'Yes, you. Come here.'

Harriett shuffled over to the suit thinking about what she could do if he grabbed her. She would run out the door and across the road to a cafe, then out the back door and off.

'Where do you think you're going?'

Harriett's voice had deserted her. 'For lunch,' she whispered.

She looked down at the cigarette. It was burning down and would soon reach the place where the diamond was hidden. It would fizz and the diamond would be exposed if that happened.

'Well, take that coat off. No one takes coats outside.'

Harriett's shoulders, which had tensed into a tight line, collapsed and she let out a soft sigh. She was just able to fling off the coat and hang it on a peg by the door before the cigarette burned too far.

'Sorry sir,' she said as she stepped out onto the pavement.

Her legs were shaking and she almost fell as she crossed the street and hurried down the pavement on the other side to the bus stop. She slumped into the bus seat and closed her eyes, taking the cigarette from her mouth, pinching it out, and shoving it in her pocket, the diamond still inside.

Back at the apartment, Sylvia was happy to see her.

'I was so worried, Harriett. I was scared something had happened to you when you didn't come back.'

Harriett took a sip of her coffee. The cup shook in her hand as she clutched it tighter, letting the heat of the coffee slide down her throat and into her stomach which was still full of butterflies.

'Sorry, Sylvia. I had no chance to come back to you.'

'Did you have to go to your warm up class?'

'No, I didn't make it this morning. Luckily for me, they don't always expect the stars to turn up.' She grinned and then frowned.

'You know, I don't want to be called Harriett anymore. I want to be Rosa. I don't know who that stranger was and I didn't see him again at that office where you followed him. So I just want to disappear so he'll never find me. Can you remember to call me Rosa, Sylvia?'

'Sure I can, Rosa. In fact, I think you are more Rosa than H …'. She stopped, then continued, '… that name that I can't remember, whatever it was.'

Harriett and Sylvia laughed together and hugged.

*

Lautaro Rodriguez sat in his office at the True Diamonds Exchange examining photos. He rubbed his moustache as he pondered his plans.

'See this, here?' He showed the photograph to Joaquin Garcia, who was sitting next to him. 'I don't know what that woman was doing, but these CCTV shots in the sorting room show clearly she was here last night.'

Garcia looked over his shoulder. 'That's her.' He stabbed his finger on the photo. 'She's the one I was following in England. She's the one who had taken the waterfall brooch, although we could never find it, and eventually it was handed in to the police.'

'Is that so? I wonder what she was looking for here?' Rodriguez tossed a folder on the desk followed by a closed fist. 'This is the folder for the man we bought the ring from. She was sitting next to him on the plane. We were able to get part of the money back from her, but not the rest. He was also the thief who took two roughs I brought back from Australia. Is he still here in Argentina?'

'I've searched but can't find him. She is our next best bet. We need to find him, get the money back and my roughs, and get rid of him. He knows too much about us.'

Rodriguez twisted in his seat, his body slammed back against the wall, his hands balled into fists. 'No one gets away with this.'

'I'll find her. I already know what she looks like. Do you want 24-hour surveillance?'

'Good. Yes. At the moment, we'll just keep track of her. We don't want her alerted to our surveillance. We want him. She's sure to lead us to him. Her last known address was here.' Rodriguez handed Garcia a note with the street name and number on it. 'Her neighbour said she'd left and gone home, but that obviously wasn't true. So this would be a good place to start.'

They separated at the front door, with Garcia sloping off towards Sylvia's flat.

Chapter 21

By the end of the fortnight Harriett was feeling safe and very clever at having changed Neville's file. She was also becoming known for her dancing. Everyone complimented her on her unique sensual style. Except Carla.

Carla was the star of the show. She did all the major adagio duets with her partner, Jose Santiago. They were known throughout the country and even throughout the whole of South America.

A millionaire five times over, Carla was now forty years old and was afraid that her time at the top was limited. Steps were becoming much harder to remember and some of them took a great deal of physical effort, whereas when she was younger she could easily do them.

One day as she watched Harriett dance a duet with Antonio, she realised she was a threat. How could she prevent her rise to fame? Jose, too, viewed Harriett as a threat to his future. He brooded on the idea of his demise along with Carla's fall from grace.

The next day at rehearsals Carla sat next to the director, commenting on Harriett's dancing.

'She's not bad, Constantino, but very naive. Not ready yet for a major role.'

Constantino turned to her. He recognised envy in Carla's voice immediately. Carla had been his find when she was only 18. After teaching her all he knew over the previous two decades, she'd become his star. She had brought him fame and fortune and he had a soft spot for her. But time was marching on.

'I don't agree, Carla. I think she has potential and an unusual talent. I've decided to make her your understudy. That's how she'll get the skills we need.'

Carla stomped off in an angry huff, leaving the company to rehearse without her. This was a mistake as it allowed Constantino to invite Harriett to stand in for Carla without a moment's delay.

Jose sighed. Carla had always been a hothead. And now she had left the gate open for a newcomer. He decided there and then he'd devise a plan to stop Harriett in her tracks – somehow, sometime – unless Carla was prepared to retire gracefully with him.

Harriett was overwhelmed. Of course she knew most of Carla's dances and could perform them satisfactorily but she needed a deeper understanding of each role.

The company stood around and gave her encouragement as she tried to bring some excitement to the dance. They could see she had talent.

Harriett drew in a deep breath. She knew she had to do better. Practice was the only way. So she began getting up early and going through all Carla's dances until she felt she understood the emotions she needed to bring to them.

Antonio came early one day and watched Harriett practising.

'Good work, Harriett. I think you're ready to replace Carla.'

'Oh, Antonio, I'm not looking to replace Carla – just be ready in case she is sick.'

'Hmm, all right,' Antonio murmured. 'Let's practice that last dance together.'

A week later, Harriett, still thinking of Antonio's words, was dreaming about being a soloist. She sat on the stage floor stretching and imagining a time when stardom would occur for her.

Carla might be completing an intricate spiral turn upstage close to the edge, falling off into the orchestra pit, and breaking her ankle. Immediately, the director will call for me to take Carla's place.

There was a sudden groaning sound that brought Harriett out of her dream state. It was coming from the whole cast. She looked up and there was Carla, lying in the orchestra pit, rocking backwards and forwards, holding her ankle and screaming in pain.

It seemed that her dream had come true!

Harriett looked around. She hoped that no one could guess from her face that this was what she had been thinking about. Then guilt overwhelmed her.

Perhaps wanting Carla to fall had made it happen. Could something that you imagined, hoped for, come true?

Before she could examine this thought any further, an ambulance arrived, and Constantino was asking Harriett to prepare for Carla's role tonight.

There was no time to lose.

Jose, Carla's partner, had left in the ambulance with Carla, so Antonio was also preparing for the role. They would dance together.

A little shiver of excitement spread through Harriett's body.

This was not the time for guilt. She pushed it to the back of her mind, where Neville also lived, and strode off to the costume department to choose something grand for the performance.

She wouldn't let anything distract her.

Calmly she did her warm up exercises and mentally went through the steps of Carla's dances.

Then it was time for makeup and hair.

Everything was completed efficiently by the company staff and Harriett felt herself being turned into a solo dancer. A star.

A knock at her dressing room door announced five minutes to curtain. Harriett took one last look in the mirror and walked to the middle of the closed velvet curtains where Antonio was waiting.

He knew how Harriett would be feeling. He had felt this way himself when he had begun his dance career. He gazed down at her, reaching out his hand to take hers.

'Are you ready to do this?'

'Yes, I think so.' Harriett's lips trembled as she answered.

He smiled. 'We'll be great! Just focus on the music.'

As the orchestra's opening chords speared the air, the curtains slid apart to reveal the starring couple in the spotlight. The music took hold of Harriett and she fell into Antonio's arms in the tango's opening lunge.

After that the night was a blur. Harriett was there for her entrances and exits and then back in the dressing room for changes of costumes. It was not until the finale when she and Antonio moved forward for their bows, that her body and mind seemed to rise to a higher exaltation. The crowd spontaneously stood and erupted into clapping and stamping that lasted for ten curtain calls. It was astonishing. Antonio and Harriett could not believe the audience was so willing to clap for so long. Surely their hands were red and raw from the effort.

At last the curtains closed and the company collapsed on the floor of the stage, talking quietly in groups.

The director appeared on stage and gathered everyone together, pulling Harriett and Antonio in beside him.

'This has been an amazing night. Harriett and Antonio are our new stars since the audience could tell how special they were. Congratulations to you all for capturing that same excitement yourselves, and responding to the audience too.'

It was all too much for Harriett.

Later in bed, she couldn't sleep. When she got up she couldn't even stand still. She phoned Antonio in his room and after hearing that he couldn't sleep either, suggested they go for a walk.

They were still awake at 5 am when the papers were thrown from trucks to the footpath in readiness for the day, and they discovered their faces on the front pages, with banners such as, 'New Stars Discovered,' and 'The Tango Company Thrills Us With New Stars'.

Harriett's dream really had come true.

*

In the hospital, Carla awoke to be greeted by Jose, surrounded by a variety of newspapers.

'I'm afraid it's not good news, Carla. It seems we have been ousted by those two dancers who are being acclaimed as new stars.'

Carla grabbed one paper and read the headlines, then screwed up the page and tossed it towards the bin.

Jose watched it miss the bin and land on the floor. He sighed.

'You know, Carla. I've wanted to retire for some time now. I'm 45 and finding it harder and harder to maintain my edge, to be as flexible as I was. I've only kept going for your sake. But it seems to me that now is the opportunity to retire gracefully from this major company. We will still be a couple that people will want to watch. A small company with the possibility of adagio stage work would suit us perfectly.'

He looked speculatively at Carla with a slight smile. It might even be the right time to get married and live happily ever after, as the saying goes, he thought.

Carla was not in the mood to agree.

But two hours later when Constantino came to tell her the news that he was replacing her with Antonio and Harriett, she burst into tears instead of throwing one of her famous temper tantrums.

*

Back at the company warm up and rehearsal, Harriett and Antonio were still in a daze. Partly from the wonder of it all and partly because they'd had only a few hours' sleep.

Later when Harriett stood outside the theatre where new banners and neon signs were already up announcing the two new stars, she spoke her name out loud – 'Rosa'.

After the success of that first night, Constantino had immediately phoned the marketing department so Rosa's and Antonio's full names would be used for all promotion in the future.

Harriett was now living a very full life as Rosa La Boca.

And as Rosa, she was determined to let her old life go and be happy with her dance partner, Antonio. They worked well together and

Rosa found him very attractive.

Why didn't I see his great looks and body before? she asked herself, as she put on the last touches of lipstick before the show began. *He seems to like me too.* Rosa was convinced that they would make a great couple.

She imagined Antonio and herself touring the world, doing exhibition dances wherever they went.

We'll have an entourage of staff who will look after the twins, baby Rosa and baby Antonio. We'll stay in the most expensive hotels and each year will have time away at our cliffside house in the Bahamas where Antonio and I will recapture our love as we frolic in the surf at the edge of the sand near our home. Neville will look on from the top of the cliff and wish he never left me. Olé! How magnificent! How poignant!

At the end of that night's show while both Rosa and Antonio were on a high from the performance, Rosa made her move.

'Come on, let's go back to my dressing room for a drink.' Since she had become a star, Rosa's dressing room had changed from the dormitory style where all the chorus changed, sharing mirrors and clothes hangers, to a suite of rooms with lounges and even a bed. She had spent some time that afternoon fluffing up the pillows and spraying her favourite perfume around.

Now was the time.

With a flick of her gown's zipper, her robe fell in a puddle to the floor, leaving her in stockings, heels and a teddy, all in black. Her eyes glittered with excitement. She was now a Spanish femme fatale.

She knew she had changed. The dancing had made her slimmer and more toned and this made her seem taller. The climate and a little sunbathing had given her skin a bronze glow. Her hair had grown even longer and was now able to be twisted and coiled into some wonderful shapes. She could move sensuously and seductively, smoothly and sexily Her cheek bones were now accentuated, higher, so that her lips appeared poutier, and her nose more aquiline. In point of fact, Harriett, the pretty local girl from Thames Row, diamond sorter by trade, looked and was now fully Rosa La Boca, a sultry model of fame and international beauty.

Her eyes beckoned to Antonio.

She carefully poured him a Caipirinha cocktail, the famous South American drink expected to start any romance. Handing it to him with long fingers tapering to blood red nails, she sidled up to him expectantly.

Antonio took a step back with his arms out to her. 'Querida,' he said softly. 'This can't be.'

Rosa looked quizzically at him. *Why is he waiting?*

'I like you, Rosa. In fact, I love you. But I lust after men.' He gazed ruefully at her.

Men! Rosa was aghast. Her thoughts of femme fatale action and marriage and twins and lust in the sand and sea, all shrivelled and died in a moment.

Later, walking home alone, she talked quietly in her head to her dad, a thing she had begun to do over recent months.

You see Dad, I've made it. I'm a star. I know, I know, that I still haven't found a nice man. But you know what, Dad? I don't need a nice man. Of course I want someone to share my successes and pitfalls with, but it could be a friend or family – if you were still alive it would have been you. I just want to be happy. If Neville had still been around I would have shared my life with him. Not because he was a nice man, even though he was, but because I love him.

Neville's face came into her mind. A kind face, a loving face, a handsome face – until it wasn't.

Harriett wiped a tear from her eyes and then, as a group of teenagers came running up squealing and asking for autographs, she became a star again.

Chapter 22

Several months had gone by while Harriett and Antonio were being interviewed by the media, had their photos plastered on every billboard and magazine and signed contracts from sponsors for perfume, underwear and sporting goods.

They were very tired but, as they said to each other when it all seemed too much, they were very, very rich.

They needed some time out from the bustle of the theatre and even each other.

Harriett decided to walk leisurely down to Sylvia's flat and say hello. It would be the first time for months that she could relax in an atmosphere that had nothing to do with dance.

She knocked on Sylvia's door, hoping she was home. The door was flung open and Sylvia stood there, baby Jacinta on her hip.

'Harriett', she cried out. 'It's so great to see you. I've followed your success all the way. Let's go down to the cafe for coffee.'

Once there, Harriett sat with Jacinta on her lap, bouncing her up and down.

'Thank goodness you haven't become one of those stars who don't want to have anything to do with old friends,' Sylvia said, slurping coffee and cake at the same time.

'I keep telling everyone that I was instrumental in you becoming a star. Most of them don't believe me, of course.' She leaned across the table and hugged Harriett. 'I'm so happy to see you. Tell me all about it.'

'I agree that you were instrumental in getting me started. If you hadn't invited me to the Milongas I would never have met Antonio.' She smiled, then the smile left her face and she became serious.

'Sylvia, did my fiancé ever come back to find me?'

Sylvia looked hard at Harriett. She looked so good, so confident, so beautiful and rich. She didn't need that fiancé. If he came back, he would probably only want her for her money, she thought. So she shook her head and changed the subject, telling Harriett of the escapades Jacinta had in trying to walk while falling over everything.

Three hours later, Harriett had to go. She gave Sylvia a big hug, promising to come around again to chat and handing her two tickets to the show. 'I hope you can get a babysitter and come see me,' she said.

As she walked to the stairwell, Sylvia called after her. 'Harriett.'

Harriett turned around with a smile, 'Not Harriett – Rosa,' she said.

Sylvia had been having second thoughts about not telling Harriett about Neville coming around to find her. Should she tell her? Would it be the right thing to do? But on seeing Harriett's happy smile and hearing her say her new name, 'Rosa', she decided against it.

Harriett's eyebrows were raised in a question.

'Nothing really,' Sylvia called out. 'Just … good luck.'

Harriett nodded and ran down the stairs to the street as Sylvia shut the door firmly behind her.

*

Joaquin Garcia slipped into a dark doorway. Had he been seen? It was stupid of him to be so careless.

Harriett stopped dead in her tracks. That man. Where was he now? The same man who had been following her in Thames Row. Surely she was mistaken.

No, she wasn't. She began to shake. *He must have followed me across the world*, she thought. *There must be a connection between the Thames Row Diamond Exchange criminals and the Buenos Aires criminals and they've found me.* Perhaps she hadn't been as clever as she thought during her midnight break-in at the True Diamonds office.

Harriett dashed down a small alley, taking several back streets to the theatre stage door.

Inside, she collapsed against a wall, breathing heavily and shaking all over.

What could she do now?

At front of stage, Constantino was interrupted by a loud bang as someone flung the foyer doors back against the wall.

Harriett had a premonition that it was something to do with her, so she ran silently along the mezzanine to the steps leading down into the foyer.

There stood the man, the limo driver, arguing with Constantino.

'I saw her come in here. Where is she?'

Constantino answered sternly. 'There is no one here called Harriett Langer. So get out. Now. Or I'll call the Policia Federal.'

Constantino firmly closed and locked the doors to the main theatre, leaving a frustrated man standing outside.

Harriett – or Rosa as she was known in the dance troupe – was terrified. She would have to leave the company and disappear.

Constantino grabbed her as she came down onto the floor.

'Who was that guy and what did he want?'

She sank to the front seats of the audience and told Constantino about the brooch and the criminal connection.

Constantino looked thoughtful. 'We can't have our star treated like a thief. I'll fix it for you. If you see him again just call me.'

Harriett was only partly relieved by this. Constantino didn't know how dangerous this man was. She needed to walk from her hotel to the theatre every day and back every evening and not be seen.

Rushing down to the basement, she began to search among the props for a disguise.

'Hello Joseph, I'm just down here looking for a disguise.'

'Hello, love. I can find you anything you want or I wouldn't be a very good costume manager, would I? he asked. Everyone loved Joseph. He was always down there sorting through the gear, repairing, ironing and, Harriett surmised, trying on a few of the dresses.

'Here, this will suit you,' Joseph handed her a red wig with a deep fringe that fell forward over her forehead. A bib-and-brace painter's suit with the cuffs rolled up seemed right. .

She crossed the road to the hotel with a group of dancers.

'Are you in disguise, Rosa?' one asked.

'Sort of,' she said, trying not to look around. 'Just thought this wig was more me.'

'You're a star now, Rosa. You'll just have to put up with the attention. Besides it's good for the company.'

By this time, they had reached the hotel and 'Rosa' slipped inside.

*

Out in the street, Garcia slumped against the wall watching the company leave the theatre.

There were several men, and two women, a red head and a blonde. But no one like Harriett Langer.

He turned to leave and came up against an enormous poster of Harriett. The dancer's eyes shone, her mouth pouted. Her body was enveloped in silver and her legs balanced on high-heels in a tango lunge. Across the top of the poster in large letters was the name, 'Rosa La Boca'.

He clawed at the poster, ripping it into a long strip. Rodriguez would be happy to see this, he thought.

Soon Joaquin Garcia was meeting with Rodriguez in his office. The air was smoky with the cigars both were puffing. Rodriguez growled.

'What have you found out? I hope it's something good.'

'I've found her. She's a dancer with the Argentine tango troupe. He threw the poster on the table. Rosa's face boldly, sensually, looked out from the curled, torn paper. She calls herself 'Rosa La Boca' now. That's why I had trouble finding her.'

'Is she meeting with this Winston Symens? That's who I really

151

want.'

'So far she's done nothing. I've hacked her mobile but she has made no calls to him at all. She's quite a star now and getting good money. I'm afraid she may have left him.'

'We'll keep on it for a bit. He might have decided to tour around the country. He's got all my money now and my roughs.' Rodriguez's face took on a cruel twist. 'I want her frightened enough to phone him. Then …,' he said softly, with menace, 'I want you to kill him.'

'Right. I'm on it.' Garcia left, going straight to the theatre. He'd just let her see him occasionally so that she'd know he was onto her, he thought.

*

Rosa was scared for every minute of every day, except when she was dancing. It took away her worries, set her mind free. But for the rest of the time, her anxiety could be seen on her face and in her manner.

Constantino was worried about her.

'I can see you are still frightened of that man, Rosa. Don't let it affect your performance.'

Harriett spent all day in the theatre with other cast members and then in disguise going to and from the theatre, and then alone in her room, doors locked and thumb ready to press her mobile for help.

Antonio became increasingly concerned about her behaviour.

'What's wrong, Rosa.'

'There's someone after me. I'm so frightened.'

'My partner could help. You need a bodyguard and he would be perfect. What about that?'

Rosa hugged Antonio. 'Thank you. That would be a great help.'

From then on, every morning Antonio's partner would wait for her at her door and in the evening usher her to her room.

Rosa stayed frightened though. It was just the way it had been in Thames Row. And it was the same man. At every turn she felt someone was there, just out of sight, watching her, drilling his eyes into her.

It had gone beyond imagination and conjecture. It was real and her body and mind were tense all the time.

I'm just dancing to stay out of danger, she thought.

*

Carla was so angry. Rosa had taken everything. She, herself, was the one that people loved and she was sure they were dismayed that someone so unsophisticated, so gauche, so new would be her equal.

She was convinced she could prove she was better than Rosa, and one day she could contain herself no longer.

She changed into one of her famous costumes, shrugged into her coat and stepped out onto the stage where Antonio was practising a new step.

Jose, who had been searching for her, stepped across her path.

'What mischief are you planning Carla?'

Pushing him aside, Carla strode up to Antonio, letting her coat drop to the floor and placing her arm around Antonio's neck.

'This is the way tango should be danced, not that insipid method chosen by Rosa.'

As Antonio backed away, she arched her back and dipped into her lunge. At the same moment Jose had reached her side and bent down to retrieve her coat from the floor.

Their heads met in the loudest crack and both of them staggered away, their knees buckling, their arms flailing about.

Jose, closest to the curtain, grasped it firmly and tried to pull himself up with it. Immediately a louder crack was heard as the strain on the curtain rings gave, and 10 metres of red velvet and golden tassels plunged onto the stage with Jose and Carla underneath.

There was silence for a moment until stage hands came running. It took another few moments to find them both in the folds of material, mostly guided by Carla's screaming and the tangle of kicking legs.

Bits of velvet were stuck to her perspiring body, and her neat bun at the nape of her neck was askew. She knew she had made a fool of herself but looked around wildly for blame.

There was Jose, standing limp, brushing velvet off his hair.

Bending towards him, pointing her red-nailed finger at him like a claw, mouth open, Carla screamed obscenities.

Still screaming, she flounced off the stage holding her head high while Jose rushed after her. This hadn't gone well. It was all Rosa's fault, according to the now enraged Jose.

*

Joaquin Garcia couldn't gain entrance into the theatre to find Harriett, or Rosa, as she was now called. He needed help.

He watched the dancers as they returned to the hotel. It was Carla's angry face and her shouted comments about Rosa that took his interest

Garcia walked up to her and offered her a cigarette. 'Heard you talking about Rosa. She's disgusting, isn't she.'

Carla drew on her cigarette and looked him over. Here was someone who seemed to hate Rosa as much as she did. 'She's a usurper. I wish I could get rid of her.'

'You can, you know. I want her out of my hair too. She's left her husband and the three children all alone. Can you get me into the theatre so I can talk to her?'

Carla drew a shocked breath. 'What a liar. She said she was single. I can help you. She's down in the basement trying on the costumes for the masked ball scene. Come with me.'

Garcia followed Carla to the side door where Carla entered her passcode. 'The basement is down those stairs and you can come out this automatic exit.' Carla disappeared leaving Garcia to creep down the stairs alone.

A vast wardrobe room opened up at a turn in the stairs. A flash of glittery tulle and a purple mask moved ahead of him. Perhaps he could catch her alone and make her tell him where the man, Winston Symens, had gone.

With one grab he had a hold on Rosa, twisting her arms behind her back and thrusting her up against a wall. 'Tell me where he is,' he growled.

But Rosa wasn't as helpless as he'd anticipated, landing an elbow into his stomach and then his ribs. She used all her skills to flip him over so he landed, winded, flat on the floor.

Garcia, who was usually able to subdue any one in a combat situation, realised he'd been outsmarted, so rolled away and rushed up the stairs and out the exit door.

Joseph, dressed as a woman, watched him go. He turned to Rosa who had been nearby, also wearing a mask. She took it off, her mouth open in horror.

'I don't know how he got in here, Rosa, but he obviously can't compete with a martial arts black belt like me,' Joseph explained. 'He must have mistaken me for you, seeing me in this dress.' He gazed down at the shimmering confection he was wearing.

Garcia, out of breath and bruised, hurried back to the diamond trader's office. He hadn't considered Rosa La Boca-Harriett Langer could be so skilled.

He decided he would have to find some other way to keep track of her movements. In the meantime, he'd keep himself busy with other work.

Chapter 23

A year after he'd landed his first modelling job, Neville had made it.

The first job, at Harrods, had been exciting and hard work. But now he was being touted as 'The Face of Harrods'. Every magazine contained at least one photo of him. Every advertisement for Harrods featured him – in Rome, wearing leather coats or with a leather wallet to hand; in Paris, wearing plum or yellow silk ties and handkerchiefs or the latest Hermes men's cologne; in Prague, wearing the latest style in boots and holding a Swarovski crystal champagne glass of bubbly.

He was a household name.

It had all happened so quickly, one week you're nobody and the next you are somebody. He had been so busy he hardly thought of anything other than work. The only thing he pined for was to see Harriett again. He had never been able to find her.

Thinking she had returned to Thames Row, which had been her home for so many years, he went to the local authorities site-directory and then, finding nothing, googled her name. When that proved unsuccessful, he widened his search to include inner and outer London and finally the whole of Britain. Almost every night he beat himself up with thoughts of how he had behaved. If only he hadn't been so angry. They could have lived happily ever after and placed the three million pounds in a suitable charity. He decided to place that money in a trust account and not spend it on himself. If he ever found her he would give it to her so she could make the decision about what to do with it.

His work life had become a great success. But he couldn't understand how that could be when he was so miserable all the time.

'They love that sultry look you have Neville, so keep it up,' was

Tom's advice.

Neville had learned from talking to Janie, that it had taken some time for the discovery of the ring. It was when he was having coffee in the cafe, now owned by Janie, that he heard the story.

'We were all terminated when the Thames Row Diamond Exchange went into liquidation. Evidently someone had stolen the Monroe ring, and insurance didn't cover it. You were lucky you had left the previous month or you would have been terminated too.'

A month! That was quite a long time for no one to notice the fake, Neville thought.

'What happened to everyone?' he asked, feeling guilty.

'Well, some people took the opportunity to travel, others got jobs in London and a few stayed here in Thames Row taking other jobs.'

'Of course, we never found out what happened to Harriett. She left about the same time as you. We all thought you'd run off together. But here you are and no Harriett.'

'Yes,' muttered Neville.' Here I am and no Harriett.'

'Janie gave him a hug. It's nice to see you again. I know the diamond exchange is trying to haul itself back from disaster and wants some of the old staff to return, but I'm happy here in my own business now. Maybe you'd like to come to dinner one night with me and we could chat over old times together. Mmm?'

Neville looked at Janie. She was nice. She had made her way after the company failed and had landed on her feet, which showed some gumption. And he hadn't had a girlfriend since Harriett. Perhaps now was the time?

'I'd like that Janie. Let's make it this Saturday?'

Saturday came around too soon. Neville had been thinking of cancelling it several times and then deciding not to. He needed to take the plunge and forget Harriett. At 8 pm he knocked on Janie's door.

There she was in a wonderful crimson dress that clung to her body in all the right places. And on her feet she was wearing those beautiful black shoes with the red velvet roses and diamante studs.

'Wow,' he said. 'You look terrific.'

'Thank you,' Janie said coyly. 'The dress is new but the shoes are ones I wore at the Diamond Exchange. I thought a little reminder of those days was in order for tonight.' She took a few steps, posing and twisting her body to one side then the other, with a smile.

'I do remember them,' Neville said. 'I remember they caused such a noise when the alarm went off, each time you wore them.'

Janie stopped walking. 'I have a confession to make Neville.' She paused.

Neville raised his eyebrows.

'I sometimes hid diamonds in the diamante studs, little ones only, and got away with it.'

Neville smiled at her triumphantly. 'I knew about that Janie. I thought they didn't pay the secretaries very well and that this could be some sort of compensation. Besides I hated the 'suits'. You don't think the alarm and I could not find you out?'

'Oh, dear,' Janie gasped. 'I thought I was being so clever. You knew all the time?'

They set off, chatting along the way, and he took her hand as they turned into the restaurant. They had a delicious meal of lemon chicken with jasmine rice, and ice cold Riesling, followed by sticky date pudding.

By 10 pm they were walking back to Janie's house above the cafe. At the stairs she turned to him. 'Would you like to come up and have some champagne?'

'Thanks Janie, It's just what I would like.'

At the top of the stairs, Janie flung off her velvet shoes and turned to Neville. 'I've never kissed a boss before,' she said.

'And you haven't now. I'm not your boss any more. In fact, you are your own boss. So here's to you.'

He lifted her off her feet and carried her into the kitchen. 'Something to drink first,' he said, wondering why he was hesitating.

'Oh, yes,' said Janie. 'And perhaps some cake. I've just made it especially for you.'

Neville twisted around to see the cake and tripped over Janie's feet as she was standing right behind him. His hands flailed in the air as he staggered forward, until one hand landed in the centre of the cake, squashing it completely so that cream and cake dripped down the bench and onto the floor.

They both looked at it. Then they began to laugh. 'I guess that's the end of any romance,' Janie said, still laughing.

Neville, looking concerned, nodded as he choked on his laughter. 'I guess that's so. Perhaps we can just be friends, Janie?'

Janie nodded as she ushered him out the door. *Just as well*, she thought as she cleaned up the cake. *Because I'm not in love with him.*

*

It was about that same time, after a year working in Buenos Aires, that Rosa-Harriett found herself back in London with the tango company, booked for a season. It had been a year of fear and tension and this old setting gave her reason to pause and reflect on her life and the physically demanding path she'd chosen.

I've been afraid for too long, she decided. She hadn't seen the limo man for many months. Either he'd given up after being beaten about by Joseph or he was too clever at staying hidden. She had kept up her disguises as protection for the entire time. Now her home country would be safer, she thought. No one following her here.

Her first task was to google lots of sites to see if there was any mention of Harriett Langer. She found nothing.

Her feelings for her home overwhelmed her so much that after she had settled into The Savoy, where the stars were being housed by the company, her first thought was to visit her real home, Thames Row.

A feeling of relief from home sickness and a sense of freedom overwhelmed her as she walked along the high street. The summer wind was strong and gusts of blossoms spiced the air. The sky was the usual white over London, with drifts of pale blue. Everything was as she remembered it except The Diamond Exchange building, which looked forlorn, empty, with 'For Rent' signs and graffiti littering the walls.

The café across the way was still there, so she meandered across, expecting to see Bruno.

She had left Harriett behind. A year and a half as Rosa had cemented her character. She now had an Argentinian way of speaking and using her hands, and a dancers' way of walking and moving.

As much as everyone was shocked and amazed to see a beautiful and alluring woman in the coffee shop, Harriett was shocked and amazed to learn that Janie owned it.

Janie came sweeping out to greet her and walked her inside. 'Hello, it's you, isn't it, Harriett? I have seen posters everywhere and wondered if it was you.'

She fussed about with coffee and pastries, engaging Harriett in conversation.

Harriett had trouble recognising Janie. The change was amazing. She now wore casual clothes and flat ballet shoes. Where were the high-heeled beauties that she had always coveted?

It wasn't hard to get Janie talking about the town and in particular the diamond exchange, the bank and the coffee shop. Soon Harriett knew everything there was to know.

'The diamond exchange suffered some hard times.,' Janie said. 'But good times came around again and they have now moved to bigger premises, where the bank used to be.'

'What happened to the bank?'

'Oh, it closed, and the bank manager is now a famous model for Selfridges.'

'Wow, what a change – from bank manager to model!'

'Yes,' said Janie, 'But that's not all. One of our very own diamond exchange security managers also became a male model.'

Harriett's mind quickened at these words. 'And who would that be?'

Janie leaned forward. 'It was Hatchet-face. He's at Harrods and, in fact, is their mascot, "The Face of Harrods".'

It amazed Harriett that she still had this frisson of excitement every time she heard Neville's name. Of course she still loved him even though she knew he did not love her back.

Harriett was interested to hear how Janie had come to own the cafe.

'Well,' Janie settled in to tell her story. 'When the Diamond Exchange failed and everyone was made redundant, I wanted a new start so I bought Bruno's café. I've always been interested in cooking and wanted to try my hand at making cupcakes and slices for a coffee shop.'

Harriett was amazed. Fancy Janie making cupcakes. Wonders would never cease. She supposed that if she could remake herself as Rosa, a dancer, then Janie could certainly remake herself as a chef.

Chapter 24

Joaquin Garcia sat at his desk waiting for the international phone call beeps to finish.

'Have you any news for me?'

'No, nothing.' The woman's voice at the other end was thin and hesitant, as fear at hearing Garcia's voice penetrated her mind.

'She hasn't talked to anyone outside the dancers and Antonio. There's nothing I can do.'

'You'll have to try harder. Follow her more closely and check her emails. I need to know soon. Don't forget you are putting your little family in jeopardy if you don't get something for me.'

He slammed the phone down and turned to Rodriguez.

'I think I'll have to go to London myself. This arrangement I set up in Argentina isn't working out as I'd thought. Especially now they are all in London.'

Rodriguez turned a pistol over and over in his hands. 'We've waited long enough on your say-so. I've almost run out of patience.'

Garcia watched the gun glint in the light, shiny, attractive and lethal. He would have to check on Rosa himself, he thought.

In London his first call to his female contact was made with just a message for them to meet.

*

Harriett and Sylvia were having tea in Regent Street. Harriett was glad that Sylvia had asked to come to London with her because she was the one friend she could count on.

'What is it, Sylvia? You are so fidgety today. Aren't you enjoying this break from work?'

'Of course I like it. I just have something to do. I have to go. I won't be long.'

Harriett watched her scuttle away, head down as she hurried as if her life depended upon it.

Harriett noticed her own face on a billboard nearby. *These pictures are everywhere, so why doesn't Neville come and find me? Because he hates me, that's why. Why don't I seek him out then?* This was harder to answer to herself. *I guess it's because I am conflicted about it. I love him but hate him because he hasn't bothered to find me. I want him but somehow I'm afraid to find him and tell him in case he rejects me. It's better not to know the answer. It's best just to stay aloof.*

Out in the warm sunshine, Harriett strolled down the street, enjoying the hustle and bustle of the crowd. She moved through an arcade and onto The Ritz on her way to Green Park.

Suddenly she saw Sylvia hurrying up the steps of The Ritz side entrance.

Harriett called to her, thinking perhaps they could have a cocktail in The Ritz bar. She hurried to catch up.

At the steps, she pulled up short. Sylvia had turned into the archway of The Ritz bar and with her was the hated limo driver.

Fear hit her again. He was here in London. The tension that she had thought was over had caught up with her again, clawing at her mind, causing her stomach to contract. Nausea overcame her and she bent over the gutter, her throat contracting and heaving.

As she straightened up and wiped her mouth, Harriett looked around her. She was confused. What could Sylvia be doing with this man?

She sidled into the bar, checking first that Sylvia and the limo man were being ushered to seats at the back. She slid into a seat behind a large pillar and strained forward to listen.

Although they were talking quietly, their voices became louder as they argued.

'You need to stay with her and watch her closely.'

'I can't do any more than I do. I'm at the theatre as much as possible but I have Jacinta.'

'You'll be putting Jacinta in jeopardy if you don't do better than this.'

'Please don't hurt her. I'll do anything you say.'

'Get back to her emails and calls. She must be meeting him here in London. Get it done. Hear me? Get it done.'

A chair scraped back and Harriett put her head down, turning up the collar of her coat at the same time, hoping that this would disguise her.

The breeze ruffled her hair as they swept by, he in an aggressive way and Sylvia quietly, and fortunately they did not see her.

Somehow Sylvia was in league with these criminals, Harriett realised. From what she had heard, they were using Sylvia to track down Neville.

Harriett made a quick call to Sylvia, saying she was going back to The Savoy and then looked for the limo driver on the street.

There he was walking quickly to Fortnum and Mason's. Following him wasn't hard as his head was down and he was in a hurry.

Ducking into the store, she could see him in the cafe section with a man who looked like one of the suits from the Thames Row Diamond Exchange.

Harriett thought they were arguing, he was poking the limo driver in the chest, his mouth open, his face red.

After a short time, they left, going in different directions. Who should she follow?

In the end she decided on the suit, the boss.

With heightened adrenalin and feeling quite clever at her manoeuvres in and out of the crowd, Harriett managed to keep him in her sights … until he climbed into a taxi.

Harriett stopped. There must be a way to find him. She turned towards the taxi rank.

'I think I left something in that taxi. Could you give me his number?'

'Course ma'am, here it is.' He handed her a company card with the taxi number in the rank.

Immediately, Harriett phoned the company. 'I think I left something in taxi 1022. Will you ask him to call me as soon as he is free?'

Fifteen minutes later, the driver returned her call. 'You didn't leave anything in my taxi,' he said.

'Maybe a man, your next passenger, took it. Can you tell me where you dropped him?'

'I took him to the Red Lion in Westminster.'

'Thank you so much.'

Harriett took the next taxi on the rank to the pub, which was squeezed between two women's fashion stores. Its windows were arched and the glass decorated with patterns. Baskets of geraniums adorned the entrance and, inside, brass lamps hung from the ceiling. She could see several well-dressed men sipping drinks. The man she had followed was in the far corner with someone she knew. Kevin Coates! The man who had run the "Using your Diamonds as an Asset" course.

Kevin Coates and the limo driver, who she knew was linked to criminals at the diamond exchange. What could that mean?

At that moment the pair rose and approached the door.

She scurried into one of the stores next door, hiding her face and bending her body to make it seem smaller.

Kevin stood on the pavement and lit up a cigarette. The match flared and Kevin took a long draw, then let it out, his eyes glancing over the store and its customers. Then he nodded to his companion and walked away. The limo driver immediately turned and walked off in the opposite direction.

Harriett let out a small groan. She whispered a 'sorry' to the shop assistant and also left – via the back door – before scurrying down the closest lane. She had come close to being caught.

*

Back at The Savoy, Harriett sought out Sylvia.

'Sylvia, what's going on?'

'I don't know what you're talking about Rosa.'

'That man you met at The Ritz. What does he want? Why were you with him?'

Sylvia staggered back and collapsed on the bed. 'How did you know? What did you hear?'

'Enough to know you have been spying on me.'

Sylvia burst into tears. 'Oh, Rosa, that man came up to me in Argentina and told me I had to find out everything you did and report to him. He said he would hurt Jacinta if I didn't do as he said.'

They both looked over at Jacinta playing happily on the floor with coloured blocks.

'So you've been spying on me since we were in Argentina? What is he looking for?' Harriett took out her phone and showed Sylvia the picture she had taken of Joaquin Garcia and Kevin Coates.

'That's him, but I don't know the other man. He wanted to know who you were seeing. He said you had broken into his office in Buenos Aires and that you had a brooch and a ring that belonged to him. He said he couldn't get back the brooch because you had given it to the police who would ask too many questions if he claimed it.'

Harriett looked at Sylvia whose eyes were desperately pleading with her.

She glanced once more at Jacinta. She had come to love her too and could understand Sylvia's predicament, even as she considered the danger she now faced.

Sylvia went on. 'He wants information about the man you came to Argentina with because he has three million pounds and some things called 'roughs' that are theirs.'

'Who are they?'

'They're criminals. I don't know, really. Maybe some sort of organised crime gang.' Sylvia whispered, burying her head in her hands as she sobbed loudly. 'He says if I don't have information soon he will take Jacinta away. I didn't know what to do.'

Harriett could see the connections now between Kevin Coates and the criminals in both the Thames Row and Buenos Aires diamond exchanges.

'Alright, this is what we'll do,' she told Sylvia, taking charge of the situation, sure that Sylvia would now follow her instructions. 'You need to give him something so he will back off a bit. I'm going to find the brooch. As for the man I came to Argentina with, he has long disappeared. I don't know where he is.'

'I said that to him but he didn't believe me.'

Harriett had a week to solve her problems while the company rehearsed on the new London stage. So she began her search right away for the brooch, which she saw as a priority to get the limo man off Sylvia's back, and ultimately her own. First up for information she sought out Janie again.

Chapter 25

Janie was pleased to see Harriett.

'The brooch. I remember when you found it and handed it in to the police. No one claimed it, so Bruno bought it, partly with the proceeds from selling his cafe.'

'Good. Does he live nearby?'

'Of course,' she said, and wrote down his address.'

Bruno certainly had made it, Harriett realised when she saw his home. She knocked on the door set in the midst of white columns and white floor tiles, as though modelled on a Greek mansion in Santorini.

'Harriett! It's you, isn't it?'

'Hello Bruno.'

'Come in, come in. It's nice to see you.' He looked a little shy.

'I remember at lunch you always had a latte and an avocado and tomato sandwich. You look wonderful! Better than when you lived in Thames Row working for the Diamond Exchange.'

Harriett shook her head. *Still gauche*, she thought. *I don't know why I ever went out with you.*

Claire, Bruno's wife, served them cups of coffee and Harriett met the couple's three children who stared at her in her exotic outfit as if she was an exotic butterfly.

When there was a lull in the conversation Harriett mentioned the brooch.

'Do you remember it?'

'Of course.'

'I'd like to buy it back from you.'

Bruno looked flustered and then tried to explain. 'At the time,

Kevin …' He paused. 'Do you remember Kevin Coates? He told me you had it but that you'd handed it into the police. But I don't have it any more. I sold it to Charles.'

Harriett sat up. 'Charles! Do you mean Charles the ex-banker, now a model?'

'I do,' Bruno said. 'Charles came by one day and said he'd heard about it too and wanted it. I was having a bit of financial difficulty at the time so I sold it.'

Harriett asked Bruno where Charles lived, and then said goodbye, promising to keep in touch, already knowing she wouldn't.

So Charles has the brooch! I need to see him as soon as possible, she decided.

Bruno watched Harriett leave. Life was not so great these days, he thought, what with three children and a wife he didn't like. It was all his mother's fault. If she hadn't been best friends with Claire's mother, he wouldn't have been ensnared in their machinations to get him married. Now look at him. He was hoping she'd go back to Italy with their children.

He fancied Harriett. Or should he call her Rosa, he wondered. A tryst in London could be the start of a new romance. So by 10 am the next day he had made arrangements to have lunch with her.

Harriett was intrigued to see Bruno again so soon. Perhaps he had more information about the brooch.

But it wasn't long before she found out why he wanted to see her.

Bruno had arrived at The Savoy restaurant early and stood to kiss Harriett's hand and present her with a posy of dark red roses.

He ushered her to a seat, placing his hand gently on her thigh and then taking it away. Harriett looked at his hand. He still had those long sensitive fingers but she was no longer attracted to them. She looked into his eyes. Still the same deep pools of brown. But she was no longer interested. Still the same pouting lips. Hmm! No, she wasn't interested. She felt slightly annoyed that she was going to turn him down, but she knew the timing was all wrong. He was a leftover from another life.

She had thought he was a great catch when she was just Harriett Langer and he owned the coffee shop. Perhaps she had been desperate to find a good man to please her father.

She had been trying to find the same love that her mother and father had enjoyed over so many years. Now, at thirty-two, famous, rich and sure of herself, things were different for Harriett.

Today she was just amused. Bruno was trying to seduce her, even though she had met his wife just the day before.

Bruno was feeling good. His mojo was back. He was sure Rosa would be ready to take him up to her room at any moment.

'Darling Harriett, you are so beautiful and I am so attracted to you.'

Harriett opened her mouth to refute this, but Bruno continued.

'Do you remember the connection we made years ago when you were just a plain little woman at the diamond exchange?'

Harriett couldn't believe it. Was this his way of seducing her, to remind her of herself as plain?

'It's still there, isn't it? The passion?'

Harriett was amazed. 'Bruno!' she said angrily.

'Yes, my dear?' He leaned towards her, expectation in his eyes.

'I'm no longer the same woman you knew.'

'I know that; it's why I like you.'

'Oh.' Harriett could think of nothing to say in response.

'Are you some sort of idiot to think I would fall for you. I have no time for some shabby liaison.'

'But Rosa, I want to marry you.'

'Goodbye Bruno. Go back to your wife and three children. I'm not interested.'

Harriett slid her chair back, stood up, and then walked gracefully out of the restaurant to the elevator and up to her room – alone.

The next afternoon, Harriett was back in Thames Row, seeking out someone else from her past.

'Glad to see you, Harriett. And glad to see you're now a star in the world of dance. I always knew you were destined for bigger things.'

'I see you've made it big in the modelling industry as well, Charles.'

Charles looked down modestly. 'Yes, I was lucky. First, winning the model contest, and then because I found a great agent.'

Harriett was curious. 'Who is your agent, Charles?'

'Do you remember Tom? He entered the contest too – and won – but in the end decided to become an agent and find jobs for others in advertising products. I think this is his real skill, running a business.'

Harriett was surprised. Fancy Tom becoming an agent. She tucked the information away in a corner of her mind. *You never know when you need an agent*, she thought.

Later, as they were settled in the lounge overlooking his garden, Charles alluded to the basis of their liaison.

'I loved our little trysts and dinners, Harriett. Did you?' He eyed her warily.

Harriett grinned at him, remembering the turret room in the hole-in-the-wall, at The Castle restaurant. 'Of course, I remember it all fondly. We could have made a great couple, potentially.'

Charles relaxed at that, and they chatted for some time about Thames Row, its people and events.

'What happened to the bank?'

'You know I won that model competition? Well, I left immediately and the next manager seemed to run that branch into the ground. The site had to be sold in the end.'

Harriett enquired about life as a model.

Charles perked up at this interest. 'Yes I seem to have made it in the big time. I'm the house model for Selfridges you know. I get lots of work and can afford this place.' He nodded as he looked around. 'It's triple the money I made at the bank.'

Finally, Harriett brought up the topic of the brooch. 'I'd like to buy it. There are great memories for me about it.'

Charles looked forlorn. I can't sell it to you,' he said. 'It isn't mine. I gave it to George.'

'George! Do you mean George who used to date Muriel and was my partner at tango classes?'

'Yes.' Charles explained. 'He's my partner, you know.'

He called out across the room. 'George, come here, will you?'

After a short pause, George came in and stood behind Charles with his hand on Charles's shoulder. Charles looked up lovingly and patted his hand.

Harriett could see this was more than a business partnership. It was a loving partnership. They were a couple.

Harriett had a quick thought back to her date with Charles. He had been amorous, but also slightly formal as though he was acting like a hero in a romance novel out a fiction novel in his approach. Perhaps that was where he got his ideas of how to behave on a date. From romance novels. Harriett looked up.

'You see,' Charles was saying. 'I love George and would give him anything. He wanted the brooch and I gave it to him. George owns it.'

Later, in her cosy bed at The Savoy, Harriett considered Charles and George's partnership. After announcing that they were a couple, George had stated firmly that as Charles had given him the brooch, he treasured it so much that he would never give it away. That now seemed to be the end of her quest to own the brooch.

But later the same day, Sylvia told Harriett that Joaquin Garcia had so far not contacted her again.

So there's still time to find the brooch! I'll continue with the idea of purchasing it. Never give up is my motto, Harriett thought. She phoned George to ask him one more time if he would sell the brooch.

'I can't,' George said. 'I know I said that I treasured it because Charles gave it to me, and that is true. But I also used it as collateral to start my own business and my business partner won't let me sell it. He believes it will grow in value and that we should hold onto it.'

'What business, George?'

'I have my own tango business. I teach tango to adults and children in school. The business is called Tango Dances R4 U. It's quite a going concern, especially now your tango company is here in London. You've helped me enormously, even though you didn't know it, Harriett.'

'Good on you, George. I'm pleased for you. But, tell me, who is your business partner?'

'You probably know him, Harriett. It's Kevin Coates. He was a diamond lecturer at one time and now trades diamonds internationally.'

Kevin Coates!

Harriett stopped feeling sad and down. 'Listen George, I'm really keen on this brooch. Do you mind if I ask Kevin if he'd like my money instead of the brooch as collateral?'

George hesitated. 'You can try. But I still might not want to sell it because Charles gave it to me.' He abruptly stopped talking. 'I don't think I mind ...' and his voice trailed off.

Harriett could hear his hesitation. Perhaps Charles was not aware of the business deal with Kevin, but maybe George wouldn't mind selling. He might only be holding out to ensure Charles would not be hurt if he didn't seem to value the present as much as he should. She would have to look into this.

Now it was time to find Kevin Coates.

Chapter 26

Kevin was angry at himself. George had been to see him that morning and talked about finance. He probably wouldn't remain financial himself any time soon.

He hefted his bags out of his car boot and placed them in his hallway. If only he hadn't visited Monaco on his way home from Europe. He'd lost two million pounds' profit that was owed to an organised crime group in Europe and it wasn't the first time he'd got into this kind of trouble. His gambling had caused him this sort of grief when he'd dropped the waterfall setting brooch to Harriett. He had gone to Paul Lowe, one of the senior 'suits' in the diamond exchange, to borrow money for a gambling debt, spied the brooch and taken it. Of course he was discovered and from that day had been owned by Lowe and the crime syndicate.

If only he had realised the Thames Row Diamond Exchange had been infiltrated by criminals, but because of his mistake and the threat of revenge, even death, he was required to carry illegal diamonds to and from Customs ever since.

Two men suddenly appeared from his lounge room – muscle-bound, pock-marked and red-necked.

'Who are you?'

'We are your worst nightmare.' They stood smiling at him with their large hands loosely holding guns by their sides.

Kevin tried to bluster through his fear. Perhaps those he was indebted to had heard that he'd lost all that money yesterday.

'You know, taking our money and not repaying it is a crime,' the biggest of the burly men said – and they both laughed. 'This time you might have your neck slashed or be executed with a bullet to the brain.'

His companion added, 'Or left to sink in the Thames in concrete boots'. Once again they laughed.

Kevin's face blanched. He was scared.

'I've got the money, boys. There's no reason to worry.' He spread his arms wide in a supplicating manner.

The two goons flicked their guns towards the open safe on the wall.

'We've already checked that out,' the big guy said.

'No, please, it's not here. I'll get it. Don't shoot. Remember, you need me. I'm the best fence you have in London. There's no one as good as me.'

'Where's the money then?'

'I don't keep money here. It's all in the bank and I can get it for you tomorrow. As soon as the bank opens.' He gave them a beseeching look, hands in the air.

The two goons glanced at each other. Their orders had been clear. Kill him if he protested.

Two shots rang out, both bullets hitting their target.

Kevin was brutally forced back to the wall, tumbled forward again, his hand to his chest, and his breath caught in his throat. Then he toppled to the floor lying there as if taking a nap, except for the gaping holes in his otherwise pristine white shirt.

The goons moved as one to nudge the corpse with their feet.

'He's gone.'

'Yeah, guess he was right about the money. It isn't here.'

Calmly and expertly they checked the room, removed the bullet cases and left.

About half an hour later Harriett knocked on Kevin Coates's door, which slowly swung open.

'Hello,' Harriett called, her tentative voice echoing down the hall to the open lounge room, with a blue-water pool beyond.

She could see Kevin's car outside, and luggage in the hall, next to a side table with a briefcase underneath and keys on top.

Maybe he was out at the pool.

'Kevin, it's Harriett Langer. I've come to talk to you about the waterfall brooch.'

Harriett's steps echoed weirdly as she moved towards the middle of the lounge, the silence seeming almost ominous. As she rounded the chair, her feet almost tripped over legs sprawled disjointedly on the floor.

She looked along the legs and up to the chest, where she saw two holes oozing blood which had crusted around their edges.

A scream caught in her throat. 'No, no, no, no.' Kevin was dead.

Her eyes focussed on the lava-like blood. This was recent. So recent that whoever had killed him might still be there, hiding, waiting to attack her.

Crashing back down the hall, bumping into the side table and sending the keys sliding, she opened the front door and ran to her car, scrambling into it and locking the doors.

Crouched on the floor of the passenger seat, she keyed in the police and with a shaky, breathless voice asked for help to come to the scene of the crime.

She couldn't see any other cars, and the quietness of the place suggested that whoever had killed Coates had left, but she stayed in her car until the police arrived.

'I came to see him about a brooch. The door was open. I thought he might have been in the pool and couldn't hear so I … I knew he was dead, but blood was still coming out … I thought the killer might be still here and get me too.'

The constable taking notes looked up. 'Who do you think the killer was?'

'I don't know. I just thought there might be someone still here.'

'The safe was open. Did you see it?'

'No, I just ran.' Harriett waved her arms in distress.

'Let me take some details then. Name first.'

For a moment Harriett was confused.

'Rosa La Boca.' Then, second thoughts. *Should I say Harriett Langer? I've come into the country as Rosa La Boca, but the police might find that my passport is false and I'm really Harriett Langer.*

She blustered through an explanation. 'My stage name is Rosa La Boca. I'm with the national Argentine tango company. Do you know it?'

'I don't want a stage name.'

'My real name is Harriett Langer.'

One of the constables went back to his car. Harriett could see he was radioing in her details. Soon he returned.

'Alright, let's get down to the station and go through this again.'

*

'What about this brooch? Is it the one you brought to the station two years ago?'

Harriett gasped. She had forgotten that they would have files about that.

'Did you kill the victim in order to steal it back?'

'No, I didn't kill him. I don't even own a gun. I was only meeting Kevin Coates again for the first time today. A friend, George, told me Kevin had the brooch. You can ask him.'

Hours later, after a tortuous questioning centred around, 'How did you kill him?' Harriett was released. She had not called any friend, only the tango troupe's office to say she would not be at rehearsals. There was no one who knew about her complex story except Sylvia and Harriett didn't trust her at all now.

Just before she was released, George turned up at the station and things changed. 'I've come to take you back to our place tonight, Harriett. I heard about Kevin when the police phoned seeking confirmation of your story.'

'Thank you so much George. I think I might have been here all night otherwise.'

As George drove back to his home, he confessed to Harriett. 'It was such a shock. Although Kevin is my financial partner, I don't know him all that well. I always thought he was mixed up with the diamond exchange. But the police are saying he was a high-roller gambler.'

'Do you think he was killed because of the brooch, George?'

'That might have been their intention, but he didn't have it.'

'Who has it then?'

'I came by earlier to get it back. I told him about your request and exchanged it for a cash pledge. So they might have killed him for nothing.'

Even in the middle of a murder investigation, Harriett couldn't help but be glad that the brooch was safe. 'I still want to buy it George. And I'd like to assist you financially for coming to my rescue.'

George smiled as he helped her from the car. 'That sounds great Harriett.'

*

Muriel loved her new job as a receptionist and secretary for the Tom Brown Theatrical Agency. She also loved Tom.

It had been a year since she'd split from George. His obsession with tango dancing had left no time for Muriel.

Thank goodness it was a friendly split as she had to work with George in the agency in his new business, Tango Dances R4 U.

She tidied the desk, filed a few papers and arranged flowers in a vase for the coffee table surrounded by comfortable lounges. Everything looked professional. She hoped Tom would be pleased when he arrived about half an hour later.

She straightened the photo of Tom that took pride of place behind her desk and sat down ready to deal with her emails.

One email stood out from the rest.

It was from Rosa La Boca, announcing she would be coming in that morning to sign the contract for 'London Tonight'.

Did Tom really love Rosa – or should she say Harriett? He talked non-stop about her. She remembered when Harriett had dated Tom. Perhaps he was still in love with her.

The previous night Muriel and Tom had had an enormous fight.

'Stop talking about Rosa. You never give it up,' she'd shouted.

'I'll talk about her if I want to.'

'You're home now and I'm sick of it.'

'This is my job. You'll just have to put up with me bringing my work home with me. You like your job, don't you? Well, you wouldn't have it if it wasn't for me.'

'You pig. You act as if I couldn't get a job without you.'

'Maybe you can't.'

'Well, your agency wouldn't be as good as it is without me.'

'You think you helped? Anyone could have done what you've done.'

'Why, you sanctimonious brute! I've held this business together from the start.'

'Just get off my back will you? I'm going for a walk.'

He stomped out of the house, slamming the door after him and not coming back until she was fast asleep.

By the time Muriel was up the next day, Tom had already gone.

Right at 9.30 am, Tom flung open the door to the Agency and with a curt, 'Morning,' strode into his office.

Muriel sat frozen at the desk.

She began to cry.

*

Once again Harriett set off for Thames Row. *I've been here so much I ought to buy a house here*, she thought.

The agency was in the square in a two-story glass building where the chemist used to be. She walked into the office foyer only to find Muriel sitting at the reception desk crying.

Muriel saw Harriett and tried to reduce the sobs to sniffles.

Harriett rushed over to her. She had fond memories of Muriel. She remembered that Muriel really wanted to have a home and babies. It seemed that being a receptionist was as far as she had got in that quest.

'Hello. Ms La Boca,' she wavered.

'Oh, forget that, Muriel. You know my name as Harriett. Remember the diamond exchange?'

'Yes,' Muriel was still wan and sniffly.

'So, what's wrong Muriel? Tell me.'

'It's Tom. I'm in love with him. I thought he loved me too. But we had a big fight about you. All he can think about is you. He loves you and not me.'

She burst into tears again as she said this.

'How do you know that Tom is interested in me?'

He's talked about you non-stop for days. He has pictures of you all over his desk. He even called out your name when …' she blushed … you know … he was dreaming.'

Harriett sat on the side of Muriel's desk.

'Tom's not interested in me personally, Muriel. He's just managed to secure the tango company for the agency. It's a big coup for him. Besides I'm not the slightest bit interested in him. So buck up. I'm sure you're wrong.'

Muriel had stopped crying by this time and was looking hopefully at Harriett with dried tears streaking her cheeks. 'Oh, Harriett. I hope you are right. I love him so much, you know.'

'I guessed that,' Harriett said dryly. 'So is he ready for me to sign the contract now?'

Just then Tom appeared at the door of his office. 'Ms La Boca, or should I call you Harriett?

'Harriett will do, Tom.'

They got down to business.

It wasn't long before Harriett had signed a contract and arranged dates, times, money and the name under which she would work. As

Harriett shook hands and started to walk to the door, she turned and said. 'You know, Muriel loves you and was scared that you had a thing for me?'

Tom was shocked. 'No I didn't. Is that why she was crying?'

'You'd better do something about that if you are serious about her' Harriett said as she left his office.

She went straight to Muriel's desk and sat on it.

'Come on, Muriel, let's find Janie. The three of us can go out on the town together.'

Muriel perked up at this and said she would arrange it straight away.

Chapter 27

Harriett met Sylvia in her room.

'I've found the brooch.' She opened the pouch and showed it to Sylvia who burst into tears again. As Sylvia wiped away the tears, her eyes gleamed. The brooch was magnificent.

'You've done so much for me, after all the horrible things I've done to you. Thank you, Rosa.'

'This is what you can do for me now. Phone this Joaquin Garcia and ask him to come to your room so you can give him the brooch. Tell him you are still trying to find out about the man. Say you need some more time.'

Sylvia nodded. 'I'm so scared of him.'

'Just get it done. I'll be out tomorrow night and don't plan to be back until the morning because I'll stay in Thames Row. So you have lots of time.'

*

Joaquin Garcia entered The Savoy via a side door climbing to Level 3 where he found Sylvia's room.

Sylvia was waiting.

'Come with me, the brooch is in Rosa's room. We can get it now because she is out all night.'

'This better not be a trick or you won't see your child again.' Garcia's face had taken on a pinched angry snarl.

Sylvia's heart hardened. 'It's over there in the bottom drawer of the desk.'

Garcia turned to Sylvia, gun in hand, grabbing her arm and pulling her towards the desk. 'You get it.'

Sylvia was thrust down towards the desk drawer. She slowly opened it, revealing the pouch with the brooch.

Garcia greedily bent down to wrest the pouch from Sylvia using both hands to prise open the cord at the top, gun back in its underarm holster. Sylvia leaned on the desk, noticing the letter opener on the leather top.

For a moment she just stared at the opener. Garcia would never let up. After the brooch it would be the money and the roughs they said they were owed. She couldn't let them take Jacinta. She had never received any restitution for the things she'd done, just threats and more threats.

Slowly her hand crept to the letter opener. She grabbed it in her right hand, turning it so she gripped the handle tight.

In an instant, before Garcia could disentangle his hands and manoeuvre the gun, Sylvia turned and thrust the knife under his breast bone and pushed upwards. When the letter opener was in his chest up to the hilt, she let go and stepped back.

Garcia looked down, then back up at her. His body began to sink to the floor, the pouch and gun slipping out of his hands.

A groan left his lips as he slowly knelt then toppled sideways his eyes still open.

Sylvia, hand over her mouth, watched and waited. Eventually Garcia's eyes closed, and his body was still.

There was no time to lose. Sylvia gathered up he pouch and, wiping down the letter opener, left it beside him on the floor.

'Serve you right,' she said as she locked Harriett's door. 'You deserve what you got.'

*

Out on the town with her girlfriends for the night, it was Harriett's shout.

Back she came from the bar again, her hands full of multi-coloured cocktails festooned with umbrellas, cherries, olives and bright little plastic swizzle sticks.

She looked over at her friends. They were having such fun, talking about lives at the diamond exchange and their plans for the future. It was a pity that most of her thoughts were back at The Savoy, wondering what was happening with Sylvia and the limo driver. She hoped that she could think of something to do next to get rid of him.

At least the two women she was having fun with were real friends. People Harriett could talk to about normal things and not be frowned upon.

She handed out the drinks and the three of them took a sip with a giggle. *I wonder how many I've had*, Harriett thought. She tried to recall, but finally gave up. Any number past three seemed to be hard to remember.

Muriel giggled. It was time to tell a joke. 'Knock, knock.' She said.

Janie and Harriett shouted out the traditional response. 'Who's there?'

'Noah,' Muriel said.

'Noah who?'

'Noah good place we can get something to drink?'

The three of them collapsed in a giggling heap.

Muriel was thinking of Tom. 'You know, there was a big bunch of roses from Tom when I got home with a note that said I was his girl and he wanted to marry me.'

This announcement led to another round of drinks with congratulations all round.

Harriett remembered George. 'Muriel I thought you would end up with George.'

'I did too at first. But then he became obsessed with his Tango Dances R4 U studio. I could see he had no thought for me. He really wanted to be a dancer the way you are, Harriett, but obviously he's doing the next best thing – teaching tango. And he's found his true love.'

Then Muriel, who could never see anyone less happy than her or without a boyfriend, asked Harriett if she had a love of her life.

Harriett proceeded to tell them the story of Antonio. 'I thought he liked me but instead he liked men.'

They giggled some more over this.

Then, looking into her drink rather sadly, Harriett said, 'I did have one love in my life but it was not to be.'

Janie and Muriel looked at each other, nodded and said as one, 'Mr Symonds'

Harriett gasped. 'How did you know?'

'We could see that he loved you and you loved him when you were both at the diamond exchange.'

Then Janie, in typical fashion, said, 'We must do something about this. You know, he's "The Face of Harrods."'

Harriett just nodded.

'We could go to Harrods and accidently bump into him. He would see you and immediately ask for a date. Or I could hold a dinner at my place and invite him. He would see you from across the room and go straight to you and give you a kiss.'

As the night went on, the ideas on how to get Harriett and Mr Symonds (or Neville) together became more outlandish.

'I could ring him and say Tom has been struck by lightning and we need him in the office and when he got there you would be at the receptionist desk. He would see you and ask you to marry him straight away, on the spot, saying he needs a good receptionist.'

They were still laughing and coming up with more wicked ideas as they hurried to catch a taxi back to Thames Row and home.

'The Thames Row Inn please, driver,' Harriett said. 'Ooh! Posh!' Janie and Muriel exclaimed together as they sped off.

*

The next morning at The Savoy was chaotic. Police were everywhere, although most seemed to be crowded into Harriett's room.

Harriett sat on the lounge in Sylvia's room with a detective. This was the second time she had been a witness to a murder. And even though the police must have been suspicious, they had no evidence that Harriett was involved in the murder, no matter how hard they questioned her. Could the two murders just be a coincidence?

'I just came home this morning and there he was.'

'Do you know him?'

'Yes. He'd been following me for a long while. But Sylvia knew him best.'

Harriett was allowed to book another room in the hotel, leaving the police to do their job. As she was still not needed for rehearsal, she phoned George to fill him in. All very perplexing, but George was fired up about another idea entirely.

'Would you care to come to my studio and show the older students some moves, Harriett?' he asked. George was hesitant about making the request of a famous star like Harriett, but had been egged on by Charles to do so.

Arrangements were made and Harriett turned up at the studio the next week. Raucous cheering and clapping from the students followed her hour-long practice session.

Harriett gave George a great compliment after all the students had trooped out of the studio. 'George, you've improved so much, I think you could be a professional. I know Carla, who used to be the star of the Argentine company, is now looking for an adagio partner. Are you interested?'

George was thrilled. 'Yes, I am. I know now that I wasn't good enough before. But I've changed.'

Harriett nodded in agreement.

'I've always wanted the opportunity to dance professionally,' George enthused. 'I'd really like that.'

*

And so they began their warm ups in the studio of Tango Dances R4 U. Harriett, who had developed an advanced warm up routine as a member of the tango company, began with leg extensions, lifts and back bends.

She had phoned Tom to see if he had any other ideas for a tango duo. She explained that she was doing George a favour and Carla had agreed to it. It was to be his entré into public performance – a high-level entry point.

'You are lucky Harriett. Harrods has just asked me if a star of the tango company can come to Harrods to sign autographs and perhaps dance. This just might suit George and Carla. It would certainly enhance the Argentine tango company's reputation, and my agency as well.

'I've chosen some music already for the trial. I hope you like it,' Harriett said. 'It's called "Poruna Cabeza" and is typical Argentine tango music. It has a wonderful ending crescendo which lends itself to a great finale.

They both sat on the studio floor and listened to it.

'I like it,' said George, who would have said yes to anything that Harriett suggested. 'Would you or Carla choreograph it, Harriett?'

'I'll choreograph it for you, George, and you can show Carla …' but then added, '… with help from you, George.'

George smiled. 'Thank you Harriett, that's very kind of you.'

They began testing steps together, considering tempo, emotion, contrasts of fast to slow, high tension to low, smooth segues from one section to another, including lifts that would suit George and allow Carla to feature.

As they went over and over each section of the dance, perfecting each movement, ensuring arms and legs and body created lines of beauty and strength, they considered facial expressions – as the tango must always be danced with both love and hate.

Three weeks later, Carla's rehearsals with George had bonded them as a pair and they were ready to perform publicly. After viewing their rehearsals, the manager Constantino was happy to give his blessing.

'I didn't know you were so good at choreographing tango dances, George,' was Carla's winning compliment.

George just smiled. He didn't want Carla to know that Harriett had designed the dance and coached him.

George had decided on a modern black dinner suit with silver lapels. His hair was slicked back from his forehead with a long ponytail down his back. He looked bold and sexy.

Carla was firmly in the character of a tango star and had chosen an orange velvet sheath with a sweetheart neckline and cap sleeves. Sheer black stockings with a silver sheen encased her long legs and blue patent leather heels finished the outfit. Around her neck and in her hair was large silver rose jewellery. She definitely felt in charge again.

The event had been advertised in the papers and on T.V. for several weeks so that hundreds of people were lined up outside Harrods to see the limousine arrive.

Inside on the first floor, celebrities, politicians and others who considered themselves the rich and famous had purchased 500-pound tickets to the event.

An entourage of bouncers and assistants swept Carla and George across the red carpet, which stretched from the car to the front door of Harrods. The store glittered in the evening light, its windows displaying a wealth of Harrods merchandise.

The dancers were whisked up to a temporary dressing room at the end of the dining area behind the stage as the six guitar players arranged themselves next to the stage and began to tune their instruments.

George was nervous. He had never danced before such an audience and with such a famous star. 'Let's warm up, George, and mark out the steps one more time,' coached Carla.

The music began.

The lead guitar played a few riffs of the melody and then was joined by the rest until a staccato of notes announced the dancers who posed together at the back of the stage.

Carla's role was played out through varying strident then sweet melodies of hate, by the woman for the aggressive man who pursued her with tenderness and power. The woman was falling for the man, only to have him turn away. And at last the two were desperately in love, finally together.

The audience response was deafening. People stamped, clapped and shouted their delight with 'olé's through four curtain calls. George was in raptures. He hugged Carla tight.

Harriett who had been backstage watching, was elated by the audience response. George had excelled himself. He would be a great partner for Carla.

Neville had been in the audience, watching closely. She had spied him with other celebrities shaking hands with George at the end of the performance while cameras flashed.

She sighed.

Later, lying back in her king-size bed in The Savoy's penthouse suite, Harriett closed her eyes and daydreamed about Neville. She imagined him holding her hand as they entered the penthouse where they lived.

He guides me towards the coffee table where a large box sits, tied up with pink ribbon.

I pull the ties and let the ribbon cascade to the floor. As I take the top off and pushing the tissue aside, I see a gorgeous pink silk negligée.

Turning to him with shining eyes, I allow him to lift the negligee over my head, letting the soft lacy folds shimmer down my body.

Neville captures me in his strong arms and carries me to the bedroom where he kneels on the bed, puffing and panting, and deposits me gently onto the middle of the quilt, among hundreds of rose petals. Dark velvety red 'Briar' rose petals, creamy pale 'Peace' rose petals, soft mauve-pink 'Queen Elizabeth' rose petals, and bright candy-pink rose petals with orange centres.

I stretch my arms above my head, taking in the rich heady perfume permeating the room, and sigh with pleasure.

Neville leans over me, sliding his fingers along my tender arms as he nuzzles my ear.

'Knock, knock,' he whispers.

Harriett opened her eyes. What was that all about in the middle of her dream?

'Knock, knock.'

'Who's there,' I whisper back.

'Neville.'

'Neville, who?'

'Neville who loves you desperately and completely.'

'Hmm.' I turn to him, then ...

'Knock, knock,' I say.

'Who's there?' he asks as he kisses my earlobe.

'Noah.'

'Noah who?'

'Noah good place to fall in love?'

How can one of Muriel's silly jokes emerge in my imagining, and change my love scene into a love joke, for goodness sake?

Harriett blinked a couple of times, in an effort to get back to the dream. *Neville smiles down at me, whispering sweet nothings. Then he leans over me with loving eyes and ...*

The shrill sound of the phone interrupted Harriett's dream.

'Hello, Harriett. Just thought I'd phone to tell you that I had a wonderful time tonight. Dancing with Carla was the best experience, the highlight of my life – except for Charles's love, that is. So goodnight Harriett and thank you for arranging everything.'

'Goodnight George.' Harriett was pleased – but her dream had disappeared. Just like the real thing. Probably gone forever.

Chapter 28

Back in Buenos Aires, Lautaro Rodriguez opened the on-line *Sunday Times* as he sat at his desk. On the screen were large pictures of George, Carla and 'The Face of Harrods', Neville Symonds.

He peered closely at it. The man next to Carla seemed familiar to him. This grainy image was like another picture he had seen. He searched his memory. *Now where was that?*

A side note mentioned Neville as a worker for the Thames Row Diamond Exchange in his early years. He clicked the link which came up with a picture of a group of men in front of a display. Neville was in the back of the picture. He read the script. Neville had set up the display of a famous ring at the diamond exchange.

This was it. He read on: about Neville leaving the company soon after, and that the Thames Row Diamond Exchange had discovered that the ring was copied.

This was the man he was after.

He phoned his men in London.

'I've found him. He's quite a celebrity. The name is different but the pictures don't lie. It's about time we had a breakthrough. He took my money and my roughs and he knows too much about us. Find an opportunity to get the money and then kill him.'

'Done, I'll get onto it.'

Did you ever find that waterfall brooch?'

'No, we went to Kevin Coates's place like you said but you should know already that he had nothing. So we finished him off.

'Have you heard from Garcia yet?' Rodriguez was concerned that he had heard nothing from Joaquin Garcia. *Perhaps he has taken the brooch and skipped. I'll have to deal with him too when this is over*, he thought. He cleared his voice and said, 'I've got another job for you, so listen up.'

He then put in a call to Paul Lowe at the London diamond exchange, leaving a message that he would arrive at Heathrow the following day.

*

Over in London, Harriett turned to page three of the paper as she sipped her coffee. There was Neville, larger than life. She turned to the article. It was mainly about Neville's early work at the diamond exchange. Immediately, she knew that Neville was in danger. If the limo driver saw this, he would know that Neville was the man he was searching for. She had to find Neville and warn him.

It was while she was on the main escalator at Harrods, admiring the Egyptian icons and artwork, that she noticed a stranger.

She rubbed her eyes and blinked. Was she right?

It was 'moustache man', who had been searching for her in Buenos Aires two years before. The one who worked at True Diamond's. The one on Sylvia's phone camera.

He still looked cruel and was intent on something or someone.

She looked in the direction he was staring and saw Neville, who must have come in to talk to the admin people about the newspaper article. He hadn't noticed 'moustache man', although she realised he probably wouldn't know him anyway. Neville moved towards the stairs leading to the office section, 'moustache man' following discreetly behind.

Her intuition kicking in, Harriett just knew that he was after Neville to kill him.

Clearly, Neville had been discovered. She had tried to cover up his file in the Buenos Aires office and it must have worked for a while. But now because of that journalist uncovering Neville's background at the diamond exchange, his background had been exposed.

What should I do? Harriett thought. She needed to go to the police.

*

'Sir, there's a lady downstairs who wants to speak to a detective.'

'Find her a constable.'

'You'll want to see this one sir. She's famous. She's the star of the tango company playing in London, Rosa La Boca.'

'Oh well, that's different. I'd like to see her.' He skipped down the stairs to the front office.

'Good morning, Ms La Boca. I'm Detective Storm. How can I help?'

'There's a man here in London who wants to kill Neville Symonds, "The Face of Harrods".'

'Really? How do you know that?'

'I know the man. I saw him in Buenos Aires and I knew he was after Neville. Now he's here following Neville in Harrods. I saw him. He wants to kill him. Here's his picture.' She found Sylvia's photo of him on her phone and thrust it towards the detective.

'Maybe he admires Mr Symonds. Maybe he likes the clothes he wears. Why would he kill him?' *She sounds like a typical theatrical person,* Detective Storm thought.

Harriett couldn't say 'because he stole a ring'.

'It's because Neville was at the Thames Row Diamond Exchange when a million-pound ring was stolen.'

'Hmm. Seems a bit thin to me. I can't investigate a man just for being seen following Neville Symonds. Sorry.'

Harriett knocked her chair backwards as she stood. She hurried to the door without a goodbye.

I'll have to investigate it myself then, she whispered under her breath.

Detective Storm watched her go. There was something about

193

her. She seemed so upset, so frantic. It wouldn't hurt for him to follow her, make sure she didn't do anything foolish. Besides, the idea of following a star like her seemed much more inviting than the paperwork on his desk.

*

Where would Neville be now? she thought. *I'll have to find him and stop the moustache man from getting to him.*

She phoned Tom.

'Brown's Theatrical Agency.'

'Hello, Tom. Do you know where Neville is today?'

'Hello, Harriett. As a matter of fact, I do. He's on the train coming to Thames Row to sign new contracts and discuss the newspaper article.'

'Right!' she said and hung up without a goodbye. There was no time to chat to Tom.

She hurried to her rental car, thankful that her frequent trips to Thames Row had resulted in her already having hired one.

Harriett hoped she'd reach Thames Row about the same time as the afternoon train.

*

In another part of London during the tango company's rehearsals, Jose was angry.

Carla had gone off with George, just like that. After all these years together through thick and thin, she could turn in an instant. But just because Jose had accidently torn the ligaments in his knee and wouldn't be able to dance for a while, it didn't mean she couldn't marry him. These were Jose's thoughts.

He grabbed Carla as she came in the dressing room door. 'Why are you doing this to me?'

Carla watched him throw her spare tights, leotard and practice shoes at the wall.

'I can do what I like. It has nothing to do with you.'

'Nothing. I have been your partner for ten years and you know I want to marry you. That's not nothing.'

'It is to me. You might have been a good partner before, but not anymore. I need someone younger who can lift and turn better than you.'

'You think George is good enough? He's not. You are just fooling yourself.'

He bent to pick up her leotard which was made of silvery material with a low neckline.

'Look at this. You are just trying to be young again and you never will.'

'How dare you. I'm still young enough to be a star, unlike you. I wouldn't dance with you again. You're showing your age old man.'

Jose stiffened, then flung his hand in a backhand slap across her face, a furious look in his eyes.

Carla's head snapped back and to the side, her arms reaching up to protect herself.

'Get out. Get out and don't come back. Go back to Argentina where you belong.'

She tottered to the bathroom and slammed the door, locking it from the inside while Jose strode out of the room, flinging obscenities in Spanish after her.

Carla hid in the bathroom until all was quiet, then came out and picked up the phone.

It was time to return George's call about the contract.

*

Jose had waited a long time for Carla. Didn't she love him? Didn't she have any loyalty to him? He had asked her to marry so many times before and she had always put him off saying, 'When we retire'. Just as he was certain that retirement time had come, George came along.

It was all Rosa's fault, according to Jose's thinking. She had been the one to usurp Carla's place and force her out of the spotlight. She had been a friend to this George person that was now dancing with Carla. It was Rosa's fault that Carla had rejected him. His blood was up.

It hadn't been hard to find a gun in the London underworld weapons trade, and it wasn't hard to find Rosa. She was always surrounded by fans and even had her itinerary posted on Facebook. Jose began to follow her. First to Harrods and then to the police station.

At first he wondered if she had spotted him and was reporting him to the police. But he felt confident that he had been quite clever at staying hidden.

After a fast car trip following her to Thames Row railway station, he stopped nearby in a taxi zone, abandoning the car, not caring if it was towed or clamped. Jose realised Harriett was meeting someone.

He rushed to the platform and positioned himself near her but still out of her sight.

He saw a man alight and then Rosa moving towards him. Jose's anger was rising fast over this high-speed cat and mouse game. Quickly he slid into the line of sight that had Rosa centred for the best shot. Now was his chance. He raised the gun.

Hot-tempered, his mind in a rage and unable to think rationally, Jose tried to focus on how he might wound Rosa where it would hurt her most – on one of those beautiful legs, the source of her income, her accumulated wealth, her fame. Let her feel what it was like to suffer an injury that would take her off the stage – just the way he had been overlooked due to injury, he thought.

What Jose didn't realise in his state of agitation was that you couldn't shoot a person – even if you only meant to injure them – in a public place in broad daylight and expect to get away with it.

Jose also didn't know that Detective Storm was also on the station platform wondering who Rosa was meeting. Storm was hoping it was Neville Symonds so that he could talk to both of them and find out.

Chapter 29

Waiting on that platform those few minutes for the train to pull in had been hard for Harriett. It was not only the alarming circumstances that upset her but the very fact that she hadn't spoken to Neville in such a long time – and that she still cared so much for him – that provoked such turmoil in her mind.

After a mechanical rumble announced the doors opening and she saw Neville, one of the first passengers to step down onto the platform, she headed towards him as he looked down, watching out for the gap between the train and the platform.

Something made Harriett turn to look to her right. 'Moustache man' from Buenos Aires was moving towards Neville too, very close to her. He must have followed Neville from Harrods, she thought. He was staring intently at Neville, his face angry and twisted. Her eyes followed his arm down to his pocket as he withdrew a pistol.

Her eyes flicked to the left, but all she saw there was a woman hurrying for the train.

Now Neville was walking along the platform, and behind him was a man pointing a gun, both straight ahead of her.

Jose! It was Jose, Carla's partner, and his eyes were locked on Harriett. He wasn't after Neville; he was after her, she realised with a jolt.

Two threats from two different positions.

Her momentum was toward Neville. If she changed direction to collide with 'moustache man', she thought she might lose precious moments and he would have pulled the trigger and shot Neville.

So she launched herself forward, arms stretched out and with her head butting into Neville's chest, she tackled him as hard as she could.

Neville crumpled as he staggered backwards falling on his back and his head colliding with the cold concrete platform. At the same time, moustache man raised his pistol and fired, the bullet singing over the now prone Neville and hitting Jose in the chest.

Simultaneously, Jose, fired at Harriett, but wavering at the last moment, his bullet grazed the arm of the woman next to Harriett. But the bullet fired by 'moustache man' tore into Jose's heart as his body twisted in agony from the impact.

With a lightning presence of mind, Detective Storm, immediately behind Harriett, raised his weapon and with a double tap to the trigger, brought down 'moustache man'.

Harriett was oblivious to the people around her. All she could see was Neville, prone, eyes closed, looking dead. She scrambled up from the platform and rushed to kneel beside him, placing her hand on his cheek.

'Neville, wake up!'

Tears streamed down her face. *Was he dead?* Yet she'd only just pushed him. She hadn't meant to harm him.

Detective Storm was already calling the ambulance and local police reinforcements and had asked the station guards to cordon off the area until they arrived.

He lifted Harriett up by her elbow. 'Come with me.'

Harriett gestured towards Neville. 'No, I can't leave him.'

'The guards are here and the ambulance is on its way. Come now.'

Harriett obeyed, and as she walked out of the station supported by Detective Storm's arm, she broke down in tears. It was all too much to bear.

When they reached the local police station, she was ushered into a room where a policewoman tried to console her.

All Harriett could say was, 'I need to know how Neville is.'

Slowly her sobs lessened and Detective Storm sat next to her to carry out an interview.

But before he could begin, Harriett wanted to know why he'd been at the railway station.

'I followed you. When you told me your story, I thought it was a bit of a fairy-tale. But when you hurried away, I could see that you might get yourself into trouble so I came after you.'

He leaned forward. 'Now tell me what happened.'

'I saw the stranger I told you about. He had a gun. Then I saw Jose. He had a gun too. I just reacted and pushed Neville out of the way so he wouldn't be shot. But I think I may have killed him. Can you find out?'

'My colleague is at the hospital now. She'll call us as soon as she knows something.

He folded his arms. 'Now tell me about the stranger again?'

'He followed me in Buenos Aires but I thought I'd gotten rid of him back here. Then, just today, I saw him in Harrods stalking Neville. I knew he was after him.'

'How did you know that?'

I believe he saw the newspaper article about Neville and had found him after all these years.'

'Why did he need to find Neville Symonds?'

'Because …' Harriett stopped. She realised she couldn't say Neville had stolen a ring and sold it in Buenos Aires. So she became vague.

'… because he had worked for the diamond exchange where the ring was first stolen and I think they thought he might have seen who stole it. They hadn't known where he was for the past two years.'

'Why would they kill him? Surely they'd want to find out what he knew about it?'

Harriett struggled for a sensible answer.

'I believe they stole it themselves. For insurance. I think they wanted to silence him.'

Detective Storm nodded. The explanation seemed valid on the surface, but by the way Rosa avoided his eyes and the vagueness of her answers, he was sure Rosa was hiding something. There were still quite a few things that didn't quite match up.

'What about this Jose? Who is he and why did he want to kill Neville?'

'He wasn't after Neville. He was after me.'

This is getting complex, he thought. 'Why?'

'He and Carla were the stars of the tango company when Antonio and I came along and took their places. He is in love with her and now she has found a new partner in my friend, George. I think Jose hates me.'

'Hmm, enough to kill you?'

'Yes, he was like that, I think.'

Detective Storm's colleague knocked and walked in.

Harriett stood. 'Is Neville alright?'

'Yes, it was just a concussion. He'll be released later today. I can take you to see him if Detective Storm is finished with you?'

Detective Storm nodded. 'You can go but I will want to see you again.'

Harriett gathered her things and followed the constable to the car.

*

Neville was awake, lying in his hospital bed. He kept his eyes closed as he considered what had happened to him. He remembered getting off the train. He remembered several loud bangs, screams and strange noises.

He remembered Harriett reaching for him.

His eyes sprang open. Harriett! She couldn't have been there. He had only seen Harriett a couple of times in the distance and on T.V. in the past six months. He must be hallucinating.

He closed his eyes again and slept – as Harriett looked through the observation window at him sleeping.

'Is he going to be alright?'

'Of course, Ms La Boca. He was concussed. We have taken scans of his brain and there is nothing wrong. We have only kept him here for observation. He can leave later today.'

'Good.'

Harriett was overwhelmed with relief. She hadn't killed him.

At that moment Neville opened his eyes. There was his Harriett looking through the window.

'Harriett,' he croaked, holding out his arm towards her.

Harriett rushed to his bedside, sank down on the bed, and took his hand in hers. 'I'm so sorry I hurt you. I didn't have time to think about what I was doing. Are you okay?'

Neville searched Harriett's eyes. It seemed that she had forgiven him for running off without her.

'Harriett, they tell me I have you to thank for saving my life. Would you come back home with me today when they let me go? I need to speak to you and thank you properly.'

Harriett nodded. She was past hating him. She needed him.

*

Neville sat on his lounge resting, while Harriett fussed around him.

'Come here,' he called softly.

Harriett fell into his arms, then leant back as he sucked in his breath with pain.

Neville shifted his weight as his penetrating blue eyes took in her beauty.

Slowly, Neville ran his fingertips through Harriett's hair, angling her face for his kiss.

At first it was soft, tentative, gentle, and then as his apprehension left him, he pulled her towards him, kissing her deeply.

Harriett melted into Neville, the fusion of their bodies claiming her mind until there was only emotion and love.

'Can we …?' Neville lifted his head and motioned towards the bedroom.

'Yes!' Harriett took a few steps, leading Neville along with her.

He lowered himself down onto the bed, Harriett following. He was breathless with the movement and stabbing pain but he couldn't let her go. He needed her close, melded to him.

A loud knocking on the door finally pierced their cocoon. Harriett sat up, a sleepy loving look still in her eyes.

Neville sat up too, as the knocking didn't stop. They gathered themselves together and moved to the door.

'Are you Harriett Langer,' one of the two burly policemen said, taking a step forward, 'Also known as Rosa La Boca?'

'Yes,' Harriett replied at the same time as Neville said, 'What's this about?'

'Harriett Langer, I'm arresting you for the murder of Joaquin Garcia.' Handcuffs clasped her wrists with a click and Harriett turned to Neville, feeling dread.

'Who is he?' he asked. 'She doesn't know anyone by that name.'

Harriett looked past the constable and saw Sylvia in the back of one of the police cars.

'Is Sylvia arrested too?'

'No, she is helping us with our enquiries.'

Harriett's body slumped. *Sylvia must be in league with the criminals and lying about me.*

Within thirty minutes Harriett was locked in an interview room with a London policeman.

'Do you know this man?' Harriett looked down at a photo of the limousine driver covered in blood and lying on the floor of her room.

'Yes, that's the man who has been following me and was going to hurt Jacinta if Sylvia didn't find the brooch and ring they thought that I had.'

'You seem to have been involved with a number of deaths

recently.'

Harriett shrugged her shoulders. It was true. Somehow the criminals had come to her doorstep.

'Did you kill Kevin Coates and steal a brooch from him?'

'No, I didn't. George had the brooch all the time. Kevin didn't have it and I only found him dead. Someone else did it.'

'Did you get Sylvia to give the brooch to this man.'

'Yes, yes I did. To help her.'

'Did the brooch disappear?'

'Sylvia said that he took the brooch and threatened her not to tell anyone.'

The constable stood and walked around the room thinking. And then he walked back to her again.

'Sylvia found him dead on the floor of your room and there was no brooch on him. Where were you last night?'

'I was out with my friends, Janie and Muriel. They can vouch for me.'

'What time did you get home?'

'I didn't go home. I stayed at the Thames Row Inn.'

'So you never went to your room at The Savoy?'

'No, I didn't. I couldn't have killed him, I wasn't there.'

This time the constable tossed another photo on the desk in front of her. 'Here is the letter opener he was killed with. Is it yours?'

Harriett gazed at the letter opener. It was hers and usually sat on her desk. Long, thin and sharp, it looked like a killing blade.

'Sylvia says you returned to your room and seemed very jubilant this morning. She didn't see him dead on the floor until later when she went to collect you.'

Harriett was silent, thoughts of Sylvia's lies, complicity or just plain greed rushing through her mind in a kaleidoscope of colours. Of blood and ghostly shapes and knives.

There was nothing new to say. Just to say it all over again.

Neville had arranged a lawyer, who joined her in the interview room, advising her to say nothing more.

Later, Neville visited her in the holding cell where she told him everything in whispers and stuttering of incomprehension.

'Why did she do this? What can I do? The story from Sylvia sounds better, more real than mine. It sounds true. And they have lots of suspicions about me because I was there when Kevin was killed and I had the brooch at one time.'

There was nothing Neville could do but hold her and repeat that he would do all he could.

A constable came to usher him out. Neville took her in his arms, whispering 'I love you' and 'Don't give up. Be strong.'

Harriett's eyes overflowed, so that her last sight of Neville leaving was blurred, as if he was in a fog forever dissipating.

Chapter 30

Harriett could not measure the days, just times for food and more interviews. She tried to keep Neville's last words in her mind as she sat by the lawyer and answered question after question:

'Did you kill Joaquin Garcia?'

'Did you kill Kevin Coates?'

'How did you do it?'

'Why did you use a letter opener?'

'Where is the brooch?'

'Why are you lying?'

Three days later, she was ushered to another room. Her lawyer took her by the arm and told her gently, 'They are letting you go.'

Harriett almost collapsed with relief, leaning against him while he steadied her.

'I can go? I'm not under arrest?'

'No, they have discovered evidence that indicates the murderer was not you. Fingerprints, timing, proof of absence, the search of your room and a guest who saw a person leave your room about the time he was killed. They were all instrumental in dismissing you.'

'What about Sylvia?'

'There is no evidence that Sylvia was the killer. But she had police permission to leave the country. She's gone. She said that you probably don't trust her anymore so she's resigned and gone back to live where she used to live.'

'What about the brooch?'

They've never found it. The most popular theory is that whoever killed her took the brooch.'

Harriett's relief was overwhelming, especially when she heard that Neville had been instrumental in hounding the police to look further afield for the killer.

A knock, and Neville stood there, looking very tired but happy.

Harriett ran to him. 'Thank you Neville. Thank you for your help.'

They clung to each other, exhausted.

An hour later, after signing lots of documents, and having her purse and mobile returned the pair stepped out into a London cool but welcome day.

A myriad of journalists who had been lounging on the station steps rushed forward with cameras flashing.

'Were you worried Rosa?'

'Did you suspect your assistant, Sylvia?'

'Will you dance tonight?'

Harriett shook her head at all the questions, and holding tight to Neville, hurried to a taxi conveniently waiting at the bottom of the steps.

'Thank goodness for this,' Harriett said, as the taxi sped off. They sat back to rest and at first watched the change of scenery on the way to Thames Row, before closing their eyes to enjoy their sense of peace.

Half an hour later, Neville looked out the window. 'Harriett, this isn't the way to Thames Row.'

He leant over the front seat. 'Driver, where are we?'

The driver turned with a grin on his pockmarked face. 'You're on your way to hell. We're taking you to our country estate and when you've given us back the money you stole, you'll be free.' This last word he said with a chortle that suggested he was lying.

Harriett and Neville sat, shocked, in the back seat. Neville turned over in his mind ways to escape, then leaned over to whisper in Harriett's ear.

'Don't bother trying to escape there's nowhere out here to escape to.'

They looked out the window. It was barren land, not a farm in sight, just turned fields and a few scattered trees.

Harriett whispered to Neville. 'We're not tied up, so can we escape out of a moving car and stay alive?'

Neville moved slowly towards the door on his side while Harriett did the same on the other side. They kept their eyes on each other, Harriett hoping she would recognise the time to jump.

The car was coming up to a sharp corner and although they were travelling reasonably fast, it slowed a little on the curve.

'Now,' Neville yelled, and threw himself at the door, turning the handle and pushing hard.

Harriett tried to do the same on her side, but the door was heavy and the angle of the car meant that she had to push upwards. With a mighty effort she managed to open it a little then, placing both feet against it, she pushed with all her might. Fortunately, Harriett's legs were her strongest ally and all she had to do was to remember the safest way to land and roll after jumping out.

Harriett careened into the grassy edge of the road and rolled down the slope of the shoulder and into some rocky rubble. She was bruised but not hurt. She searched for Neville. He had the more difficult job of landing on the asphalt in the middle of the road.

He landed on his hip and thigh and grunted in pain as he rolled over and over. As soon as he could, he sprang up and looked for Harriett who was also trying to jump up after her very rocky landing.

The driver screeched to a stop and reversed so that he was near to where they had landed. The window slid open and he aimed his pistol at them.

'Run, zig zag.' cried Neville. And Harriett, obeying mindlessly, curved first one way and then the other.

Bullets sprayed around them but none connected. *It must be working*, thought Harriett, cresting a small rise and falling down the other side into a gully, with Neville following.

There was silence for a moment. 'He must be out of ammunition.

We need to go now before he can re-load,' was Neville's conclusion.

They stood, heads down, and set off running again, Neville hobbling and holding his side where his hip had struck the road. A stand of trees bordered a fence line.

'There,' Neville pointed. 'If we run along the fence it will surely lead to a farm of some sort.'

Still zigging and zagging, they kept their eyes glued on the trees and ran. They heard sounds of crashing from some distance behind them and then bullets again zinged near their heads.

'Harriett keep your head down.' Neville croaked. His voice thick with panting.

They reached the tree line but could see that the fence was old, falling down and it led nowhere.

'We'll have to make a stand for it.'

'How?' Harriett asked, looking around. 'There's no time.'

'Behind a tree,' Neville told her quietly, and stepped behind the nearest. Harriett did the same.

There was a moment when the driver stopped to look at the seemingly empty area, his gun waving from one side to the other, aware of a possible surprise attack.

Harriett thought the escape was hopeless as they wouldn't be able to run forever and the man would soon catch them in such open country. She decided their best chance was to help Neville with his plan.

She stepped out from behind her tree, saying haltingly, 'I give in.'

The driver automatically turned towards her and in that moment Neville sprang from his tree, tackling the driver below the knees and bringing him down to the ground. The gun flew from his grasp and Harriett ran to get it, while Neville began to punch his assailant in the ribs and face.

He was very strong, muscly and an experienced fighter. As Neville rained blows on him, the driver got in a few hard-hitting and well-placed punches to Neville's head and stomach.

Neville was losing the fight.

Harriett, with the gun in her hand moved around Neville to aim at the driver but found she could not be sure of missing Neville. So in a last effort, she rushed into the fight head on, swinging the gun in an arc and bashing the driver on the head with the steal butt.

The driver went down in an unconscious heap, and Harriett, hands still gripping the gun, bent over her knees, panting and groaning.

Neville, also reeling from the attack, moved to Harriett and grabbed the gun, aiming it at the driver.

'What can we do, I don't want him to wake up? He's stronger than us. He might have other weapons on him too.'

Neville approached the driver, keeping just out of his way in case he was foxing then, reaching forward, he gave him another clout on the head.

'That should do it,' he said, relieved. 'Let's go back to the car and drive to the police station.'

'What about him?'

'It's too far to drag him to the car and put him in the boot and we don't have our phones on us. This is the best we can do.'

Harriett agreed and they trudged back, every now and then looking back, fearful that the driver was coming after them.

Once they'd informed the police, the driver, still unconscious, was recovered from the field, taken to hospital and later charged with kidnapping.

Detective Storm looked at all the files which had involved Harriett. It was a complex story but she always seemed to be on the side of the angels. He shook his head and concluded that there was nothing further to pursue, either about the deceased Jose Santiago, the 'moustache man' now known as Lautaro Rodriguez, nor the woman who was shot in the arm.

After speaking to Carla, who blamed herself for enraging Jose, that was the end of the the inquiry. Rodriguez was also dead after his shot had missed Neville Symonds.

They would keep track of Mr Symonds and other criminal connections Rodriguez seemed to have, but following up on that lead would just be on the back burner. He closed the files and tossed them into the out basket.

Chapter 31

Neville was conflicted.

Things had gone back to normal after the attempted kidnapping. That is, the man appeared in court and a trial date was set, Harriett was busy recuperating and dancing, and had little time to see Neville and he was also busy doing the same at Harrods. It seemed that everyone loved their story of crime and violence, but it kept them away from each other.

He knew he was different now as was Harriett, but he still recognised the essential Harriett: smart, kind, loving and sweet-natured.

Neville sighed. He wanted her, and his sleepless nights had led to a plan. He would do two things. Learn to tango, and buy back the Marilyn Monroe ring to present to her when he asked her to marry him. Buoyed by his plan, Neville phoned George.

'George,' he said. 'I want Harriett back in my life for good. She loves to dance the tango so I'm hoping that I can learn a bit of what you know to impress her. What do you think? Can you keep this a secret, George?'

'Of course' said George, pleased to have such a star learn at his studio and excited because he knew Harriett would love it.

Next, Neville phoned a gem dealer he knew. If anyone knew where he might find the Marilyn Monroe ring it would be him.

'The Monroe ring!' The dealer's voice sounded amused. I remember when it was displayed at the Thames Row Diamond Exchange before they found that it had been replaced by a fake. But I do know where it is. I've seen it.'

'Where?' Neville asked.

'In London. In the main showroom of the Thames Row Diamond Exchange.'

'You mean that it is here in London, at the diamond exchange and I didn't know?'

'They reclaimed it some time ago but I don't think they want to sell it. They've made more money by just displaying it.'

It was at that moment that Neville's rage at the diamond exchange criminals surfaced. He didn't want to buy it. He wanted to steal it and ruin them. It had cost him Harriett's love, three million pounds, and nearly their lives. He wanted payback.

Back home, he thought about how he could do it. Shortly after, Neville told Harriett about his plan.

'Neville, this is dangerous.'

Janie and Muriel were soon in the know and their reaction was positive. 'Don't be silly, Harriett. We know the risks and we want to help. The diamond exchange treated us and everyone else there like dirt when they first folded. Besides, we've listened to Neville's idea and it's a good one.'

With that, Neville held out his hand with a ring in it. It was exactly like the Monroe ring.

'How did you get it. Did they sell it to you?' Harriett was excited.

Janie and Muriel laughed. 'That's not the real ring. That's a copy,' Janie guessed.

'Not again,' Harriett groaned.'

*

'You have three minutes before the alarm stops,' Neville said. 'And do you have your special shoes, the ones with the glass ruby studs?' Neville winked at Janie. She smiled and agreed.

'Harriett, do you have the money we need?'

'Sure,' Harriett said.

'Muriel, you've got the most to remember. Have you got the car keys, the key to your friend's locker, the disguise, the umbrella, the extra clothes and most of all, the gun?'

'Got the lot,' Muriel reassured Neville. 'I've also been practising shooting at a small target so don't worry about that. And, I've discovered there is no ricochet with the glass.'

Janie turned to Muriel. 'How did you learn to shoot, Muriel?'

'We had a farm, so I learnt there. Dad was a crack shot and was keen for me to be as able as my brothers. And I was.'

Harriett frowned. 'How do you know that the bullets from Muriel's gun will shatter the glass?'

Neville explained again. 'Paul Lowe was always a cheapskate. When he designed the Diamond Exchange office in Thames Row he used only the minimum bullet proof glass. I've googled the display room at the Central London exchange and found he's used the same type of glass. And it's been there for so long – it's old. There are much more modern theft-proof options today but, luckily, he's not using them. Bullet proof glass can flex instead of shatter. But at this thickness, ¾ inch, that is UL752 Level 1, it only takes three shots from a 9mm gun to pierce it. Muriel has a 50 calibre automatic Magnum pistol with armour piercing rounds that she will aim at the glass and pull the trigger as many times as she can handle the weight of it. That should blow the glass out and allow her to get her hand in and snatch the ring.

'But will the glass cut her hands?' said Janie.

Muriel butted in, 'No, the glass flexes in when the bullet hits it and the glass turns into pebbles that rain down on the floor. A bit like windscreen glass when a car is in an accident.

'What about the bullets and the cartridge casings? Won't the police be able to tell with their forensics who owns the gun?'

'Good questions, Janie,' Neville observed – and Janie looked pleased. 'Muriel has found a black market pistol that has been used before. While the police can tell from the bullets and casings what type of gun they came from, they cannot pinpoint the exact gun unless they can find it and put a round through it to find a match for the bullets. Muriel, of course, is going to get rid of the gun.'

'Even then,' Muriel added, 'if they could ever find the gun, it's almost impossible to match the bullets as the barrel of the gun changes over time with wear and tear, scratches from cleaning and usage.'

'What about Paul Lowe, Harriett. Will he be there tomorrow as we planned?'

'He'll be there,' Harriett stated firmly. 'But doesn't he know you, Neville, from your days at the diamond exchange?'

'No, Harriett. Although he was the designer, he only worked in Central London.'

'Okay, everyone …' Neville took charge. 'Let's review the environment we have to work in.'

'Here's how it looks,' Harriett said. 'As you know, the street is a cul-de-sac with an arcade at the end. The shops are tiny and close together as they date from the Dickensian era, built for the poor of London. But with a few tweaks and restoration and refurbishment, they have become a glamour zone. The diamond exchange is at the end of the circle, flanked by a dress shop and an art gallery. Inside the diamond exchange, the floor is covered with a diagonal striped plush carpet of black and grey stripes. The walls are covered with an old gilt flock wallpaper and a curved glass counter sits four steps from the sliding doors, which open swiftly when one is about three steps away from them, so no one has to hesitate to walk in. Each of the diamonds in this counter is displayed individually on a gold and black velvet plinth. Nothing is below 50,000 pounds. Behind the counter is a stand with a Swarovski vase shaped like a wave. It is similar to the "Under the Wave" painting by Katsushika Hokusai. At each point that the waves break on the vase, they are set with clusters of rare pink diamonds.'

'To the right of the doors are the three glass display cases set into the wall. In the middle is the ring.'

'What about the security guard?' Muriel asked.

Harriett continued. 'Some of the more modern jewellery shops have amazing security. Some you can only get in with an appointment and after speaking through a voice machine at the door. But even then there have been some famous heists. One heist was successful with an underground tunnel and one with a phalanx of bikies crashing into the shop and swiping what they could.'

'Once again, because Lowe is a cheapskate, he has forgone any real security,' Neville explained. 'The guard in the shop is required to come with Lowe to the office to count any cash and sign for it. So he's away from his post at that time. There are only four steps to the display boxes and then back to the doors. The alarm goes off if the display cabinets are breached or if the sales person presses the emergency button.'

'OK then,' Neville said. 'We all know our roles. All we have to do is remember our timing.'

All eyes looked soberly at each other. It was really happening.

On Saturday.

Chapter 32

The four conspirators were in the car when it was parked in the multi-storey carpark near the arcade.

Muriel took the keys with her as she would be driving home. Then they walked down to the ground floor of the arcade.

Muriel walked down to the end of the main alley and to a staff entrance. Quickly she entered and walked down the hall past toilets and cleaning store cupboards, and into the main room containing the staff lockers. Muriel's friend had lent her a key to her locker and the staff entry as Muriel had said she wanted to shop without having to carry all her bags around. Muriel left a shopping bag with goodies bought from Dior in the locker.

It was early morning. The shops were just about to open so the only employees who could be seen were cleaning windows and rearranging goods. There were no customers around.

Outside, the alley looked cold, dim and lonely to Muriel. At the end, where two bolsters prevented cars from driving down, she could see the openness of a street parallel to the alley. It was the street she needed.

Muriel looked down at her attire. Sneakers, black tights, a black long-sleeved shirt and a black wool balaclava which rested like a round collar on her shirt. In her pocket were gloves and a coloured scarf. She opened the umbrella and held it close to her head and shoulders so her face was hidden. It would allow her to quickly pull up the balaclava when needed. The hidden gun bumped against her hip as she walked.

Down at the diamond exchange store, Harriett, Neville and Janie were introducing themselves to the thirty-something male sales assistant behind the counter.

The counter curved around the room and a lift in a corner led to offices upstairs.

'Is Paul around?' Harriett enquired. 'I've come to see him. I'm Rosa La Boca and I have an appointment.'

The sales assistant phoned Paul Lowe who came down within minutes.

'These are my friends,' Harriett continued. 'Neville Symonds, who's known as "The Face of Harrods", and Janie, his fiancée. They are here to look for an engagement ring while I complete my business with you.' Neville shook hands and Janie smiled sweetly.

'You've come to the right place,' Lowe boomed. 'I'll give you a good price on our diamonds, for any friend of Rosa La Boca.'

'Wait,' said Rosa. 'The security guard needs to come with us. It's not that I don't trust you, Paul …. But … I want a signed statement that I've paid the right amount.'

Lowe nodded to the security guard to come with them.

Soon Neville and Janie were looking at rings. The sales assistant had placed a black velvet mat on the counter while Janie looked at the stones inside the cabinet.

'We'll either choose a ready-made ring or a diamond for you to create a setting. What would you like, darling?'

Janie looked up at him. 'I'd like one of these two diamonds, darling.' She turned to the sales assistant. 'How much are these?'

The sales assistant, gloves on his hands, took out the two Janie had pointed to and placed them on the mat. 'Madam has good taste,' he said. 'The first is a mere 1 million and the second is 1.6 million.'

Janie's face fell. 'Oh darling, I didn't know they were that expensive. Is it too much?'

Neville hesitated. 'Oh go ahead, darling. We only get engaged once.'

At that moment pandemonium broke out. A black clad figure came hurtling into the shop brandishing a large gun. Janie shrieked and quickly ducked her head into her arms on the counter then swept them up to her ears as the black hood of the fierce looking fellow glanced at her. She staggered back towards the sliding doors which opened immediately, screaming loudly, with her hands to her mouth.

'Keep still and no-one gets hurt,' the harsh voice yelled.

The sales assistant kept his cool. His eyes were riveted on the hooded thief, but he bravely slid a small step to the right and pressed the red button under the counter to alert the police.

The black clad figure turned to the display cabinets and shot at the middle one, then reached in and grabbed the ring sitting among the shattered pebbled and flexed glass.

With a quick turn, the thief was out of the shop, knocking Janie out the door and onto the ground. The alarm wailed.

For a moment all stood still, then Neville shouted, 'I'll get him,' and raced after the thief who was heading for the alley. The sales assistant, not to be outdone in the bravery stakes, followed.

At the sound of the commotion from downstairs, Harriett, Lowe and the security guard hurried to the lift and rushed into the showroom.

By this time Neville had caught up to the thief and was trying to wrestle him to the ground. But with a swipe of the gun butt, Neville collapsed, after first staggering into the sales assistant who had just arrived and was preparing to run into the alley. Neville latched onto the man and they collapsed on the ground together.

The assistant sprung up, twisted around and tried to peer down the alley. It was empty. So he turned to Neville and helped him to stand. The two men hobbled back to the shop doorway, Neville with a cut, and blood on his forehead and both of them with grazed shins and hands from their fall. Neville rubbed his forehead and thought how too much method acting had turned Muriel's head.

Several men from the nearby shops had also run up to Neville, one even running into the alley, but on finding it empty, had slowly walked back to the street. Several other shopkeepers and early customers cowered in the shop doorways out of danger.

Meanwhile, the thief had run into the alley and behind the

dumpster where the balaclava and gloves were removed and a bright coloured scarf was taken from her pocket and flung around her neck. Checking that no one was following, she walked casually to the staff entrance and slid into the first toilet inside. Sneakers, balaclava, gloves, and scarf were piled on the floor with the gun on top. Next, the black top was reversed to expose a multi-coloured outfit in swirls of orange and blue. Holding the gun hidden in the bundle of clothes, Muriel walked down to the lockers and took out the bag she had left there. Then she took out her lovely blue high heels and stepped into them. Over on the opposite wall was a mirror where Muriel did some repairs, added make-up and fluffed her hair into spiky bangs of red streaks. She was ready to walk out to the multi-storey carpark and drive home. She felt elated that everything had gone off so well.

Neville had played a major role in the drama. At the height of the fracas he collapsed against the counter, and then called out in a stifled voice, 'I couldn't get him. But I managed to wrestle the ring from him.' He held out his arm and opened his palm. There was the ring winking brightly.

Paul Lowe rushed over, while the security man turned off the alarm. Lowe grabbed the ring from Neville's hand. 'Thank goodness,' he said. 'It's priceless.'

A police car screeched to a halt and two large policemen alighted. They perused the scene, then walked towards the diamond exchange.

Lowe immediately stepped forward. 'Paul Lowe, the manager. Thanks for coming so quickly. I was upstairs with a customer and security so I don't have any real knowledge of what happened, but my sales assistant has. He'll tell you.'

The assistant explained. 'I was helping two customers with their purchase when a thief wearing black came in waving a gun. I really couldn't tell if it was a man or a woman. I immediately pressed the danger button.' He looked towards Lowe to see if he was taking note of this bravery. 'The thief shot at the glass display and reached for the ring inside. Then he ran out and I ran after him but I couldn't catch him.'

The largest policeman looked at Neville, startled to recognise him, and then at Harriett. 'Mr Symonds, of Harrods, and Ms Rosa La Boca, the star of the tango show. Nice to meet you both. What are you doing here?'

'I was the customer,' Neville replied. 'Rosa had decided to invest in the diamond business, and I was buying an engagement ring for my fiancée … and …

'Where is she, sir?'

'The thief knocked into her and she fell on the cobblestones outside. I believe the sales women next door are helping her, as she's in shock.'

They all looked outside and saw Janie sitting on a chair near the door of the dress shop. She was re-buckling her shoes that must have come loose in the fall. Her opened clutch purse, with several items spilling from it, lay on the gravel outside the doors to the diamond exchange.

One of the policemen went over, reached for the purse, picked up the lipstick, powder, comb and other items and snapped it shut. He walked over to Janie and gave her the purse.

'Mr Symonds has been quite a hero,' Lowe interrupted. 'He chased the thief and although he did not catch him, he retrieved the ring, and here it is.' Lowe opened his hand where the ring lay in all its glory.

'Is anything else missing, sir?' the largest policeman asked, looking at the assistant.

'No, the cupboard under the counter was locked and the only two things out on top are still here – two diamonds that Mr Symonds was examining.'

'I think we had chosen the 1.6-million-pound diamond just before the thief burst in,' said Neville. 'I'll pay a deposit now of 10,000 pounds to hold the diamond for us, and the rest when we come back next week to choose a setting. I think my fiancée has had enough for one day.

Paul Lowe agreed with the requirement that the showroom be

closed for the forensic team to gather any evidence of the crime, and that the sales assistant, Neville and Janie would all need to go to the station to sign a statement.

They climbed into a police car, Neville helping Janie who was still quite shaken. Everyone was ushered into separate rooms to be interviewed and sign statements. The largest policeman spent some time with Neville, then asked sheepishly for an autograph for his daughter who shopped at Harrods regularly. It was about 5 pm by the time Neville and Janie, still feeling excited but tired, arrived back in Thames Row to meet Muriel and Harriett.

They looked at the ring that Janie now had in her hand and the two diamonds from her shoes, that she had swiped from the counter and replaced with two fake ones. They were all excited about their scam.

'Let's not get too exuberant,' was Neville's sage advice. 'That's only Part One. Wait until next week.'

Chapter 33

The following weekend Neville and Janie were again in the London showroom of the diamond exchange.

Crowding around outside was a clutch of media personnel with cameras and microphones. A security guard, with arms outstretched, kept them back from entering.

Paul Lowe had been there to greet the couple, and was quite concerned about the media trying to crash into the shop.

'Somehow, and I don't how, they became aware of my visit to you, Paul,' Neville said. 'Sorry about that. I'm hounded wherever I go.'

Neville walked over to the counter. 'I have a friend meeting me here who is a diamond expert, just to make sure I am buying a quality diamond. Ah, here he comes now.'

The small man in a grey suit and glasses was walking down to the shop. 'Paul, I'd like you to meet Marcus Evans. Marcus, this is Paul Lowe, the manager of the Central London store.'

The two men shook hands both of them acknowledging to each other that they knew of each other's reputation.

'My fiancée and I have chosen one of two diamonds for her engagement ring,' Neville explained. 'I have asked you here, Marcus, as I don't know much about diamonds and want an expert opinion of their quality.'

Evans moved closer to the counter where the two diamonds were displayed on the black velvet mat. He put his loupe to his eye and began to examine them. Lowe stood nearby with the sales assistant, quite content that they would find nothing wrong with the diamonds. All this time, from the shop doorway the media were taking photos of Neville and Janie, who were holding hands and beaming at each other. In fact, creating quite a beautiful photo opportunity.

Suddenly, Marcus Evans put the two diamonds down and announced in a loud voice, 'These diamonds are fake.'

Immediately there was a frenzy of chatter from the media group. Reporters, photographers and camera operators were forging forward, microphones thrust in front of Marcus and Neville. Paul Lowe stood open-mouthed until the media turned on him and began asking their questions.

'Do you often cheat your customers?'

'Are you just cheating Symonds, "The Face of Harrods", because he says he knows nothing about diamonds?'

'Did you expect the expert not to notice the fakes?'

'What else is fake in the store?'

Neville spoke quietly to one of the media. 'I am most disappointed in this store. It had a reputation that I thought was excellent. Now …' he shook his head sadly, '… I won't be shopping here again.'

Soon Neville, Janie and Marcus Evans were on the way home while the media rushed back to their departments to prepare their news stories.

The news broke online almost immediately and by that evening the papers were full of stories of the fake diamonds. Neville, Harriett, Janie and Muriel were sitting around a table at Janie's cafe. With TV on the news channel in the background, newspapers were spread out in front of them, showing large pictures of Paul Lowe and Marcus Evans. They were waiting for the 6 pm news break. The anchor came on to give the audience a taste of the night's top stories. There was Neville hugging Janie, then Marcus Evans pronouncing the diamonds were fake, then Paul Lowe open-mouthed, trying to deny everything. The news script damned the Thames Row Diamond Exchange and Lowe. Neville and Janie were heard to say they would go somewhere else for their engagement ring.

'Now we can celebrate,' Neville announced with a big grin.

'My spies tell me that Paul Lowe seems to have disappeared and the store is closed. Those in the know think he has gone to Buenos Aires. Either that, or the criminals he seems to be aligned with have done away with him.'

*

Neville stood at a bar in The Savoy surveying the splendid scene. Tom had gone all out to advertise his agency even though it was a personal occasion, his own engagement party. Enormous posters of the stars in his agency graced the walls.

Muriel sidled over to Neville, pleased that he was on time.

'I like the decorations,' Neville said, nodding towards the one nearest him which happened to be of himself.

'Hmm,' Muriel said. 'I wanted more photos of South America but I didn't win that argument. At least the tango company posters of Harriett and Antonio keep to the theme.'

Neville grinned. 'I think you've fallen on your feet, girl.'

'I have, haven't I? A great job and a boss who's the love of my life to boot. I am lucky.' She was beaming. 'Anyway, Harriett will be here later after the show and I plan to get you two together. Just be here at this bar when I need you.'

She sashayed away to greet more guests.

Janie too was taking in the ambience of the party. She had provided the catering and was very satisfied with the results: plates of Spanish paella and small dishes of vegetables with sweet onions, spicy red peppers, tomatoes, eggplants and other culinary delights with unpronounceable names. And, if anyone was drinking, Zarangollo and Escalivada. Little chocolate brigadeiro cakes were set out on cake stands among fruits of all descriptions.

Janie thought about the two diamonds that she had rescued in her shoes from the diamond exchange. No one from the criminal gang seemed to want to claim them. George was busy learning new dances

224

with Carla while Charles watched each performance with lots of 'olé's and 'bravo's. Muriel and Tom, of course, were busy becoming engaged.

Janie thought about the new diamond exchange building which used to be the bank. It was now empty and was a very handsome structure. It seemed that there might be an opening for her there. Business and making money was one thing, but cooking wonderful cakes was her passion. The building was just right for an expanded cake company. She'd woken one night to the idea of little cakes, decorated with look-a-like diamonds on top. They would become her 'Diamond Range' and would be sold on-line and could be delivered anywhere in the world. She sighed in delight at the plan.

Waiting by the bar, Neville took a sip of his cocktail and closed his eyes, letting the vision of Harriett's face come into his mind. Such a beautiful face. Sculpted cheekbones, a clear brow, soft lips, masses of thick brown hair. He almost groaned out loud.

If only he hadn't stolen the ring all those years ago. If only his anger hadn't caused her such pain. They might even have still been working at the Thames Row Diamond Exchange, not talking to each other.

Muriel was back by Neville's side, to draw him out of his reverie.

'Time to go, Neville.'

'Where?'

'Up to the top of The Savoy. Specifically, Harriett's suite.'

Neville walked with Muriel to the lift. As she pressed the button for the top floor executive suite, she hoped her plan was going to work.

Chapter 34

The last act of Rosa's very last show in London was coming to an end. Rosa would soon join her friends at The Savoy bar.

The audience was clapping, stamping their feet and calling out 'Rosa' and 'Antonio' over and over again.

Rosa moved forward to Antonio and they posed, ready for their last dance on the London stage.

Her black lace bodice, scattered with diamantes, hugged her body to the hips, flaring out in the lightest of blood red chiffon waves.

Head to his chest and her eyes gazing up at him, he dragged her across the floor, one toe only on the ground, until he stopped for three, four, five beats, while her skirt curled and dipped in the dying moment.

The music accelerated, and they swirled across the floor with kicks, twists, turns and tension-stilled poses. Then, with a final knee flex and double leg twist, Rosa floated to a finish, displaying her as wanton and sensual as at the beginning of the dance.

The last night of the Buenos Aires tango troupe's London season had come to an end. It had been magnificent. They now had a lay-off for one week before starting at the Paris Opera for a European tour.

It had been a long day and an exciting evening for Harriett and she was exhausted. There had been many people to thank and meet after the show, followed by an end of tour party. She had stayed with Antonio until it was over. Now she was among the tango company performers arriving at the engagement party and she and Antonio were at the centre of the group, still graciously shaking hands and smiling.

She moved to the bar and took a sip of an icy Moscato, letting it run down her throat to cool all the nerve ends of her body. It was just like

Janie and Muriel to choose a South American theme with the appropriate drinks and food for the engagement party.

She was keen to see George and Carla dance.

An announcement called everyone to the stage area and the music began.

George and Carla moved into each other's arms and began to move sensuously across the floor ready for the main dance to begin.

Things were going well until Carla spied Rosa. Why was she here and getting all the attention? Even George had noticed her and smiled beatifically.

He whispered in Carla's ear as they completed a few turns. 'Rosa's here, Carla. I'm so thrilled she's come to see us. She was my first partner and helped design this dance.'

Carla, who hadn't known about Harriett's role in the choreography, pursed her lips and squinted her eyes. Carla straightened her back even more to become the star she had always been.

It was then she noticed George glancing over her shoulder instead of at her. Her body became hot and her limbs out of control.

Suddenly she was stamping on George's feet and swinging away from him, pummelling him with her fists. The audience was silent. What was happening?

Carla leant down to the tray of a passing waiter and threw a champagne at George, who was standing bemused. His lovely dance was ruined.

Charles jumped up onto the stage and encased Carla in a bear hug, dragging her off to a corner.

Harriett seeing the problem and George's distress, skipped up the steps to the stage and took up a position with George.

Immediately the orchestra struck up and George floated with Harriett into a preparation step and then into a dance.

The lights dimmed and Harriett and George danced with abandon. After the clapping had died down and Charles had congratulated them both, George spoke quietly to Harriett. 'This is all due to you,

Harriett. Thank you. I guess I won't be partnering Carla now.'

'Sorry, George. Still, I'm sure you'll find another partner.'

'Charles said that too. He thought it was wonderful. He said I am more …' here George stopped and blushed … 'affectionate when I dance.'

Harriett laughed. 'Good on you, George. Find a new partner and keep it up.'

They laughed at the double entendre.

Just then Janie and Muriel came rushing up, with Muriel pressing Harriett into action. 'Harriett we need to freshen up again. Could you take us up to your penthouse, please?'

'Of course,' Harriett said, 'and then I might say goodnight. I'm very tired.'

The three friends got in the lift and Muriel, who had been holding Harriett's key card, gave it back to her to swipe.

When they arrived at the penthouse floor, Harriett swiped her key card and pushed the door open, just as Janie and Muriel backed away, calling out, 'Enjoy your evening, Harriett.'

Pools of light flooded the penthouse floor, and the shadow of a well-built man stood in the half light.

Harriett immediately knew who it was. Neville.

She stood still, bemused.

'Neville,' she whispered.

'Oh, Harriett, I've yearned for this moment.'

Harriett answered softly. 'Me too.'

'I just want to apologise for everything.'

Harriett closed her eyes.

'I am so sorry, so sorry, Harriett. I was angry when I left you in Argentina and everything that has happened since seems to have stemmed from that. I went back for you, you know, but Sylvia told me you had gone. So I went home too. Besides, I know now how Sylvia can lie.'

'I learnt to tango. What else could I do?' Harriett brushed a curl back from her face.

Neville took a step towards her. 'And I know how wonderfully you dance. I really thought you had forgotten about me.'

Harriett shook her head. 'I thought you hated me and didn't want to know me.'

Taking another step closer, Neville said, 'I wish we could go back to that night in the hacienda in Buenos Aires. Can we go back, Harriett?'

Harriett took a deep breath. She didn't want to go back to a time when she was nobody. She liked being confident, creative, a person of wealth and importance. A star.

'Perhaps we can't, but we could try going forward instead.'

Neville took another step to meet Harriett, the small space between them filled with tension. He reached out his hands to her shoulders and lightly stroked her arms, pulling her close to him.

'I love you.' Neville's closeness affected Harriett's equilibrium. She could not speak. She was frozen in place. She felt she had no will of her own. So she nodded.

Neville pulled her hands around his waist, then moved his splayed hands across her back and into her hair. Pins flicked to the floor as he combed his fingers into the bun at the nape of her neck, loosening the knot and letting her thick, silky hair cascade down her back. Neville buried his face in her tresses.

'I love your hair, Harriett. I love the way it falls into my hands and how it smells so fresh and sweet.'

He tenderly cupped her cheeks and angled her mouth to his. Gently he rubbed his lips across hers, back and forth, until both of them were shaking with a need that consumed them, until the pressure of his lips increased into a deep, deep kiss.

Harriett felt her limbs becoming limp as Neville poured all the feelings he had into his kiss. He wanted her to know and understand the depths of his love.

Harriett wound her arms around his waist and held on.

Here was the Neville she loved. She had been wanting him here beside her for two years and here he was, real, solid and loving.

The pain that had lodged in Harriett's chest for all this time began to dissipate. Here was a new beginning, a femme fatale opportunity with just one man, Neville.

Time seemed to stand still.

Images of herself and Neville catching planes together, him waiting at the stage door for her to finish the show and lots of loving in their high-rise apartment seemed to be vying with images of her walking the floor with a crying baby while Neville heated milk in a saucepan and brought her nappies and wipes.

Her mind was caught in her dream.

Neville took the plunge. He had been practising his tango steps with George for two lessons. He cleared his throat, tentatively. 'Do you want to dance?'

He moved to a tango position with his arms holding Harriett's.

Automatically, unconsciously, Harriett moved into a tango stance too. Neville took the first five sliding steps then turned right and left and into a dip. He stopped.

Shocked out of her daydream of planes and babies, Harriett asked, 'You can tango?'

Neville nodded bashfully. 'Just a bit. Still learning.'

'For me?' Harriett replied.

'For you, my dear. I want to tango through life with you.' He laughed at the silliness of his statement. Harriett grinned back at him, searching his face, until they fell to kissing again, softly, gently as if to move on to the whole body might be too much to bear.

But then Neville's restraint broke.

Swiftly he lifted Harriett up in his arms and carried her to the bed. With little effort, he knelt and placed her in the centre, following on with his body. Harriett stretched her arms up and giggled.

'What?' Neville said.

'I had a dream about this. You were in it. Only you were puffing and panting trying to lift me onto the bed which was covered in rose petals.'

Neville smiled. 'Hmm! Puffing, was I? Not now. But maybe the rose petals next time.'

'Will there be a next time, Neville?' Harriett asked dreamily.

'Yes Harriett. Lots of next times. I want to be with you.'

Harriett paused. Had he thought about her job, her life?

Neville read her thoughts. 'I know, darling. You are a tango dancer who flits around the world. But I can model anywhere.'

He set to kissing her and running his hands down her body, getting to know it all over again. Clothes disappeared and their bodies finally fused together in love.

Afterwards, he rolled off the bed and reached into the pocket of his trousers lying on the floor. He pulled out a small jewellery case, took from it an exquisite setting, raised her left hand, and onto her ring finger placed the ultimate symbol of his love.

Harriett looked down with tears in her eyes.

'My ring,' she whispered.

She looked from the ring to Neville. Her hand came up to his face and she traced his chin and lips with her fingers. She loved his face. It was so strong and noble.

Neville, who had always been able to read Harriett's thoughts said, 'This is the best day of our lives.'

And Harriett, who could always read Neville's thoughts added, 'And even better than diamonds.'

From the same publisher

An extraordinary
relationship

Early in **Leo Ryan**'s career as a counsellor he became aware of the number of female clients being abused by their husbands/partners/boyfriends and was determined to help. This book highlights his conclusions, making it possible for most people to bring on the changes needed have a great relationship.

Category: NON-FICTION – HOW-TO BOOK – RELATIONSHIPS

Angela's Anorexia:
the story
of my mother

A son's story of the debilitating illness, anorexia nervosa, that his single mother suffered from throughout his childhood. The mother and son formed a close bond and the boy's description of their life together is filled with both joy and sadness. A true story showing the boy's experience of growing up fast in Australia and New Zealand, caring for his mother while coming to understand her sickness and his need to develop an independent spirit early on.

Damian Cooper has written a straightforward, honest and loving account of his boyhood, set against a poignant parallel story of his mother's excessive focus on body image, food, diet and exercise.

Category: SELF-HELP/EATING DISORDERS AND BODY IMAGE

ARCO:
the legend
of the blue vortex

An exciting new story from first-time novelist, **Ferdinando Manzo**, ARCO explores man's battle with the sea in an attempt to seek solace.

The story is set in two different eras: on the high seas among ancient pirates and in contemporary Europe ravaged by war. The legend of the blue vortex – a door into another world – is the central focus of both periods.

An adventure story, it also raises philosophical questions about love and the purpose of life.

Category: FICTION MAGICAL REALISM/ROMANCE/FANTASY

Burma My Mother
And Why I Had To Leave

Myanmar's future is informed by its past – and BURMA MY MOTHER tells it like it is.

A valuable story of living through good times and plenty of bad in Burma, now known as Myanmar, before an escape to a new life of freedom.

Author **Sao Khemawadee Mangrai**'s husband, Hom, was imprisoned for 5 years, and his father was shot and killed sitting alongside independence leader, General Aung San, when he was assassinated.

Khemawadee grew up in a Shan state in the north-east of Myanmar, previously known as Burma, and now lives in Sydney. Her sad memories are also infused by the beauty of the country and the grace of Myanmar's Buddhist culture.

Category: MEMOIR

Drenched
by the Sun

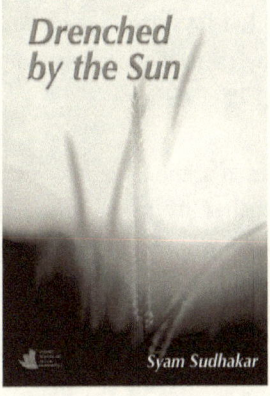

I, who prophesy
by reading the stars and the wind,
now think of that country ...

Syam Sudhakar 'has an eye for the strange
and the uncanny and a way of building
translucent metaphors,' according to leading South Indian poet, K. Satchidanandan.

An award-winning poet who writes in English
and Malayalam, Sudhakar is based in Kerala, teaching and researching Indian poetry.

Category: POEMS

Night Road to Life

Themes of the sea and the emotions, particularly the deeply felt joys and melancholies experienced by men, are a touchstone of NIGHT ROAD TO LIFE.

Ferdinando Manzo's thoughts are not bound to fluidity; they fly to the greatest heights of exhilaration in poems such as, *The sky above us*, which displays 'a mantle of stars that burns in my heart' and in the evocative lines of *Eclipse*: 'the moon rose, bright between the eyelids of the night'. Even the constellation Andromeda is given due recognition, breaking her chains and ready for revenge, before another poem *The voice of the universe* explores 'a hidden legend as far away as waves in outer space'.

A distinctive quality of this collection of poems is its musicality – the sounds of words carefully chosen, and their rhythms. The pleasing effect of the sensuality of sounds, ranging from gentleness to the drama of sex, is in tune with the gamut of human emotion.

Category: POEMS

Reported Missing

Di Harding's novel is set in a very contemporary Sydney, taking in multi-layered sights and sounds, from the northern beaches to performances at the Sydney Opera House.

The plot spans the complications of what a woman must consider if she is to save her children from domestic violence. And the main character has good reason to hold fears for her life.

What would you do if your daughter was missing and you thought your son-in-law was somehow involved? Is there someone who could help you, or would you take matters into your own hands?

She does, and so the terror begins – from vile and personal harassment to life threatening acts, until she is ready to commit murder.

Her obsession with killing grows in her mind until she begins to plan and plot. Can she actually do it? Then something shocking happens to make up her mind.

The story ends on an upbeat for a new life ahead for the family.

Category: DOMESTIC VIOLENCE
CRIME FICTION/SYDNEY NOVEL
AUSTRALIAN FICTION

Road
to Mandalay
Less Travelled

'The Road to Mandalay Less Travelled' by **Ingrid Raj** provides research on a selection of Anglo-Burmese writing published from the period of British rule in Burma up until 2007.

What Raj shares with us in this study is the knowledge she gained about the value of social resistance achieved through writing. Both fiction and non-fiction texts are included in arguing a case that these might be viewed as tools of often ambivalent resistance against oppressive regimes, both local and colonial.Her research deserves a wider readership than was initially provided, and to this aim Sydney School of Arts & Humanities presents the work as its first publication in this new category of Essays & Theses.

We hope that specialist researchers as well as members of the general reading public take this opportunity to learn more about the culture of the people of Myanmar through their unique approach to storytelling, based largely on their religious understanding, their rich store of folk legend and their chequered history.

Category: MEMOIR/LITERATURE/BURMA-HISTORY

Road to Rishi Konda

'ROAD TO RISHI KONDA' by **Geetha Waters** is a memoir of insight and charm, with a serious educational purpose. The author recalls delightful and stimulating stories from her childhood to throw light on the work of the philosopher J. Krishnamurti as a revolutionary 20th century educator.

At once fascinating and enchanting, Geetha Waters' stories centre on a girl growing up in Kerala and Andhra Pradesh in the '60s and '70s.

These youthful tales are underpinned by Geetha's deep understanding of childhood education, based both on her academic studies and in practice in her daily life as a mother and childcare professional.

Written from a child's perspective, the tales of awakening to life offer the reader an opportunity to appreciate how all children learn, as they draw on a deep well of curiosity that needs to be respected.

Category: BIOGRAPHY & AUTOBIOGRAPHY
PERSONAL MEMOIR/EDUCATORS

The Dark Side of the Opera

In this collection, **Ferdinando Manzo** plays with language, teasing out meaning and tempting the senses. His poetic approach is akin to the Buddhist path where happiness is gained through an understanding of negation.

From the earthly to the stellar, each poem holds the reader in suspense until the final moment.

Category: POEMS

What's in a Name?
20 People - 20 Stories

This collection of short stories will appeal to readers who are attracted to snapshots of the human condition. While set in Australia, the stories reflect universal themes. They range over a number of genres from crime to science fiction, from human weakness to human strength, and capture pockets of life with uncanny accuracy and sensitivity.

The author, **Lawrence Goodstone**, is a retired public servant who spent his professional life writing for others. With a background ranging from teaching to immigrant services as well as assisting in the delivery of the 2000 Olympic Games in Sydney, he is now in a position to write for himself and create stories from a life well lived.

Category: FICTION/SHORT STORY/SYDNEY STORIES
FICTION/AUSTRALIAN FICTION

Jiddu Krishnamurti World Philosopher
Revised Edition

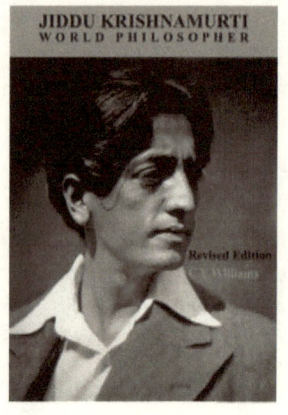

The life of the 20th-century philosopher Jiddu Krishnamurti was truly astonishing. As this new updated edition shows, people from all over the world would gather to hear him speak the wisdom of the ages.

Biographer **Christine (CV) Williams** carried out research over a period of four years to write this ebook account of Krishnamurti's life. She studied his major archive of personal correspondence and talks, and interviewed people who knew him intimately.

Krishna was born into poverty in a South Indian village, before being adopted by a wealthy English public figure, Annie Besant. As an adult he settled in California, travelling to India and England every year to give public lectures that inspired spiritual seekers beyond any single religion.

Category: BIOGRAPHY